A CASE

OF

WITCHCRAFT

BY

JOE REVILL.

Paperback: ISBN 978-1-78092-009-2
Mobipocket/Kindle: ISBN 978-1-78092-010-8
ePub/iBook: ISBN 978-1-78092-011-5

Published in the UK by MX Publishing Limited,
335 Princess Park Manor, Royal Drive,
London, N11 3GX.

www.mxpublishing.com

Cover design by Staunch Design,
11 Shipton Road,
Woodstock,
Oxfordshire, OX20 1LW.
www.staunch.com

TO
THE
ETERNAL
BELOVED.

CHAPTER I.
FRIDAY, OCTOBER THE TWENTY-SEVENTH, 1899.

"I do not know if you can help me, Mr. Holmes; but I am sure that, if you cannot, no one can!"

The speaker was a pale but resolute blonde in her late thirties, tall and slender, dressed in an unfashionable suit of powder-blue, with leg-o'-mutton sleeves. The white band of her hat was slightly soiled by the London rain. She was good-looking in an aristocratic, faintly equine way, and evidently in considerable distress. From her card, Holmes knew her to be Miss Emily Tollemache, the resident of a vicarage in Devonshire.

"Some tea, Mrs. Hudson! And you, my poor young lady, pray come and sit by the fire. This afternoon's weather has been most inclement." He motioned her towards the armchair from which he had risen on her arrival. When she was comfortably seated, he moved the little room's third armchair, which was of wicker-work construction, to a position equidistant from her chair and that of his friend Dr. Watson, whose apparent lack of chivalry was excused by the bandaged leg which rested on a footstool.

"I suppose, gentlemen, that you have heard of my father, the Reverend Mr. Melchior Tollemache?"

"A folklorist of some renown, I believe."

"Some years ago I read his book on were-wolves!" added Watson. "The breadth of your father's erudition is matched only by the grace of his style—although in that work I found his subject-matter to be somewhat gruesome."

"Indeed. It has ever been my father's aspiration to shine the light of scholarship into the darkness of primitive superstition, and by exposing it to diminish its power. Yet now I fear that he himself has fallen into that dark world, and that its age-old horrors have destroyed him!"

"You speak figuratively?"

"No, Mr. Holmes: my father is missing, and may, I fear, be slain—at the hands of Devil-worshippers!"

"Calm yourself, dear lady, and tell us the facts which have led you to so extraordinary a conclusion."

"Very well." She breathed deeply. "I shall tell you all that I know, although to explain all that has happened I must begin far back, and tell you of my father's research.

"For more than two years the Reverend Mr. Tollemache has been studying the folk-tale of *Cinderella*. When he first read the many variants in Miss Cox's collection, he believed that he could distinguish three different types of the tale; and these he supposed, from their present distribution and their characteristic narrative elements, to have originated independently: one in Asia, another in the Mediterranean region, and a third in Northern Europe—although these three original tales have undoubtedly been somewhat confused with one another by story-tellers over the centuries. That which most interested him was the Northern *Cinderella*, as represented primarily in the folklore of Iceland and Scandinavia. Are you acquainted with such tales, Mr. Holmes?"

Holmes shook his head. "My investigations of the real world have left me little time for studies of fantasy."

"Of course. One forgets how obscure such matters must appear to all but a fellow-student. I should say, then, that these Northern stories differ greatly from the *Cinderella* that you may have encountered in the nursery. Their central character is the daughter of a petty King, who marries for a second time after the untimely death of his wife. His new Queen—who is usually said to be a Witch—comes with a daughter of her own, and the two girls soon become rivals for the affection of both the King and his people. Those who dislike the black-haired Queen refer to her as 'The Crow', and, naturally, to her daughter as 'The Crow's Daughter', by which name the tale itself is often known. Rejected by her infatuated father, the persecuted Cinderella-figure is sent into a lonely exile, from which she is eventually rescued by the intervention of a handsome young King, who marries her and places her upon the throne of her father's Kingdom, while her stepsister and stepmother are deposed and punished, rather horribly."

"Indeed: that resembles rather a chapter from some Dark-Age historian than one of the Grimms' fairy-tales."

"Just so, Mr. Holmes. Although fantastic or supernatural elements are present in many versions, the basic story sounds like something that could well have happened in the real world. My father's intuition told him that it had indeed done so, and he set about trying to determine exactly when and where these events had occurred. For months the village postman would bring us almost daily correspondence from foreign scholars, and parcels containing maps, dictionaries, or volumes of folk-tales in uncouth languages. At length, by putting together various clues in the stories, Father deduced that the tale had originated very early in the Viking Age, and that its setting had been in the Northern Isles, most probably upon the largest of them, Trowley" (it rhymed with *holy*), "whose very name appears to signify 'the Isle of Witches'."

"So it does," said Holmes; "*Trolla-ey* in the Old Norse, if I am not mistaken."

Miss Tollemache gave a quick smile, the first that Holmes had seen from her. "Papa's first thought was to write to the clergymen in those parts, but few responded to his letters—and those who did were most unhelpful. So he decided to visit the Island himself, to see if any recollection of the story might persist among uneducated people there.

"He went up to Trowley ten days ago, and since then I have received two long letters from him, the last of them written on Sunday. We are very close, and he always says that explaining something to me helps him to understand it better. His letters were mostly concerned with the progress of his researches."

"Have you brought these letters?"

"Naturally, Mr. Holmes. But I will tell you briefly of their purport. He found the local clergy as unhelpful in person as they had been in correspondence. Generally, the natives seemed either ignorant of the story or unwilling to discuss it. The local antiquarian said that he had no knowledge of such events; that if they had ever happened, it must have been in the days before the first Earl of Trowley had been appointed by the Norwegian King—and of that distant time there survived no record, even in the sagas of the Icelanders. The trail seemed cold; but, knowing that ecclesiastical records often contain material of interest to the folklorist, my father went to search in the archives of the Cathedral, and there he found something remarkable."

"And what was that?"

"In the books of Church Discipline, from the sixteenth and seventeenth centuries, there were several references to men and women being fined or publicly humiliated for telling *The Tale of the Witches*, or *The Tale of the Two Witches*. Most remarkably of all, my father discovered an Episcopal letter, written in good fifteenth-century Latin, part of which decreed: *Let the Tale of the Witches be told no more, for those that delight in it are mostly Witches themselves, who would rejoice to see the Church of Christ overthrown and the Reign of the Crow restored."*

"This evidence seems remarkably supportive of your father's hypothesis! I suppose that there can be no suspicion of... creativity?"

Miss Tollemache appeared to be considering this idea for the first time, but she did not seem offended. "To be absolutely honest, as befits a vicar's daughter, I don't know; but I shouldn't have thought so. Father likes to spin hypotheses, but he *is* a proper scholar: that is, a seeker after truth. Rather like you, Mr. Holmes. Surely you would not plant evidence in order to secure a man's conviction—even if you believed him to be guilty! I'm sure that Father would feel just the same about forging documents in support of a favourite hypothesis."

Holmes did not consider that to be a definite *No*, but he was inclined to accord the old gentleman the benefit of the doubt.

"So," Holmes said, "we may suppose that there were once real Witches on Trowley: a society of people apparently opposed to the Christian religion, who told this folk-story as a kind of sacred myth, sympathizing, not with the Cinderella-figure, but with the two Witches who were her enemies; people who longed for the return of the Reign of the Crow just as the early Christians longed for the coming of the Kingdom of God. Perhaps all these things were so, three or four centuries ago. But what makes you think that the Cult still survives, and that it is in any way connected to the disappearance of your father?"

"As to the survival of this devilish Cult my only evidence is my father's growing belief in it during his days on the Island. He felt that some of the people with whom he spoke knew more than they were prepared to tell. Since Witches were executed there as late as the last century, it seems quite reasonable to me that the Cult might have a few adherents yet. And if we grant that there be Witches on Trowley, they must surely be the obvious suspects, because my father was poking around, trying to uncover their well-hidden secrets. And, of course, he is a Christian priest, and as such would make a particularly acceptable sacrifice to the Fiend whom they worship. All that gives me hope is this: I have learnt enough about Witches from my father's books to know that one of their major festivals is approaching, and that on such an occasion a human sacrifice is often performed: I refer of course to Hallowe'en, which (as you doubtless know) falls on Tuesday night. I believe that if the Witches have taken my father they will be keeping him alive until then, so that they can slay him at midnight and take a ghastly communion in his flesh and blood!"

"It is a plausible hypothesis, although a most disturbing one."

"And most would think me mad for suggesting it! That is why I have come to you, Mr. Holmes. I knew that you would take me

10

seriously. What I don't know is whether I can afford to pay your fees. We are quite poor."

"My dear Miss Tollemache! If I were to take this case, then, out of respect for a fellow-seeker after truth, I shouldn't dream of charging you a penny," said Holmes. "But I question how useful I can be. Is this not rather a matter for the Police, with their search-warrants and their tracker-dogs? What can I do in this case that they cannot?"

"The Trowley Police appear disinclined to do anything at all. I have corresponded telegraphically with their Superintendent; he claims to have made thorough enquiries and found no evidence of foul play. He remarks that it is not unusual for people to go missing from the isle, because to fall from the shore is very easy; and those who do so are often carried out far to sea, never to be seen again."

"Did you share with him your suspicions about the Witch-Cult?"

"I did, and was told that there are no longer any Witches on Trowley. I felt a hint of mockery in the reply."

"Nevertheless, the Superintendent may be right. Perhaps there are no Witches; perhaps your poor father went out for a walk and fell into the sea. It is a simpler explanation, which would seem to be favoured by Occam's Razor."

"Yet the other explanation cannot be ruled out."

"No: I think we have to take that seriously."

"And so there is a chance that my poor father will be sacrificed to the Devil in four days' time, while the local police look the other way."

"A chance, yes."

11

"Then, Mr. Holmes, what you can do is to go there, find him, and save him. Or if I am mistaken, and this Witch-Cult has no existence outside my imagination, I implore you to discover what has happened to my poor father, because I really need to know."

"Very well: I will do my best for you, Miss Tollemache; although sadly at present I am but half a detective, since my other half, Dr. Watson, is temporarily *hors de combat*."

"A Jezail bullet," said Watson, "from the Second Afghan War, was cut to-day from this sore old limb."

"Most unfortunate, Doctor! I wish you a speedy recovery. Yet I am sure that, even without your valuable assistance, Mr. Holmes is still the man best able to deal with this matter."

"I am most gratified by your trust in me. To details, then. How old is your father?"

"Sixty-five."

"Is he in good health?"

"Tolerably, for a man of his years."

"No fits or dizzy spells?"

"Nothing of that kind."

"No mental instability, nor problems with his memory?"

"Absolutely none."

"You have brought a recent photograph?"

"Naturally." She handed it over.

Holmes studied the face: strong and even a little grim in appearance, with downturned mouth, the old clergyman was short-haired and clean-shaven, with few obvious wrinkles, save for the pair that flanked his mouth, and the two beneath his eyes. One's dominant impression was of great intelligence.

"Where was he staying on Trowley?"

"He was renting a cottage on the outskirts of the main town, Cunningsborough. I have brought the address, and a letter of introduction to the landlady, a Mrs. Rendall, who was also serving as my father's housekeeper, though resident elsewhere. She it was who discovered his absence yesterday morning, when she arrived to prepare his breakfast."

"So your father must have vanished on Wednesday night." Holmes paused for a moment, considering the lengthy journey on which he was about to embark. It would involve taking the sleeper-train to Edinburgh to-night; then, to-morrow, a train from that city to Inverness, and another from there to Thurso; a coach-ride to Scrabster, where he should be in time for the evening ferry (at six P. M., he seemed to remember); then, after what would probably be quite a rough crossing, another coach-journey from the port at Storwick to the Island capital.

"If I recall my Bradshaw, I may not hope to be in Cunningsborough much before nine P.M. to-morrow. The hunt may commence no earlier than Sunday morning, by which time the trail will be cold indeed."

"If my theory be correct, Mr. Holmes, you will have three days in which to find my father—and I pray that you will find that time enough."

* * *

13

After Miss Tollemache had returned to her hotel, Holmes donned a top hat and a long black overcoat, and took a hansom down to Piccadilly, where he went into Hatchard's bookshop, just opposite the Royal Academy. The shop was one of his favourite places in London: he liked its decorous, Late Georgian design, the orderly arrangement of its departments, and the sense which one had in there that it was possible, by walking a few steps and reaching out one's hand, to access reliable information about almost any subject in the world. He climbed the beautiful wooden staircase that rose through the centre of the shop, and entered the department that housed books relating to the study of Mankind.

"Have any good scholars written lately on the subject of Witchcraft?" he asked the assistant behind the dark-oak counter. Holmes was fond of this slightly scruffy fellow, Josiah Mercer: clearly an impoverished autodidact whose intelligence and love of knowledge far exceeded his worldly ambition, content to serve as a lowly acolyte in this temple of knowledge. Mercer was in late middle age, fat, pale, and remarkably ugly, with a bald, shaven head, steel-rimmed *pince-nez*, a greying beard of the 'goatee' kind, and a surprisingly benevolent smile.

"There's two that come to mind, sir. A few years ago the President of the Folklore Society, Mr. Gomme, published a book called *Ethnology in Folklore*. There was a fair bit about Witchcraft in that. Mr. Gomme's idea was that it was a hang-over from very ancient times: that it had been the religion of the pre-Aryan people in Europe, which secretly survived the Aryan conquests and persisted until the Middle Ages, or even later, among what you might call the lowest of the low."

14

"What were his sources?"

"Quite diverse, as I recall, sir: modern folk-customs, ancient writings, the customs of the Hindoos and the savages—he makes a great heap of facts, then shows how they all fit together, and finds a pattern in them. It's a bit like solving a puzzle—or what you do in your line of work, sir."

"Yes, the analogy had occurred to me, Joe. That sounds just the sort of thing I need. Do you have it?"

"Yes, sir."

"What's the other one that you mentioned?"

"That's a strange one, sir! Mr. Leland, an American gentleman, has just published a book called *Aradia*, that's supposed to reveal all the secrets of Witchcraft in Italy. He says it was a Pagan Cult that was carried on, among criminals and such, right into the Middle Ages—and even down to the present day, here and there. He says further, that he met a real Witch, who taught him everything she knew about the business—for a price."

"Leland. Yes, I know his work. He was the first scholar to transcribe the Shelta language of the Irish Tinkers, and he wrote a useful account of the customs of the Gypsies. If any man could find a real Witch, and win her trust, I expect that Charles Godfrey Leland would be the man. I should be most interested to read his new book. What are the other gentlemen saying about it?"

"Some like it, sir; others say that it don't seem quite right. Some even say that he might have made it up himself to fit in with his theories."

"And what do you think, Joe?"

15

"A bit of both, sir. Some of it seems all right, and some of it smells kind of fishy. I wouldn't say that Mr. Leland had made anything up, but it seems to me as if the girl who told him most of this stuff wasn't entirely on the level."

"Has he written anything else on this subject?"

"Well, sir, a few years ago, he brought out a book called *Etruscan Roman Remains in Popular Tradition*, and there's quite a bit about Witchcraft in that. The gentlemen thought that one to be a more respectable work of scholarship."

"And you?"

"Oh, it was good, sir, and quite interesting: a lot of stuff about spells and charms and stories that have survived from Pagan times in Italy. But the new one is a view of the Witch-Cult from inside, and that makes it more... *exciting* reading."

"Are you using the word *exciting* as a technical term?"

"Well, to be candid, Mr. Holmes, there is a fair bit of... carnality, in the book. He says they worship in the nude, and have wild orgies once a month. That's perhaps why sales have been a little slow. But no, sir: that wasn't really my meaning.

"I meant *intellectually* exciting. The thing is, if Mr. Leland's right, or even half-right, the Witch-Cult was a proper religion, like Christianity—only different, with a Goddess instead of a God, and a topsy-turvy system of morality. Even if, as some of the gentlemen think, all of this should be nothing but old Mr. Leland's fancy, I still find it entertaining to contemplate, rather in the way of Mr. Nietzsche's late works. But you know that my views are a little... advanced, sir?"

"I always take that into account when considering your recommendations, Joe. In this case you have made another sale. I'll take the *Roman Remains* too. Now, have you anything on Witch-Trials in Trowley? Or indeed on Scotch Witchcraft more generally?"

"Well, there's Sir Walter Scott's old book, of course, sir: *Letters on Dæmonology*, or whatever it's called."

"I read it years ago."

"Oh—another, more recent, comes to mind, sir: *Vestiges of Paganism in the North-East of Scotland*, by Mr. McKay. That has a little about Trowley, I believe."

"Yes; and that will be enough. I shall have only a day to study."

"Would you like these delivered, Mr. Holmes?"

"No: I'll carry them. Just tie them up with some string for me, Joe."

* * *

As Holmes rode back in his hansom, he saw one of the new motor-cars pulling in to the kerb on his right. He found it interesting to observe how these vehicles were ceasing to resemble horseless carriages and taking on a shape of their own. This one, for example, had a little flat-roofed cabin around the driver and his passenger, and a large glass window in front; its red-spoked wheels were much smaller than those of a cart; and its engine was placed in front, under a metal carapace, rather like a head flanked by the two eyes of its headlamps. This was not a mere wagonette with a motor attached, but a vehicle of quite a different species. Such evolution in little more than a decade!

What marvels of progress this nineteenth century had exhibited! And here, in London, he always felt that he was living in the very epicentre of that progress, surrounded as he was by the ever-multiplying proofs of Man's growing mastery over Nature. Mastery over Man's own, primitive Nature, too; for London was proof that people of very different kinds could co-operate in an orderly and rational way for the common good. Of course, even here, in the greatest city on Earth, there were occasional eruptions of primitive Nature, in the form of crime; Holmes had been fighting against it all his life, labouring to purify his city of its pollution.

But now he was to go far beyond the charmed circle of civilization, to a desolate and backward Northern Isle, there to confront, perhaps, a group of people who worshipped the principle of Evil itself, whether in the form of Satan or that of a Pagan Goddess.

To Holmes, both of these figures were equally mythical: in the course of his forty-five years, he had come to believe that all supernatural beings were idols created by men's minds. In general, the deities symbolized various aspects of the real world: thus, as he had learned in school, Venus might stand as a symbolic representation of love, or Mars of warfare. In the same way, the God of Christian civilization, Holmes considered, was a symbolic representation of the values of that civilization; the Devil was the representation of what that civilization most abhorred. Holmes believed in civilization, but he did not believe in God, except as a symbol.

Nor, of course, did he believe in the Devil. He could, however, see that those who did believe in such a being, and worshipped him, would be dangerous foes indeed: like the Thugs of India, they could

18

lie and kill with an easy conscience. Although there might be no literal Devil, such people would certainly be Devils in human shape.

As the great nineteenth century neared its close, Holmes appeared to be going on an adventure in which he would confront Evil in its purest form. He was going to the cold north, in the dark time of the year, and he was going alone. Thoughts of *Beowulf* came to his mind, as he wondered if he might not return from this quest. Well: every man had his time, and there were worse ways to die than sword in hand.

But perhaps this trip was a wild-goose-chase: there might well be no Witches on Trowley, and he, in searching for them, might be playing the part of Don Quixote, tilting at windmills which he mistook for giants. If so, Holmes was going to make a fool of himself in front of the people of Cunningsborough; but as they were a long way off, and without influence in the Metropolis, he did not greatly care. Not even Watson would be present to witness his humiliation. The world would never smile over the story of Sherlock Holmes's ridiculous hunt for non-existent Witches in the dark Northern Isles.

* * *

"Take my service revolver, old chap."

As usual in his interactions with Watson, it was necessary to read a good deal between the lines.

You will still be protecting me, Holmes said, without words, taking the gun and packing it in his suitcase.

"John," he said aloud, looking into Watson's eyes. "Along with my will and all the legal papers, I have left you a private letter, which my solicitor will deliver to you in the case of my death; and you need not open it even then, if you do not wish to do so. It contains nothing of a legal or professional kind, just some material of a personal nature, which may or may not be of interest to you. In either event, I would implore you not to let it survive long in your custody. Read it and burn it, or burn it unread."

"You have my word on it; but I hope that I'll not be seeing that letter any time soon."

"The chances are that there is a perfectly mundane explanation for the disappearance of Mr. Tollemache; and that there have been no Witches on Trowley for a very long time. Either way, I shall put my not inconsiderable talents to the task of ensuring that, by this time next week, I am again seated by my own fire-side, in the comfortable presence of my oldest, dearest friend."

"Amen to that!"

CHAPTER II.

THE MAN IN BLACK.

Holmes liked the idea of the sleeper-train: you went to sleep in one city and awoke in another. In practice the confined space of the little compartment and the motion of the train often made him uncomfortable, and sometimes that discomfort gave rise to nightmares. To-night they were bad enough to wake him; though, in the exasperating way of most dreams, they faded rapidly, and, in a matter of seconds, were beyond his recollection. He lay on his bed in the darkness, somewhere (he estimated) in the West Riding, and could only vaguely recall a few images of a cave, a naked woman, and a crow; and for some reason these recollections were permeated through and through by a feeling of almost unbearable horror.

But at length he managed to fall asleep again; and this time slept fairly soundly, until roused by the knocking of the guard as the train approached Edinburgh.

Holmes dressed his lanky frame in clothes appropriate to travel in Scotland: a tweed suit with an Inverness cape. On his head he put a deerstalker cap, like that in which Mr. Paget had so often drawn him. All of these garments were made from the same tweed: he liked to co-ordinate.

After his ablutions in the station washroom, there was time for a good breakfast in the buffet: porridge, fried eggs and bacon, toast and marmalade, washed down with a cup of strong tea. Thinking that he might not eat again until late in the day, he bought a thick bar of chocolate from a vending-machine on the platform.

Before Holmes boarded the train for Inverness, he slipped the guard half a crown in the hope of ensuring a compartment to himself, and was assured of this, "Sae lang as the ither compertments arenae full, sir!" These first-class carriages were rather agreeable spaces to inhabit, with their dark panelling, red plush seats, and sepia photographs on the walls: the *décor* put one in mind of a gentleman's club. A silent compartment would be an ideal place for Holmes to do his research.

At first it seemed that he was going to have the solitude that he desired; but people kept getting onto the train—and, just before the time of departure, a young man in black, with a cane, a silk-lined cloak, and a top hat, entered the compartment. He took the seat farthest from Holmes, on the opposite side, putting a small hamper on the luggage-rack above it, and laying his hat and stick upon the empty seat next to his own. The two men wished each other a good morning, after which the newcomer sat, closed his eyes, and seemed to fall asleep. That was fine with Holmes, who wanted to get on with his reading; but he couldn't help casting a glance at the handsome young man and making a few deductions about him. He was well-educated, and almost certainly English, from his accent. Rich, even something of a dandy, from his clothes: the well-cut striped trousers and black frock-coat, the brocade waistcoat and the green bow-tie. Judging by his soft collar and his rather long, floppy, dark hair, he was the kind of æsthetic young man who probably fancied himself as a poet—and might even be one, since his face was not that of a fool.

22

Some intuition told Holmes that this gilded youth was no stranger to Uranian practices. Well—no need to pursue that line of thought.

On, then, with his reading. The books that he had bought at Hatchard's lay beside him on the seat. First the little green one, Gomme's *Ethnology in Folklore*. A glance at the index showed him that there were about twenty pages devoted to the subject of Witchcraft. He looked at those first, then read enough of the preceding text to grasp the author's thesis; then he read some more, and read the Witchcraft passages again; and then he formed his judgment.

It seemed quite plausible. Gomme argued that one could distinguish two strata in British folklore: one coming from the aborigines of the Stone Age, and the other from that of a more civilized people, the Aryans, who had conquered them in prehistoric times. The descendents of the conquerors had become the upper classes; the descendents of the aborigines had become the peasantry. These two strata were certainly to be found in India, where Aryans were known to have conquered and subjugated non-Aryans in the second half of the second millennium B.C.; Gomme argued that in Britain, similar causes had produced similar results, at around the same time. He thought that Witchcraft was basically the old religion of the conquered people, which had survived into mediæval times as a secret society.

What Gomme said about Witch-practices was mostly rather grisly, involving the use of human body-parts—either as ritual food, or in ceremonies of magic. From Holmes's time in Tibet, he recalled how certain eccentric yogis had been thought to gain supernatural powers from such practices; the peasants had been really frightened of those

23

men. It was easy to imagine a similar situation in Britain's own dark past.

Gomme said also that Witches made dolls and stuck pins in them, as a ritual of cursing, and that they sold winds to sailors in the form of knotted cords. This sounded credible enough: essentially the same old trick that modern charlatans were still playing with their hocus-pocus and their lucky charms.

More disturbing were the stories of animal victims being torn to pieces alive and eaten raw in non-Aryan rituals. Could such a fate be in store for the Reverend Mr. Tollemache?

Holmes next took up McKay's volume on Scotch folklore. Again, he went first for the references to Witches and Witchcraft. McKay was of the opinion that there had been real Witches, poor folk and criminals mostly, who formed an underground society which held riotous meetings in secret locations. *It would appear*, wrote McKay, *that, a hundred years after the Reformation, a fully organized Cult was still operative in at least some parts of the North-East.* He remarked on the nudity and sexual license which characterized their meetings.

If there were anything religious about this business, it was religiosity of a perverted kind, which involved paying an obscene homage to the naked form of the Devil, or that of Nic-Nevin, *alias* 'The Queen of Elfhame', as the Goddess of the Witches was known in North Britain. This latter figure McKay thought to be perhaps an ancient Goddess of the Underworld, since the dead were often said to reside in her realm, along with the fairies. He seemed to accept the testimony of accused Witches that their Deities used to manifest themselves in physical form at meetings, in order to receive homage; but he offered the rational explanation that real priests and priestesses might actually have impersonated these supernatural beings.

There were a few other passages in the book about Witches, mostly dealing with their spells (again involving body-parts, dolls, and pins); and once with the old Scotch custom of burning a Witch, in effigy, on the night of Hallowe'en, in order to break the power of the Witches in the coming year. Could this, Holmes wondered, have been the origin of the English custom of burning the Guy? McKay had, of course, looked for survivals of the Cult, and found only a few poor, ignorant, solitary women, scraping a living by exploiting popular belief in their supernatural powers. There were no more Sabbat meetings, and never would be again. McKay was happy about this.

Of Trowley, he noted that it had a particularly dark reputation among the Scots, as an Island full of Witches. The actual cases of Trowley Witchcraft that he described had little that was distinctive about them, however, although Holmes did observe that at least one of them seemed to involve the surreptitious administration of poison rather than anything apparently supernatural.

The controversial *Aradia* was the next book to receive his scrutiny. It was a slim black volume, with a delightful illustration on its title-page (designed by Leland himself) of a time-worn Norman doorway, looking like the portal to Fairyland. The text that followed was surprising. Joe Mercer's expression came to mind: this did indeed seem 'topsy-turvy', compared to Christianity. The first twist of the Witches' religion was that their Supreme Deity was female: the old Roman Goddess of wild Nature, Diana, of whom it was here written:

Diana was the first created before all creation; in her were all things; out of herself, the first darkness, she divided herself; into darkness and light she was divided.

Hardly less important was Diana's daughter, the eponymous Aradia: a kind of female Messiah, who had appeared on Earth, long ago, in the form of a beautiful maiden, to teach the ways of Witchcraft to the poor and oppressed. These Italian Witches had worshipped a Dyad instead of a Trinity: instead of the Father, the Son, and the Holy Ghost, they had adored the Mother and the Maiden! Holmes was reminded of the Crow and the Crow's Daughter in the northern tale.

Unlike *Diana*, *Aradia* was not a classical name: Leland suggested a derivation from the Biblical Herodias, wife of Herod and mother of Salome. One might have thought that *Salome* would have been a more appropriate name for the Goddess in her Maiden form; but Holmes recalled that the Bible did not call the dancing-girl by name, and that writers of the Middle Ages had generally referred to both the girl and her mother by the same appellation, *Herodias*; so that probably Leland's etymology was correct, but the Maiden rather than the Mother was meant. How was that for 'topsy-turvy'?—a religion that put Salome in the place of Christ!

Did its veneration of a Biblical character mean that this Witch-Religion was a mediæval (or post-mediæval) invention? Not necessarily: Holmes knew that the Voodoo of the Caribbean had incorporated elements of Christianity into its decidedly Pagan practices, and he considered that mediæval Witchcraft might well have done the same. Perhaps Herodias had been adopted from Christianity in the Middle Ages; or perhaps, as often happened in Voodoo, a

26

Pagan deity had come to be worshipped under a new, Biblical, appellation. He recalled from his schooldays a poem by Horace, describing how the Witches of Ancient Rome had invoked the Goddesses Diana and Proserpina. Could *Aradia* be a new name for Proserpina (*alias* Persephone): the classical Maiden-Goddess and Queen of the Underworld? It seemed very likely. Such a borrowing of a biblical name for an ancient deity did strongly suggest that a real Witch-Cult had survived into the Christian era, still vigorous enough to appropriate and re-imagine an iconic figure of the new religion. The fact that Leland himself seemed not fully to understand the origin of the name *Aradia* spoke for his sincerity: despite what "some of the gentlemen" were saying, the old scholar could hardly have invented all this!

All the same, Holmes was not entirely convinced by the book. If one paid people for information, as he knew to his cost, they sometimes made things up; and much of the material here seemed just the kind of thing that a clever but uneducated woman might fabricate to suit the tastes of the investigator who was paying her. Holmes did not believe that Maddalena herself had been initiated into the hypothetical secret Cult, as her description of its meetings did not ring true where it mattered most, in the details; and, given such unreliability in Leland's main informant, one could not be entirely sure of anything in his book. Taken as a whole, the material in *Aradia* suggested to Holmes that there may have been Goddess-worshipping Witches in Italy at a fairly recent date, but certainly did not prove that there were any there at present. He could see where Leland had gone wrong: the man had a pet theory, and was over-eager to believe

27

evidence that seemed to confirm it. A sad end to the old scholar's career: to be made a fool of by a pretty woman!

* * *

By this time the sun was high in the sky, although rarely visible through the blanket of cloud that lay over Scotland. Rain streaked the windows, sometimes beating noisily, reminding one of the primitive wilderness that lay outside this little capsule of nineteenth-century civilization. As the carriage rattled along, the young man in the corner woke from his slumbers, stretched, and looked around him with interest. His eyes were brown.

"Permit me to introduce myself, sir," he said. "My name is Crowley—Aleister Crowley." It rhymed with *Trowley*.

"Holmes—Sherlock Holmes." They rose to shake hands.

"The famous detective! Well, Mr. Holmes, I am very glad to make your acquaintance! May I invite you to share my humble meal?" He took the hamper down from the luggage-rack and opened it, to reveal (in napkins laid upon a bed of straw) half a dozen rolls, four scotch eggs, four chicken legs, and four cold roast sausages wrapped in bacon. Fastened to the lid was a flask of Chianti.

There were, Holmes noted, two glasses. "It seems that you were expecting my company?"

"One never knows whom one might run into on such a long journey as this. I had no expectation of meeting you in particular, Mr. Holmes, but I did entertain some hopes of an interesting encounter over luncheon, and they have certainly been fulfilled. Let me tell you, sir, I am quite an admirer of yours! I read some of the accounts of your investigations written by your companion, Dr. Watson, when

28

they were published in the *Strand Magazine*; and from those I formed a conception of you as one of the cleverest men alive!"

Holmes laughed and looked down. "Dr. Watson is... a romantic. I am intelligent, certainly; but there are plenty of men whose intellects are equal or even superior to mine. My sole distinction has been to devise a method for finding out the truth, and to apply that method, rigorously."

"You are too modest, I am sure, sir. Pray help yourself to food and drink!"

The food was tempting, and Holmes thought that he would take a little, as was only polite in the circumstances. Both men began to eat, and continued to do so throughout the ensuing conversation.

Crowley swallowed a mouthful of Scotch egg. "It seems from your reading, Mr. Holmes, that at present your search for truth is leading you into territory which may be more familiar to me than it is to you."

"You are a folklorist, Mr. Crowley?"

"No, sir: I am a practitioner of Magic."

"A performer?" It was not out of the question for a stage-magician to be a gentleman; and there was something a little theatrical about Crowley.

"I am speaking, sir, of High Magic, the art of the Magi: the secret science taught by men such as Christian Rosenkreuz and Hermes Trismegistus. I am an initiate of an ancient fraternity, whose purpose is to preserve and cultivate that primordial wisdom. You may think of us as Guardians of the Grail."

Holmes was not as surprised as Crowley would have liked him to be. It was fairly well known that a few occult societies were operating in London's West End. Holmes had always considered them as a genteel kind of racket, in which wealthy young people and spinsters of a certain age paid charlatans large sums of money, and in return had their heads filled with silly, old-fashioned ideas about such pseudo-sciences as astrology, alchemy, and the Kabbalah—or even wilder nonsense, supposedly from the East. The lure in all this was the promise of supernatural powers, but somehow these never seemed to manifest themselves in the real world. Crowley had fallen somewhat in Holmes's estimation.

"I've read about those old wizards, and the miracles that they used to perform. Can you do anything like that, Mr. Crowley? Could you, say, turn my sausage into gold, or levitate this wine-glass? No? Then how about conjuring spirits? Could you summon up great Cæsar's ghost and have him sit with us here and talk Latin?"

"Such an operation would require solitude, fasting, and extreme concentration."

"The very same circumstances that might incline some men to hallucinate, in fact! Do you have personal experience of that operation?"

"Yes, I have performed it many times."

"And have you seen spirits?"

"Yes."

"Did you see them as you are seeing me now, with your physical eyes, or in your mind's eye?"

"The latter... mostly. Well—entirely, if I'm honest. But what's seen in the mind's eye can seem very real; and I certainly wasn't consciously imagining these beings. It seemed as if I were perceiving them, using something other than my physical senses."

"What kind of spirits are we talking about, exactly: ghosts, demons, angels, fairies—djinn?"

"All of them, and more: Enochian spirits, for example, and elementals."

"Did they have anything of consequence to communicate: anything that might make a reasonable man conclude that they were not mere phantoms of your brain?"

"A great deal that was of consequence to me, Mr. Holmes, though mostly of a personal nature, about my spiritual quest. But that is the only thing in which I'm really interested, and so it's the only topic upon which I enquire."

"You have never been tempted to ask for racing tips, or other useful information about the real world?"

"Look at me, Mr. Holmes! Do you think that I give a fig about such things? I am rich enough to do anything that I want for the rest of my life; and I find that, deep down, all that I really desire is spiritual attainment. I have just acquired a house in the Highlands, for the purpose of performing a mediæval ritual of High Magic, from the Book of Abra-Melin the Mage. Very few men have ever had the money, the time, or the dedication to do this. It will cost me six months of abstinence and prayer, but by the end of it I should have achieved the Knowledge and Conversation of my Holy Guardian Angel, and then, according to the Book of Abra-Melin, I shall have the power to work miracles of the kind that you requested from me—

and greater ones, too, should I choose to. I shall be a kind of living saint, or living God, if you like."

"A powerful ritual indeed; and yet you say that few men have ever performed it. What happened to the others?"

"History does not record their deeds. I suppose that some of them may have been the great wonder-workers of yore: men such as Apollonius of Tyana, Merlin, or Count Cagliostro. Perhaps even Christ himself."

"So what proof have you that this process will work?"

"I am choosing to accept Abra-Melin as my *guru* for the time that is necessary to give his method a fair trial. Some things one has to take on trust, until experience confirms them."

"...or fails to."

"Yes: agreed. You know, Mr. Holmes, when I was a little boy, my father told me about the noxious properties of nettles, and how they had to be avoided during our country walks. He asked me, 'Will you take my word for it, or will you find out through your own experience?'—and I chose the latter. I dived head-first into the nettle-patch, and came out stinging all over. But I never was stung by a nettle again. That's how I am, sir: I have to try things. So, yes, you may be right. Perhaps next year I shall discover that the long ritual has accomplished nothing, and then I shall very probably revert to being an atheistical Materialist in the manner of the Baron D'Holbach; but for now I am giving the magical interpretation of reality a trial. And perhaps it will work for me."

They smiled at each other. Holmes had no doubt that the year 1900 would see Crowley's hopes in this matter disappointed; but, although the young man might be mistaken, he was certainly not irrational.

"I believe that you are the first wizard whom I have ever met socially, Mr. Crowley. You said that my reading-matter was more your kind of thing than it was mine, didn't you? So, tell me, what can a wizard teach me about Witchcraft?"

"My understanding, as an initiate, is that in most ways it was the opposite of High Magic, although it utilized some of the same techniques."

"The opposite: how?"

"The aim of the White Magician is to transcend the earthly and the physical: to become Godlike, through self-discipline, contemplation, and decorous ritual. The way of the Witch, as I understand it, was to annihilate the ego through a combination of horrifying experiences and bestial pleasures: using obscene rites to merge with sub-human Nature. In India, the Brethren of the Left-Hand Path follow a similar course even to this very day. Instead of God, they adore Nature in the form of the terrible Demon-Goddess Kali, who dances naked, carrying a man's severed head. Sex and Death, Mr. Holmes, Sex and Death: that which the Saints of all religions shun, the Witch adores!"

Holmes remembered the ruthless, seductive Salome, whose memory had lately proved so attractive to the decadent writers, like Huysmans and Wilde; and he thought that he could understand why Italian Witches called their Dark Goddess by the name of *Aradia*.

"That fits rather well," said Holmes, "with what I have already learnt; and inspires a conjecture as to what happened in the rituals of

33

the Witches. My intuition tells me that when they slew a man in sacrifice, their priestess would dance naked with his head, impersonating their Demon-Goddess, and receiving adoration from the other Witches as the very embodiment of the ambivalent power of Nature!"

"That has the ring of truth to me, sir! I can almost see her dancing so as you say it: the blood bright beneath her dainty feet!"

He looked rapt, unmistakably adoring. Holmes had learnt something about Crowley which, he suspected, was not yet clear to the young man himself: part of him was powerfully attracted to the Dark Side. Holmes could imagine Crowley falling from his holy quest and joining in the bestial rites of the Witches. But, of course, everyone had a dark side—even Holmes himself! This beautiful young Lucifer had not yet fallen, and might never do so.

But—whispered the voice of suspicion—might Crowley not have fallen already? Might he not be actually a Witch, or an agent of the Witches, sent here for some nefarious purpose? Could it be mere coincidence that had brought this young wizard into the carriage of a man on a quest for Witches?

"Do you mind if I smoke?" Holmes asked, opening his silver case and taking out one of Sullivan & Powell's Turkish cigarettes. He had purchased a box of a hundred in the Burlington Arcade after his visit to Hatchard's.

"It doesn't bother me in the slightest, sir. In fact, could I have one? Thank you so much!"

"It is one of my idiosyncrasies, Mr. Crowley, that I like to smoke in silence. I find that if I converse I lose all the pleasure of my cigarette.

34

A wise man from the East once told me: 'When walking, only walk; when drinking, only drink'. For my own part I would certainly add, 'When smoking, only smoke.' I find that one cigarette enjoyed mindfully is more satisfying than a dozen consumed inattentively. May I ask you to respect my oddity in this?"

"By all means: I shall gladly join you in your smoking-meditation, sir. We shall blaze away like two Bodhisattvas, sharing the bliss of the Sullivan: *Sullivananda*, as one might say!"

They both laughed at the little joke—mostly because they knew that few people would have been sufficiently learned to appreciate it.

Although Holmes did derive some pleasure from the exquisite cigarette, he did so rather absently, as he continued to consider the possibility of Crowley's being in league with the Witches of Trowley. He saw some strong objections to the idea. If there were Witches on that Island, they were probably ignorant peasants of the lowest order: hardly the kind of people with whom a fastidious young gentleman like Crowley would mix. Nor would such humble folk have had any way of knowing that Holmes had been hired to investigate them, let alone what train he was travelling on—unless, of course, they really did possess supernatural powers. And he was not ready to believe that. Crowley's talk about 'High Magic' had seemed sincere enough, if a little wrong-headed. In all probability the young man was exactly what he seemed to be: an aspiring White Magician. He was actually proving to be quite an interesting informant. Holmes could imagine a bright future for the boy, once he had seen through all this mediæval nonsense about magic and angels.

"So," said Holmes, as they stubbed out their Sullivans, "you have told me how Witchcraft differs from High Magic. What are their similarities?"

"Well, I have heard that the Witches used geometrical designs, involving crosses, stars, triangles and circles, rather like the pentacles of High Magic; but that they used them in a different way. I believe that one part of their use was to mark out places of sacrifice: the victim's blood was spilt onto the design."

"The Voodooists of the Caribbean have a similar custom. *Vévés*, they call such patterns there."

"Do you know much of Voodoo, sir?"

"I am not entirely unacquainted with the mysteries of the *obeah* and the *wanga*," said Holmes, and chuckled. "Perhaps we may speak of such things later—for I gather that you are going all the way to Inverness. But for the moment I should prefer that we talk about Witchcraft, a subject upon which your knowledge could prove useful to me."

"Well, then—another point of similarity is that the Witches used ritual as a way of achieving altered states of consciousness. Their rituals, like ours, involved chanting incantations in an unknown tongue, and the performance of certain symbolic actions—most importantly, eating or drinking, as a sacrament to make the celebrant one with a deity. We White Magicians dance, sometimes, but Witches danced a great deal. Our dances are slow and dignified, while theirs were riotous and lewd.

"And I've always understood that when the old stories talk about Witches leaving their bodies and flying through the air, what they

36

really mean is something like what my Order calls 'travelling in the spirit vision' or 'astral projection'. That's really a form of meditation, in which one induces a light trance-state and goes on an intense imaginary journey, sometimes flying through space, sometimes conversing with deities and fantastic beings. As I said about conjuring up spirits, what one sees, one sees in the mind, but it feels like perception rather than imagination. I understand that Witches often used certain drugs to induce a deeper trance. The book of Abra-Melin tells of its author's encounter with a Witch in fifteenth-century Germany. She used a narcotic salve so powerful that the experiences which it induced were as vivid as those of real life; but her visions of distant places and people turned out to be false, based on fancy rather than experience. Later Witches of whom I've read used the same kind of salve so that they could more vividly imagine themselves engaging in imaginary debauches—quite an addictive activity, by all accounts. We use the technique for spiritual advancement, but for them it served as an escape from reality."

"Do you believe that Witches had any real supernatural powers?"

"I think not. According to the teachings of my Order, the best that they could accomplish in that line was but an illusion. Reason would suggest that the fear of bewitchment might be enough to kill some suggestible people; and that perhaps some Witches knew the secrets of hypnosis, which can be used both to cure and to curse."

"...and to make people see things that are not really there! Yes! Such a supposition might account for the widespread fear of the Evil Eye, as well, if its origin were the rational dread that a man might feel for the gaze of a hypnotist. Well, I shall be safe from that, at least: experience has proved that I cannot be hypnotized."

"Am I to understand, Mr. Holmes, that you expect to be encountering Witches?"

"Strange as it may seem, I think that I may meet some very soon."

"What—here in Scotland?"

"Upon one of the Northern Isles."

Crowley smiled. "I'd guess that would be Trowley."

"Do you know of any survival of the cult there?"

"Not really, sir. I was just thinking of the reputation that the Island has among the common people on my estate. I've seen my ghillie turn down a friendly woman's advances because she came from Trowley; and when I asked him about it, he said it was a well-known fact that most of the women up there were Witches."

"Perhaps they were, long ago. The research of the Reverend Mr. Tollemache would suggest that in the Dark Ages the Island was ruled by a real Witch-Queen, who appears to have been as diligent in the promotion of her religion as was King Ahab's bride in the Land of Israel. So perhaps the whole Island did once bow the knee to Astarte, or Nic-Nevin, or whatever the Demon-Goddess's name was in that time and place. But this northern Jezebel's reign was brief, and came to a terrible conclusion."

"Was the lady eaten by dogs?" asked Crowley, looking strangely interested.

"Eating came into it, but it was worse than that. According to Mr. Tollemache, the Witch-Queen of Trowley was tricked into devouring the flesh of her own murdered daughter, and then told what she had eaten; after which they killed her too."

Crowley took in a sharp, audible breath. "Like Tamora, in *Titus Andronicus*."

"Yes, or the Greek story of Thyestes; but I have heard of such cases in real life, too. If one is perfectly ruthless, and one wishes to cause extreme grief to the parent of a beloved child, it is an obvious course to follow."

"What a horrible end! The lady has my sympathies, no matter what her crimes: such a thing shouldn't happen to anyone. Didn't poor Oscar say something to the effect that, when one reads history, one is appalled not so much by the crimes of the wicked as by the punishments inflicted upon them by the righteous?"

"Yes; and I know what he meant, of course: I too have the sensibilities of a modern, civilized man. Yet, without such distressing severity in ages past, the development of our civilization might not have been possible. In the case of Trowley, even the terrible death of the Queen, and the subsequent slaughter of her most devoted followers, were not enough to destroy the evil Cult that she had founded there; more lenient methods could scarcely have been expected to succeed."

"You believe that the Cult survives there to this day?"

"I think it possible. Mr. Tollemache certainly came to think so, during the last days that he spent on the Island before his disappearance. His daughter believes that the Witches have taken this venerable scholar, with the intention of sacrificing him at their Hallowe'en ceremony; and she has engaged me to rescue him."

39

"I cannot help but think it odd that you would venture on such a potentially dangerous mission alone."

"Alas, Dr. Watson is currently indisposed; but, although the Trowley Police appear to be both indolent and complacent, I am sure that they will give me as much assistance as I need, should there prove to be a real crime that needs investigation. The British Bobby is not the most imaginative of men, but he is generally a stout fellow at heart. One can hardly blame him for not taking seriously an allegation of Witchcraft at the end of the nineteenth century!"

"I suppose not," said Crowley. He drew an inch of bright steel from his cane, showing that it was a sword-stick, with a long, rapier-like blade concealed inside the black wood. "But should you require the assistance of one who understands such things, Mr. Holmes, my sword is at your command!"

CHAPTER III.
THE ISLE OF WITCHES.

"I hardly know what to say, Mr. Crowley. It is certainly an honourable offer, but I am uncertain whether I may honourably accept it. I wonder whether Dr. Watson's stories may not have given you a romantic view of my work. In reality, it can be more difficult, more tedious, and often more dangerous than one might expect from reading of my adventures in the *Strand*. For example: if there really are Witches on Trowley, they are quite likely to seek to eliminate anyone, such as Mr. Tollemache or myself, who is endeavouring to expose them; and so, if you assist me in this investigation, you may actually *die*."

"Death holds no terrors for me, sir. My mother raised me to be a timorous lad, but over the last decade I have trained myself to be brave, by doing all the things that I most feared. I have climbed mountains, and stared death in the face many times. He and I are old acquaintances. And, if the teachings of my Order be correct, I am an eternal spirit in a fleshly casing, and so death is nothing to fear; indeed, to perish in a noble cause may be greatly to my benefit in a future existence."

"I know too much about the brain to believe in the spirit. Every new discovery in the field of neurology makes me more certain that we human beings are merely intricate machines of tissue and bone, for whom death is the final end. So to be responsible for the extinction of a young life, full of promise, would lie heavy on my conscience."

"Let us grant, for the sake of argument, that the Materialist conclusion be correct—still, every finite existence must have a termination, and to go down fighting is as good a way as any for an English gentleman to make his exit from the world! Many young men of my age have been cut down this year in Africa, giving their lives in the endless battle between our civilization and those who would seek to undermine it. Should I show less courage than the 'Soldiers of the Queen'? To take that risk is part of what it means to be a man, is it not, sir?"

"Hmm," said Holmes, and nodded. "You have no experience of this kind of work, I suppose?"

"No; but I am intelligent, and willing to obey your orders without question."

"That counts for a great deal, believe me. There is, however, the delicate matter of confidentiality. My client engaged me in this case; she did not engage you."

Crowley raised his right hand, as if in a courtroom. "I give you my solemn oath on all that I hold sacred, and (what is more) my word as a gentleman, that I would reveal nothing which I might learn in the course of this investigation to anyone whatsoever, unless you should specifically instruct me to do so."

Holmes considered. Reason counselled that he accept this offer, yet on some deep level it felt wrong to him—as if it were an act of infidelity to put this handsome youth in Watson's place. On the other hand, he was sure that John would want nothing more than his safe return, and Crowley's assistance could make that more likely. It seemed best to acquiesce, for the present at least; if things did not work out, he could always send the young man away.

"Well, then: it is agreed. I thank you, Mr. Crowley."

* * *

The rest of their journey passed fairly smoothly. In Inverness, Crowley purchased a carpet-bag and some necessary items, and sent a telegram to his servants telling them that he would be away for a few days; then the two gentlemen took the north-bound train to Thurso— a town of which they saw little, since it was already pitch-dark when they arrived. A carriage-ride took them to the ferry-port, and a sturdy little steam-ship bore them further northward for a couple of hours across the rain-lashed seas to Storwick.

It was shortly after eight when they walked off the pier, tired and hungry. It was like leaving a train at a rural station, with porters, a fence, and a guard at the gate. A row of carriages stood outside.

"Is there anywhere that we might dine before we take a carriage to Cunningsborough?" Holmes enquired of the guard on the way out.

"Aye, sir: yonder!" He indicated the painted window of a shop selling "FISH & CHIPS" on the waterfront. The writing had been done in a rather elegant *Art Nouveau* script, with ornamental flourishes. Holmes was delighted to see what looked like a fragment of the great Metropolis so far from home. The shop's interior was a whitewashed room lit by a couple of oil-lamps on brackets. The room was divided by a low counter, behind which a cauldron of hot fat bubbled over an open fire, in a wide, vaguely mediæval fireplace. A pretty, dark-haired, young woman, with big brown eyes and a lilting accent, took their orders and their sixpences, and served their meals in folded newspaper. Holmes showed Crowley how to sprinkle salt and vinegar over the food before taking it over to a shelf at the side of the room, where they ate standing up. This local version of the dish was as good as any that Holmes had eaten in London, even in the excellent fish-restaurants of Mr. Isaacs: tender cod in a crunchy batter, and thick chips, fried golden-brown on the outside but white and fluffy within. Such fare was new to Crowley.

"By Jove, sir! I've paid five shillings for a meal and not enjoyed it half so much!"

And back he went for another portion of chips; although Holmes suspected that this was done partly in order to flirt with the serving-girl. From her looks and her shy smiles she seemed charmed by the smart young gentleman's attention.

* * *

"That girl in the chip-shop," said Holmes, as their carriage rumbled through the night "—do you plan to see her again?"

"I don't know, sir. I rather enjoy flirtation for its own sake, regardless of the consequences. In this case, it's certainly possible that I might come back, some time, and attempt to take our acquaintance to a deeper level. She was quite a stunner."

"But what future could there be in such a relationship?"

"Probably not a long one, but—I should hope—one which would be extremely pleasurable for both of us. I should take care to leave her in no worse case than that in which I found her."

"Hmm."

44

"Do I detect a note of disapproval, Mr. Holmes? Perhaps it's a generational difference: I know that twenty or thirty years ago the fashion was to pretend that no one ever engaged in sexual activity of any kind. My generation may speak more frankly, but I don't believe that we fornicate any more than young men have ever done.

"It seems to me, sir, that sexual desire is part of Human Nature—as natural as hunger and thirst. We cannot abolish it, and so we must seek to gratify it in a civilized way. If I were to take that girl by violence, to seduce her with false promises, or to make her pregnant and desert her, I should rightly be considered as a scoundrel; but if the two of us should merely give each other a great deal of pleasure, and do each other no harm, what is there in that transaction to which any reasonable man might object?"

"Such a liberal attitude seems strangely at odds with your spiritual aspirations. Did you not tell me that the Operation of Abra-Melin requires strict continence?"

"Indeed it does, as part of the method necessary to produce a particular result. If one wishes to swim the Channel, one follows a certain training-*régime*; to climb the Matterhorn one follows another. To attain the Knowledge and Conversation of one's Holy Guardian Angel, apparently, one needs to be chaste. I shall find that the hardest part of the Operation, to be sure—but as yet I haven't begun it."

"So you may pray with St. Augustine: *Domine, da mihi castitatem et continentiam, sed noli modo!*"

They laughed together.

"Do you not consider the sexual impulse as something which we must subdue in order to be fully civilized?"

45

"No more than we must subdue our appetite for food, sir. A civilization which abandoned either of those pleasures would soon become extinct. I grant you that for certain men, seeking to achieve certain goals, it may sometimes be better to be celibate, or to go hungry. For most of us, however, sex is a necessary part of life; and the only question is, whether a man's sex-life shall be something befitting to a gentleman or to a brute. What we must rise above, I think, is not sex but brutishness, in all its forms."

"I have always tended to see the sexual act as rather a brutish thing in itself."

"How sad! That means you never did it properly. It really can be the most exquisite pleasure—better even than Wagner!"

"Perhaps. But I think that there are some who are cut out for other things than intimacy: men to whom the pleasures of love must always seem less interesting than the resolution of certain intricate problems—in Higher Mathematics, say, or in Strategy. I'm thinking of such men as Newton, or Kant—the younger Pitt, or Dr. Watson's hero, Gordon of Khartoum. Such men remained celibate because they had other work to do: work that came more naturally to their unusual brains than the work of building and maintaining an intimate relationship.

"The more intelligent Yogis and Dervishes whom I observed in the East were men of this type. Of course, for want of science, those Holy Men had none but theological questions to contemplate; but that was all they needed to keep them happily engaged for years, contemplating the precise meaning of Emptiness or the absolute transcendence of Allah!

"Here in the West, too, many of our sages have been men of a similar kind; and no doubt you have divined that another example of the type is riding with you in this carriage. Insofar as sexual desire is a factor in the lives of such men, it is what it was for St. Anthony: something which they are obliged to overcome, if they are to achieve their *telos*. We are not all made alike, Mr. Crowley. As Blake says, *One Law for the Lion and the Ox is Oppression.*"

"Indubitably, sir. *And Wisdom is justified of all her children.*"

* * *

As the carriage rolled into Cunningsborough, it drew alongside a group of smartly-dressed young men and women standing on a corner beneath the bright lantern that hung outside a public house. As the carriage paused there, waiting for another vehicle to pass, Holmes's eyes were drawn to one of the group: a young lady with a mass of the most glorious auburn hair. She wore it up, of course, as a grown woman had to do, in public; it was partially covered by a low-crowned, flat-brimmed hat, with a long hat-pin. Her face was pale, and perfectly proportioned, with a small, rather aquiline nose, and delicately curved, coral-pink lips; her slender, black-robed figure was the very quintessence of elegant femininity. The greatest of her charms, however, lay in her bold, intelligent eyes. She looked into the carriage, and met Holmes's gaze; and she smiled at him. He felt as though he'd taken a hit of some powerful drug: the effect was highly pleasurable, but rather unsettling. Not since his last encounter with Irene, nearly a decade earlier, had a woman affected him in such a way.

The carriage moved on, into the darkness, and Crowley murmured: "There was a face Rossetti should have painted!"

"I'd have thought that Klimt would have been the man to do justice to her."

"You're right, of course: I'd pay good money to see that. You are not insensible to female beauty, then, Mr. Holmes?"

"I enjoy looking at all beautiful things. Desire does not come into it, for me; at least not generally."

"The late Miss Adler?"

"Yes; but there are things of which one does not speak. I think that you understand me, Mr. Crowley."

"Of course. Please forgive my presumption."

"Absolutely."

The carriage stopped. The driver dismounted, to let down the steps and open the door for his distinguished passengers.

The Royal Hotel was a fairly modern building, in an austere Scotch version of the French Renaissance style, with twin towers. The *décor* inside was mid-Victorian: there were oil-lamps, carpets on the floor, and heavy, dark furnishings. The desk would not have looked out of place at a similar establishment in London, and the desk-clerk spoke the Queen's English—or something very close to it. There was no problem about finding a room for Mr. Crowley, as no other guests were currently in residence. Both gentlemen being tired, they went straight to their separate rooms, and soon fell fast asleep.

* * *

Holmes went out for a walk before breakfast, trying to get his bearings in the town. He was again dressed in his tweeds. In the

48

morning twilight there was no rain, although one could tell that it was coming.

The Hotel stood on the seafront, facing the north, and the modern stone-walled harbour which was the home of the fishing-fleet, and the place from which boats sailed to the more northerly Islands—and also to Norway, the Scandinavian Kingdom of which these islands had once formed part.

To the west there extended a narrow embankment of earth and stone, stretching almost completely across the bay, and separating the wild ocean from the large body of more placid water which the locals referred to as the 'Little Sea'. A road of sorts led along the top of the embankment to what looked like a corn-mill at the far end. It seemed a sensible idea to make use of the power of the water in that narrow channel, Holmes thought; although the mill would need a wheel that worked in both directions, because of the changing tides.

The 'Little Sea' must have been the original harbour, back in the Viking Age. He wondered if the embankment had been built by the Norsemen. Although his geology was limited, he thought that it looked rather like a natural formation: perhaps the remnant of an ancient lake-shore. So the Vikings, or the Picts before them, might have cut the channel over there and connected the sea with the lake, thus forming the original harbour. Ingenious!

The Old Town, lying to the south of the new harbour and the east of the 'Little Sea', looked as if it had been planned along Scandinavian lines, but executed using local techniques and materials: a long, twisting thoroughfare of simple, slate-roofed stone houses, aligned with their gables facing the street. Behind the houses were long yards and vegetable-gardens. The most remarkable buildings in the Old Town were the impressive Romanesque Cathedral and a couple of ruined palaces, which must once have rivalled it in splendour.

The other places of worship were two mean buildings erected by rival Calvinist sects, and a tawdry Romish church. There were quite a number of modern, brick-built houses: the more imposing dwellings congregated in an extension to the east of the Old Town, the poorer housing to the south. Most of the public buildings were of recent construction, built in a plain, respectable Victorian style which would not have looked out of place anywhere in the Empire. On Holmes's ramble he observed a small Police Station, a Town Hall, a Masonic Lodge, and (sole example of the Gothic Revival) a large educational establishment, the Borough School. This lay in the south-eastern quarter of the town, on the road that led to the infamous Gallows Hill, on whose summit so many supposed Witches had been burnt alive. The juxtaposition of modern civilization and fairly recent barbarism was a little uneasy.

The little town felt to Holmes like an Outpost of Empire: a place in which a thin veneer of Britishness had been superimposed on something wilder and more ancient. The locals spoke such a strange, archaic dialect that it was hard to understand them; and they seemed wary of strangers. A Dane, thought Holmes, must feel like this when he visits Iceland.

* * *

"What shall we do to-day?" asked Crowley, over a plate of excellent kedgeree.

Holmes looked out of the window. "I'd say that we should purchase umbrellas, if I thought that such a transaction were possible in this Calvinist land on a Sunday! But perhaps the Hotel may be able to provide us with something.

"Apart from that, our first task will be to see Mrs. Rendall, and to inspect the cottage where Mr. Tollemache was staying; we may find clues there which the Bobbies have overlooked. We shall have to speak to those gentlemen, too. I shall also attempt to arrange an interview with the local antiquarian, a Mr. Brown. It seems probable that these enquiries will produce some leads for us to follow."

"Might it not be better to go among the common people and seek for rumours of Witchcraft?"

"I think not. Mr. Tollemache went among the common people and found no one willing to tell him anything, so far as we can tell, although it seems that he may have alerted the Witches to the potential danger of his presence. We may be driven to follow such a course if nothing comes of our initial enquiries—but not to-day, I think."

* * *

Mrs. Rendall was small, very old, and as wrinkled as a walnut. As a sign of her widowhood she was dressed completely in black, from her simple head-scarf to her high-heeled boots: the very stereotype of a Witch, thought Holmes, were it not for her obvious simplicity and goodness. The cottage to which she led them lay a little to the north-east of Cunningsborough, at no great distance from the Island's eastern coast. She carried an umbrella of her own, while the

51

investigators shared a large one loaned to them by the obliging desk-clerk; Crowley held it.

"Mr. Tollemache's daughter believes that he may have been abducted by a band of Witches," said Holmes. "What do you think of that idea?"

"Och, I niver haard o' sic a ting! Mair likely da pør gen'leman went oot for a waak o'er yonder, bi' da sea, an' tummel'd doon. A gust o' wind'll easy catch a body unawares—an' if dare's naebody aboot tae hilp a man, he'll nae live lang i' da caald sea."

It seemed to Holmes that most of the Islanders sounded rather like Swedes or Norwegians who had learnt to speak fluent English, of a sort, in the Lowlands of Scotland, but still retained the accent of their native tongue. Of course, the ancestors of these people had spoken Old Norse, a few centuries earlier. He wondered if local accents elsewhere might preserve the sonority of long-dead ancient languages. Might an Irishman hear the sound of Pictish in the Gaelic of the Highlands, as an Englishman heard the sound of Norse in this Island's speech?

The muddy track that led to the cottage did indeed continue along to the coast. He planned to explore that later; but now they had reached the gate of the cottage, and he paused to pay close attention to the footprints on its flag-stoned path. Although the rain had blurred them somewhat, his expert eye could still discern a number of interesting features.

"Observe, Mr. Crowley. The prints there seem plainly to be those of a Policeman's boot, like those which our London Bobbies wear—and there is the same pattern, but in a slightly larger size. At least two

Policemen came and went here, going back and forth more than once. Well—nothing surprising in that, since we know that the Trowley Constabulary have been conducting an investigation of their own! Here we see prints which match those of Mrs. Rendall's high-heeled boots—and there some others, made by a gentleman's galoshes, which a process of elimination would suggest must be the track of Mr. Tollemache himself. You will observe how his track is clearer going into the house than coming out; which suggests to me that he went inside, removed his galoshes, and left them for a while, before putting them on again to come out: the mud having dried a little in the interval."

"Amazing! Had you not pointed these things out to me I should never have seen them."

"What interests me most is what we do not see."

"Whatever can you mean?"

"There are no other tracks than these; and so no tracks which might be those of Witches, come to abduct Mr. Tollemache."

"And so, perhaps, there were no Witches, and no abduction."

"Perhaps. It does look rather as if the old gentleman went out of his own free will. Let us see inside, Mrs. Rendall!"

The cottage was of primitive construction, with walls of stone, plastered and white-washed, and a thatched roof covered with a network of rope and heavy stones—to keep the thatch from blowing away, Holmes supposed. But the windows, although small, were properly glazed; and, inside, some effort had been taken to make the place comfortable. The parlour, which they entered first, held two upholstered, spoon-backed chairs and a writing-desk with an old dining-chair drawn up to it. There was a large oil-lamp on a stand, a rug of vaguely oriental design in front of the fireplace, and a framed reproduction of Landseer's *Monarch of the Glen* hanging on the white-washed wall above.

"Dis was mi' bridder's hoose, lang syne. Noo I mak' a few shillin's bi' lettin' it oot tae da gen'le-folk at come tae see da sihts o' Trowley: dat's why it looks sae bonny, ben."

"Indeed," said Holmes, "you have furnished it most elegantly, given the means at your disposal."

He crossed to the desk, looking through its drawers and finding nothing of importance. The large sheet of blotting-paper that lay on the writing-surface, however, was of considerable interest to him. Deciphering the inky traces would be a long job, but they clearly formed the blurred reflexion of a letter that had been written quickly on a single sheet of foolscap paper. It was a much briefer epistle than either of the two that Miss Tollemache had given him; and, because of the speed of its composition, the whole page had still been fairly damp when it was blotted. He thought that he could discern the traces of the familiar salutation: *My Darling Emily*. So here was a message which had not reached its addressee. Good: if someone had thought the letter worth suppressing, the chances were that it would contain some useful information. He folded the sheet up and placed it carefully in his wallet, for further study at the Hotel.

That was about all that he could find in the way of clues, however. The notebook in which Mr. Tollemache must have written up his research was conspicuous only by its absence; and all that could be divined from the Reverend gentleman's belongings was that he had been planning an imminent departure, as almost all of them had been packed in his Gladstone bag. If Mr. Tollemache had left here of his own free will, he must have thought that he would return before morning, as he had left his razor and his toothbrush ready for use on the wash-stand. The faint footprints of the Policemen were visible in every room, so it seemed that they had made a thorough search. Perhaps they had removed anything of interest, or perhaps there had been nothing for them to take. Anyway, there seemed to be nothing more to be gained by lingering in this place. Holmes thanked the good old woman, and gave her half a sovereign for her trouble. Her gratitude was pretty to see.

"If dare's anyting mair at I can do for yi', while yi're on wør Island, Mr. Holmes, I'm at yør service!"

"Well—since you mention it, Madam, the most helpful thing that you could do for us at the moment would be to tell us what you know of Witchcraft here, and tell us where we might find an actual Witch, if we should wish to speak to one."

"Och! Dare's nae sic a ting on Trowley. Lang syne, afore my time, dare were monny, I've haard. Day were folk at didnae follow da true religion, an' wroht aa' manner o' mischief tae Christian folk wi' dare Godless charms an' spells. Wicked tings day did, in dare meetin's; tings at a gød Christian woman sødnae even taak aboot. Bit dare's nae Witches on Trowley da noo. We burned da maist part o' dem, an' da rest deed as idder folk dee, an' noo dare's nane."

* * *

Holmes and Crowley followed the muddy track that led to the coast. To their right and their left lay a flat landscape, divided into small fields by dry-stone walls; but there was little to be seen of either crops or beasts at this time of year. Although the track was well-trodden, here and there it was possible to make out a point of interest.

"See the distinctive marks of the Policemen's boots—and there the prints of Mr. Tollemache. What do you notice about them, Mr. Crowley?"

"They all go one way."

"Very good! It looks as though Mr. Tollemache went down to the coast, and did not return."

"And nor, surprisingly, did the Policemen!"

"You are right: that is something of a puzzle. But we may find an explanation further along."

They walked in silence for a few paces, then Crowley said:

"Are not those the prints of Mrs. Rendall?"

"They're very similar, but I'm not sure. It's a common style of ladies' boot. On the other hand, Mrs. Rendall's feet are unusually small, and those are about the same size. But whoever made these prints was moving quickly, almost running—and I can't imagine the good old woman being quite so nimble on her feet."

"Your powers of deduction amaze me, Mr. Holmes! But if that's another woman's print, must we not ask whether some of the prints which we took to be those of Mrs. Rendall, at the cottage, were not rather those of this other? Might not this swift-footed 'Atalanta' be the Witch who was invisible to us before?"

"A good question indeed! These prints are not clear enough for me to be able to determine any significant differences between the two pairs of shoes, and so the answer must be that I cannot tell. Your

'Atalanta' must be under suspicion—although I suspect that she may be no more than a high-spirited maiden, skipping innocently in her play, and having no connexion to the disappearance of Mr. Tollemache."

The edge of Trowley was unspectacular, here at least: the land just stopped, falling steeply away in a near-perpendicular cliff. The fall into the sea was not, Holmes thought, enough by itself to kill a man; but, as Mrs. Rendall had said, no one could live long in those cold waters. The path split into two, going north and south along the coast. The sea broke against the shore, and gulls called above.

He looked for Mr. Tollemache's track, and found it going south— but not for very long. After a few yards it seemed to disappear; although such was the state of the path that one could not be sure that the footprints had not been obliterated by others. The prints of the Constables' boots, however, continued to be visible after those of the folklorist had apparently ceased. If anything, they seemed a little deeper and clearer than before. The feminine tracks of 'Atalanta' were still in places detectable, too. At the point where Mr. Tollemache's footprints ceased, there was a patch of disturbed mud.

"Was this the place where the Reverend gentleman fell into the sea?" asked Crowley.

"Such a hypothesis seems highly plausible."

"One has to wonder whither he was bound, and for what purpose."

"Perhaps he had the same destination as the two Policemen."

"Or that of 'Atalanta'?"

"Let us see where they were going."

The Policemen's tracks continued south for a good way, then turned west, inland, along a less-used path leading to a large, walled garden. They were not the only tracks on this path, but they were certainly the clearest and the most recent. Still: here and there, and half-effaced by rain, one could discern the tracks of 'Atalanta', and of at least one other female pedestrian. The stone wall around the garden was very high, and topped with broken glass; the door was firmly locked, and knocking brought no answer.

"The two Policemen's tracks go in, and do not come out," said Crowley, "while those of 'Atalanta' seem to enter and return. Somehow, those people managed to open that door."

"They must have had more luck with their knocking; or else they were expected. Or perhaps they had keys of their own. The Police might well do so—and so might a trusted servant."

"Speaking of such things, Mr. Holmes, I was rather expecting you to carry a set of skeltonic keys which would open any door, as if by magic!"

Holmes smiled. "I have nothing made to fit so ancient a lock as this. It must be mediæval."

"I could easily climb over the wall, sir."

"I'm sure that you could, Mr. Crowley. Perhaps I might even contrive to do the same; and we may yet be driven to such an expedient. But I should prefer to try other means first. Bill Sikes's methods are generally frowned upon by the authorities, and our being under arrest would severely limit our ability to fulfil our obligations to our client. But what d'you make of this?"

On the door was an ancient symbol engraved, clearly at no recent date. It looked like a letter 'K', with the lower diagonal omitted, and a dot placed in the gap between the upper diagonal and the upright stem.

"Does the sign mean anything to you, Mr. Crowley?"

"Not a thing, I'm ashamed to say, sir. Can you enlighten me?"

"Not greatly. I believe it to be a letter of the old Runic alphabet, or *Futhark*, used by the Norsemen in these parts; and if I'm not mistaken it is the letter 'G'. But what that means in this context is more than I can tell."

"I have read that runes were used in magic. Perhaps it is a spell. Could this be an abode of Witches?"

"You go too fast. A rune may be used for magical purposes; but then again, it may not. And not all magic is Witchcraft, as you should know better than most. But here comes a pedlar upon the coast path. Do you think that you might catch up with him before he passes, and enquire of him whose property this is? I fear that am growing too old to run."

Carrying the umbrella, Holmes walked down to the coast at a comfortable pace. Before he reached it, Crowley came running back, clearly excited to be the bearer of interesting news.

CHAPTER IV.

THE FURTHER VISION.

"He says that it's the Monksdale estate: the Provost of Trowley himself, a Mr. Grimson, lives there!" Crowley pronounced the man's name as it had been said to him, 'Greemson'; but Holmes knew the spelling from his research.

"Well, I suppose that explains what the Policemen were doing: no doubt coming to report on their search for Mr. Tollemache. Perhaps they have a key to that door; or perhaps the Provost was expecting them. They would naturally have left by the other exit from Mr. Grimson's estate, leading to the town centre, where their Station is located. Since *Grimson* appears to be an Old Norse name, I think that we have an innocent explanation for the runic 'G', as well. No doubt the family have lived in that house since the days when runic markings were commonly in use—as they are still in some parts of Scandinavia."

"Might it be that Mr. Tollemache was also on his way here?"

"It is possible; although he might have knocked on that door in vain had he turned up unannounced, as you and I did just now. But perhaps he didn't know that; or perhaps he had made an appointment."

"An appointment with the Provost? Would Mr. Grimson not have mentioned this to the Police, after the disappearance of Mr. Tollemache?"

"One might expect so; but over the years I have discovered that people do not always do as one might expect, for all kinds of reasons. With or without an appointment, it seems a plausible hypothesis to me that Mr. Tollemache was coming this way in the hope of communicating with the Provost. As to what he might have wished to discuss, one can only speculate; but there seems a high probability that it had some connexion with his belief that a living Witch-Cult still flourished here on Trowley: an idea that was becoming something of an obsession with him, if one may judge from his correspondence."

"Might one further speculate that he was pushed from the cliff, by someone eager to silence him?"

"Again: possible. But Occam's Razor would favour a gust of wind. Anyway it seems less probable that he is currently alive than that he perished on Wednesday night, alone in the cold sea. I wish that I might have better news to bear to his poor daughter."

"Of course," said Crowley. "But if he was pushed, who do you think pushed him? Could it be our 'Atalanta'?"

"I think not. Probably that unknown lady was not involved in the disappearance of Mr. Tollemache—but if she were, I think it would more likely have been as a lure, sent to draw him to the coast, where someone else killed him. Few women have the heart for murder: their Sex finds its natural fulfilment in loving and nurturing Life, rather than in destroying it."

"So you imagine that a rough with a bludgeon was waiting for Mr. Tollemache when 'Atalanta' brought him here?"

"Yes—or perhaps the Reverend gentleman had made an appointment to be here, hoping to meet a real Witch, and met his murderer instead; and 'Atalanta' was just an innocent young lady who happened to be in this place at another time."

"Well, I think that she must have had something to do with it. She was certainly on the path that leads to Mr. Tollemache's cottage; and she may have been at the cottage itself. Doesn't that look rather suspicious?"

"Not necessarily. We do not know that she was at the cottage, and there might be any number of innocent explanations for her presence in the lane. She might, for example, have been a maid of Mr. Grimson's, on some legitimate errand. She may have been a tradeswoman, delivering produce; or even a daughter of the house, out for a walk."

"You can't date the prints with any precision, then, Mr. Holmes?"

He shook his head. "They are too much eroded by this infernal rain."

* * *

The Sergeant on duty in the Cunningsborough Police Station was a handsome, sandy-haired man with a large moustache, of the Kitchener style. Instead of a Policeman's helmet, he wore the Scotch equivalent, a military-style *képi*, like a high-crowned pillbox with a curt black-leather peak; the cap was made of navy-blue serge, like the uniform, and bore the elegant silver badge of the Trowley Constabulary. That this man had been a soldier was obvious; the medals on his tunic's breast showed that he had served with honour in several conflicts, including the Zulu War of twenty years earlier. It was interesting to see that the Sergeant's idea of working on a Sunday was to sit at his desk in the Police Station reading a good book; even more interesting to note that his idea of a good book was *The Time Machine*, by H. G. Wells.

He was very near the end, after the death of Weena, in the section where the Time Traveller, broken-hearted, goes on a journey to the very distant future, witnessing the slow extinction not only of human-kind but of all life on Earth. Holmes remembered vividly the image of that terminal beach, bathed in the red glow of a vast, dying sun that no longer appeared to move through the sky, as the Earth had ceased to rotate: a Hellish landscape in which there were no living things but lichens, liverworts, and a dark, round thing like a football with tentacles, which flopped about on the edge of the blood-red sea. Wells' story began as an entertaining philosophical dialogue about the Fourth Dimension, but it soon modulated into a lament for the ultimate futility of human endeavour in an uncaring Universe.

"Powerful stuff, is it not, Sergeant?"

"Aye, sir—and fine writing, too." The Sergeant's English was good, no doubt as a result of his military service. He was about fifty now—perhaps a little less. "Do you think that the world will really end like that?"

Holmes gave a little smile.

"After I read the story, I racked my brains to think of a way in which such a sad conclusion might be avoided; and, at length, I found one. Consider, Sergeant: in the course of this century, we have seen a remarkable development of machinery, which is already beginning to perform not only physical tasks, but also actions that we must classify as mental in nature. In the nineteenth century we have made machines which can add, and subtract, and calculate logarithms; in the twentieth, I believe, we shall construct more complicated devices capable of playing chess, or of translating from one language to another. Given not centuries, but *millennia* of technical development, is it not a virtual certainty that one day we shall develop machines which are capable of performing all the functions of a human brain: mechanical intelligences the equal of our own?"

The Sergeant nodded. "Aye, sir: I can see that such a thing is likely enough to come about, in the fullness of time; but what would be the consequence?"

"Most importantly—to us—that beings of flesh and blood, such as ourselves, would no longer be necessary to the existence of the intelligent machines, which could take over the design and manufacture of their own future generations. Eventually the Thinking-Machines would improve themselves in ways which no human mind could imagine, becoming a species as incontestably superior to us as we are to dogs or monkeys. Mankind may well become degenerate and decline into extinction, as Mr. Wells envisages; indeed, all biological species must do just so, in time. But even after the end of Man, the upward path of progress could still continue, in the higher civilization of the Thinking-Machines. They might well leave this planet on Star-Ships, travelling to explore the Cosmos, and so contrive to prolong their existence long after our little Earth is burnt up; quite possibly, for ever. The knowledge and the power of such beings would seem Godlike to us: their Art and their Music inconceivably lovely. Now, that to me is a more inspiring prospect than the one presented by Mr. Wells!"

"I'm reminded of what Zarathustra says about Man being a bridge between the Ape and the Superman," said Crowley; "but I don't think that Nietzsche ever imagined a metallic Superman."

"He did say that the Superman would be *hard*, though, sir. He laid great stress on that, as I recall." The Sergeant chuckled. "I think that, when he had his wits about him, he would have found this gentleman's idea as interesting as I do!" To Holmes he said: "You should write a Scientific Romance of your own, sir!"

"Perhaps when I retire."

"I look forward to that day, sir—with no offence meant!"

They laughed together.

"You strike me as something of a free-thinker, like myself, Sergeant."

"Aye, sir: I suppose I am."

"Is that not a little unusual in a Policeman?"

"Well, sir, in my experience it's a little unusual in any walk of life. But here I am, and I am a Policeman, and most folk seem to think that I'm fairly good at it."

"I deduce from your lack of Masonic insignia that you are not one of the Brotherhood. Neither am I. Good men have sometimes urged me to join, for what seemed like good reasons. But admirable as the fraternity may be, in many ways, the thought of swearing by a God of whose existence I was doubtful, to obey without question the orders of men whom I had no reason to think were any wiser than myself, just didn't feel right to me. Was it the same for you, Sergeant?"

"Not quite that, sir. Such an attitude as yours would have kept me out of the Police Force or the Army, too! But to be in the Masons a man has to give up a good deal of time and money. The mumbo-jumbo side of it would be very tedious for me, and the company would be just the kind of men that I see every day at work. Frankly, sir, I'd rather be at home by my own fireside of an evening, with a good book, my pipe, and a wee dram."

"So you must be rather the odd man out on the Force?"

"Not really, sir: we're not all Masons here. Sometimes I do feel that I'm not quite in the Inner Circle, as you might say; but then I don't want to be. I've no ambition to be Superintendent. A quiet life behind the desk here till I retire is good enough for the likes of me."

"And your life is quiet, I expect."

"Aye, sir: there's not much crime on Trowley. There's a lot of drinking, and sometimes trouble comes of that, especially on a Saturday night; but rarely anything more serious than a black eye or a broken bone. Certainly there's no Napoleon of Crime for you to combat here, Mr. Holmes!"

"You recognize me?"

"I've often read the *Strand Magazine* at the Library, sir. I recognize your manner."

"You cannot have recognized me from the illustrations, as they are a very good likeness of the artist's brother Walter. I am rather uglier in real life, am I not?"

"Hmm. Less conventionally good-looking, perhaps, sir, with that great aquiline nose and those small, close-set eyes—but hardly ugly! You look like what you are: a man of great intellect."

"Thank you, Sergeant ..."

"Flett, sir."

He rose, and they shook hands.

"But this is surely not Dr. Watson?"

"Permit me to present my assistant in this investigation: Mr. Aleister Crowley."

"Pleased to meet you, sir!"

"Charmed." Crowley gave his hand; Flett shook it and then resumed his seat.

"An investigation, you say, Mr. Holmes? There can be only one matter I can think of that might have drawn you here: that of the unfortunate old clergyman. I understand that Miss Tollemache is having a hard time believing that her father could have been snatched away from her by something so random as a gust of wind. Up here it's normal for folk to go missing like that from time to time; but I suppose that it's not so in Miss Tollemache's world. It's easy to see why the lassie might want to believe that her father was still alive—but really, Mr. Holmes: you can't for a moment believe all this nonsense about Witchcraft and human sacrifice, can you?"

"I have seen things quite as strange as that in the dark places of the Earth. What may be the case here on Trowley, I cannot tell; but I do not believe that such events as Miss Tollemache imagines are by any means impossible. There is much evidence for the former existence of Witches in these parts; and a relatively short span of years has passed since the last burnings on Gallows Hill. For all I know, the Witch-Cult may still survive here, just as the Zar Cult lingers in the Soudan, despite the strict prohibition of it by the Mohammedan theocracy there."

"The Zar Cult, sir? I've heard of that, though it goes by other names in other parts of Africa. I know that it's a woman's thing, where they sneak off to dance and feast together, but I never really knew what the point of it was. Is it just fun and games, or is there something else at the bottom of it?"

"In the Soudan, I heard that beneath the 'fun and games,' was the worship of an old Pagan Goddess, whose name was a closely-guarded secret—although once it was whispered in my ear. The Zar Cult is actually so similar to Witchcraft that I think it must be another branch of the same ancient religion. Fanatical Mohammedan *régimes* have persecuted these vestiges of Paganism every bit as vigorously as the Christian Churches have done here; so, if the one Cult may still survive, why not the other?"

"Well, sir, with respect: this is not Darkest Africa, and just because we're remote from London doesn't mean that we're savages. I don't think that you'll find any evidence of Witchcraft on Trowley, however hard you look; but you're welcome to try. Welcome as far as I'm concerned, that is, for I fancy that some of my colleagues may take a less favourable view of your investigations. We Islanders are, if you'll pardon the tautology, a very insular people. I must warn you that many of us don't take kindly to strangers coming and—as it might vulgarly be expressed—sticking their *lang nebs* into our private business."

"Some of your colleagues have such an attitude?"

"Most, I should say, sir. And of course none of them would wish to see the revival of that old *canard* about this Island being a hot-bed of

Witchcraft. But I don't suppose that you'll find any more evidence for such a thing than we have done."

"Perhaps you could tell us what form the official investigation has taken."

"Well, sir, Mrs. Rendall came in about breakfast-time to report the gentleman missing from his wee house, so Constable Scollie took her key and went straight over there to look around."

"Alone?" said Crowley. Holmes kicked him lightly on the shin. Sergeant Flett smiled.

"No, sir: he met Constable Irvine on the way, coming off of the night shift, and they went together. They both gave statements about visiting the house and searching for clues."

"What did they find?"

"Nothing of interest in the house, Mr. Holmes. But they did observe Mr. Tollemache's footprints going from the house down to the coast path and terminating abruptly on the cliff-edge. We all knew that there had been strong winds on Wednesday night. Putting two and two together, it wasn't hard to work out what had happened. The only mystery about it is what the old gentleman was doing on the cliff in the middle of the night; and that we shall never know, for only he could have told us, and I fear that he will speak no more."

"And you informed Miss Tollemache of this conclusion?"

"We did, sir; and she came back with the most amazing allegations about Witches and cannibal feasts. I think the general opinion was that the poor young lady had gone a wee bit crazy with grief; but to humour her, the Constables went out and talked to everyone they could find who'd spoken with old Mr. Tollemache recently."

"Who were these people?"

"Mrs. Rendall, obviously, sir; then there was Mr. Brown, the antiquary; Mr. Bailey, the archivist at the Cathedral; Dr. Strange, the Head-Master of the Borough School; and Miss Reid, the Head-Mistress there. There may have been others that Mr. Tollemache had spoken with, but none whose names we knew; and these seemed as good a set of witnesses as we might reasonably hope to find."

"Did their testimony throw any light on the matter?"

"It seemed to rule out suicide; they all agreed that the old gentleman was very lively in his last days, full of enthusiasm for his wild theories about Witchcraft and folk-tales."

"Did they all think his theories wild?"

"I got that impression, from what the Constables said, sir. Of course, I wasn't present at the interviews; but I'd be surprised if any of them was too keen on the idea that our wee Island had once been the realm of Cinderella's wicked stepmother, or that she'd founded an unspeakable Cult here which might still endure to this day! What Island would want such a reputation as that?"

"Quite so, Sergeant. I should like to speak with these local worthies myself; and also to your Provost."

"Well, sir, I can tell you that you'll not speak with the Provost to-day, for he'll do no secular business on the Sabbath; and the same goes for Mr. Bailey, too. There are still many here who take their religion very seriously."

"Dr. Strange, Mr. Brown, and Miss Reid not being of that number?"

"Och, the Doctor's earnest enough, but he's what they call a Liberal Christian; Mr. Brown is a great admirer of Voltaire. Despite their differences, they seem to like each other well enough, for they regularly dine together. In fact they both dined with Mr. Tollemache last Sunday night.

"As for Miss Reid, the difficulty is that she's a single lady under thirty, and living alone, so you can't very well call on her, nor invite her to visit you, unchaperoned. Probably your best plan would be to meet her at the School, to-morrow—just as Mr. Tollemache did, last week. If you bother to question her at all, that is. What she had to tell us didn't amount to much: Mr. Tollemache had discussed with her some of his notions about Witches and old wives' tales. I think that she only talked to him to be polite, the way that shop-women do with tedious customers.

"Mr. Tollemache had a much longer conversation with Mr. Brown and Dr. Strange, so you might find them more interesting to talk to; and they should see you with no problems. The Doctor lives in the School-House, and Mr. Brown has a bungalow in the new extension: number 23, Sinclair Street."

* * *

Holmes and Crowley walked eastward in the rain. Holmes was annoyed; Crowley, embarrassed.

"Do you know the regulation about trying to bribe a Policeman?"

"It wasn't a bribe—he'd already served us. It was a tip, like the half-sovereign that you gave to Mrs. Rendall; and I meant it kindly."

"Of your kindness I am sure; and I suppose that Sergeant Flett must have seen it too, since he let us go with no more than a reprimand. But your good intention does not change the fact that you have made a grievous *faux pas*. One does not give money to a Public Servant for carrying out his duty: one has already paid him, as a tax-payer. To offer anything more for his services is to suggest that one requires something extra in return; and an honourable man like the Sergeant would naturally find that suggestion abhorrent."

"Well, strictly speaking, sir, I *haven't* paid Sergeant Flett: the Trowley Police are funded out of local taxes. It's an independent Force, not even inspected by the Home Office. And from what I've heard of this place, a lot of Trowley-men still don't think of themselves as British, or even as Scots. So I thought that the system would work as it does abroad: where the Police expect a little something for serving a foreigner."

"You have visited Russia, I see," Holmes said, in the language of that country. He smiled a little.

"Yes," answered the younger man, in the same soft tongue. *"Two years ago. But in my experience the Russian Police expect money from everyone!"*

"Ah! It is indeed difficult to maintain a serious level of righteous indignation in the face of charm such as yours, Mr. Crowley. Nevertheless, your well-meant action has rather soured our relationship with a man who might have been a useful ally. In future, if payment is appropriate, I shall make it. And please leave the questions to me, too."

"Did you consider my single question equally ill-judged?"

"In this case I don't think that it made any difference. I'm rather good at spotting a lie, and I believe that Sergeant Flett was telling us the truth—or what he sincerely believed to be so. But in other circumstances such a question as yours might have influenced a witness's testimony. Asking so promptly whether Constable Scollie had gone alone, for example, might have alerted Sergeant Flett to the fact that we knew more than one Policeman to have been at the cottage; and, had the Sergeant been a dishonest man, he might have changed his story accordingly. It's surprising how such a small thing can make a crucial difference in a testimony. I have been interrogating people for twenty years, and I am generally considered to be rather good at it. Please leave it to me from now on."

"You're my captain, Mr. Holmes. I shall be content to obey, to learn, and to admire!"

"That sounds like an excellent approach to our professional relationship."

"It must be Dr. Watson's, I think."

"Yes: and it has worked well for us."

They walked in silence for a little way.

"You wouldn't have any *hasheesh* on you, would you, Mr. Crowley?"

"As it happens, I have something rather remarkable in that line, which was sold to me in Edinburgh as a Nepalese Temple Ball."

"Many things are sold as such which have never been in Nepal, or in a temple; but most of them are of good quality. May I have a little, please?"

"Of course: I'll cut you a piece when we get back to the Hotel. I didn't know that the Herb Dangerous was one of your vices, sir."

"No, I don't suppose that you would: I learnt the use of it during my years in the East, and Dr. Watson has not written about me since my return. Anyway, I should hardly describe it as a vice, since, as you must know, the intoxication brings with it no demoralizing physical addiction, such as that which comes with the use of morphine or cocaine. Excessive consumption of hasheesh can make a man lazy, and sometimes rather eccentric, admittedly; but I can take it or leave it alone, and I generally take it only for the sake of my work. The drug has a peculiar effect upon my brain, enabling me to see patterns in things. I expect that I shall find your Temple Ball useful in the task of deciphering Mr. Tollemache's last message."

"Do you need a pipe?"

"No, I have brought one. But I thank you for offering; and for the hasheesh; and, indeed, for all your help in general. I do appreciate it, Mr. Crowley, although it might not always seem so."

Crowley smiled. "I think that we might drop the 'Mr.', don't you?"

"The problem with that, young man, is that I am twenty years your senior. We may hardly be 'Holmes' and 'Crowley' to each other, may we? And if you should say, 'Mr. Holmes' and I, 'Crowley', we should sound like a gentleman and his valet. So on the whole I think it better for us to stick with the 'Mr.'s. We are two gentlemen combining to achieve a common purpose: although I have seniority, you are not my servant, but a voluntary collaborator. It is appropriate for us each to show respect to the other, Mr. Crowley."

* * *

Mr. Brown's parlour was pretty much as dark and cluttered as the one at home in Baker Street. It was a fair deduction that their host was a bachelor, or a long-time widower; Holmes thought the former, looking at him across the book-lined room. Mr. Brown bore a disconcerting resemblance to the late Professor Moriarty, with his

74

large, balding cranium and somewhat cadaverous face; but he seemed affable enough. He spoke perfect English, with a slight Scotch accent, more like that of Edinburgh than the Island speech. A Master's Degree from that city's University hung on the wall. Holmes's intuition told him that this was a man of whom great things had been expected, but whose actual career had been something of a disappointment: that having failed to become a nationally-recognized scholar, Mr. Brown had settled for being (as the saying went) 'a big fish in a small pond.' His specialist knowledge might, however, be very useful in solving the current problem; and he seemed like an intelligent observer.

"I never met the Reverend gentleman myself," said Holmes, "but when I heard Sergeant Flett talk about him I formed the impression of a decidedly eccentric figure, perhaps even a man suffering from some form of paranoia. I never had that impression from his daughter: to her, he was the very embodiment of rationality. So I wonder what you made of him, sir?"

"Well, Mr. Holmes, poor Mr. Tollemache was unquestionably a very wise and learned man; but he was growing old, and perhaps no longer quite the careful scholar that he once had been. After a lifetime spent in the careful study of his subject, he had come up with a Big Idea which he desperately wanted to prove correct before he died. I wouldn't have called him paranoiac, but there were some similarities with paranoia in the way that he twisted evidence to support his theories. For example, when he asked Mrs. Rendall about Witchcraft on Trowley, she just said that there were things of which one should not speak, and he took that as meaning that she knew a great deal about it, but didn't choose to tell—perhaps for fear of the Witches, or perhaps because she was one!"

They all laughed.

"But, said Holmes, "do you have no faith at all in Mr. Tollemache's theory that the Witch-Cult might still survive here?"

"Well, I certainly can't prove it to be false; but that's generally the way with theories that involve secret societies! All I can say is that I'd need more evidence than he had before I'd believe it."

"What was his evidence, exactly?"

"As far as I could tell, it consisted mostly of impressions: how a serving-girl had looked at him when he mentioned the Crow's Daughter; how a friendly fisherman in the tavern had suddenly turned cold and distant when the conversation turned to Witchcraft: that kind of thing. He was always looking for someone who'd own up to being a Witch, but I never heard that he'd found one."

"The evidence of such impressions as you mention may be extremely valuable in the uncovering of well-kept secrets: from a momentary expression, the twitch of a muscle or the glance of an eye, a practiced observer may often discern a person's inmost thoughts. And did not Mr. Tollemache find written evidence, in the Cathedral archives, which appeared to support his theories?"

"Yes, he told me about that. I don't know quite what to make of it. I suppose that all it really proves is that, two or three centuries ago, one way of casting suspicion on someone was to accuse them of telling this 'Tale of the Witches'; but whether anyone ever really told it, or what it might have been, we can't know."

"You were not familiar with these documents?"

"No: I've never seen them, that I can recall. But then popular culture isn't really my area of interest. Politics and military history are what I like to study, not 'the short and simple annals of the poor,' and their silly superstitions."

"It seems to me that the documentary evidence which Mr. Tollemache discovered suggests that an underground, anti-Christian Cult existed on this Island in fairly recent centuries. Can that be of no interest to a scholar who is himself said to be somewhat critical of the Christian Religion?"

"Should I, as an educated skeptic, feel any kind of intellectual kinship with savages who broke every Christian commandment in their wild orgies? Should I make common cause with the Mad Mullah, the Khalifa, or the Boxer fanatics of Shan-tung, because they too are enemies of Christianity? Folly is folly, Mr. Holmes, no matter what label it chooses to wear; and no kind of folly is very interesting to me. In the case of Trowley, I'm inclined to believe that, even if an anti-Christian Cult ever flourished here, it has long been extinct. All of the local Witch-Trials that I've investigated look like cases in which innocent people were framed by their enemies and then tortured into confessing. This whole matter of Witchcraft is a shameful page in our Island's history, and not one on which I care to dwell over-much."

"I can understand that, of course; but you must also understand that the nature of this case makes it necessary for me to take Mr. Tollemache's hypotheses seriously, and to investigate the possibility that real, living Witches have abducted him."

"Yes, of course I see that you must look into it. Why don't we make virtue of necessity by having you to dinner to-night with myself and

Dr. Strange? We could tell you all that passed between ourselves and Mr. Tollemache, and answer any other questions that you might have, over one of my André's fine meals. I have some interesting old Port. And I should very much like to be able to say that I had dined with Sherlock Holmes!"

"I have no evening-clothes," said Crowley.

"Oh, never mind, young man," said Brown—but before he could conclude his remark, Holmes had interjected:

"The Hotel will undoubtedly be able to provide you with some. One of their waiters is much your size. And I am sure that Mr. Brown is not going to take offence however my good friend appears here this evening, are you, sir?"

"Well—no, of course not."

"Very well, then. What time d'you dine?"

"Come soon after seven. We'll have a little drink before-hand."

* * *

On the way back to the Hotel, Holmes saw the lovely red-haired woman once again, walking with a female companion in the opposite direction, on the other side of the street. In daylight her hair looked brighter, streaked with copper; her skin was flawless alabaster; and the shape of her body in that tight, black suit was enough to catch the attention of any man. Even the grace with which she carried her umbrella seemed curiously attractive. He could not help staring at her; and again she responded as no lady should, by returning his gaze and smiling. 'I know that you desire me,' she seemed to say, 'and I rather enjoy it.' But no word was spoken, and in a moment she had passed, and was gone.

CHAPTER V.
IN A GLASS, DARKLY.

"Good afternoon, gentlemen!" said the desk-clerk, rising to get their keys. This one, the day-clerk, was called Forsyth: a good-looking young fellow of about twenty, thin-faced and light-haired. "You'll have found the umbrella useful, I'm thinking."

"Yes, thank you," said Holmes. "We may yet have further need of it, as we are going out this evening; and in consequence of that we have another extraordinary demand to make of your excellent establishment." He explained Crowley's need for a suit of evening-clothes.

"That should be no problem, sir. I'll have Mr. Gibson's suit sent up to Mr. Crowley's room after luncheon. Will there be anything else?"

Holmes hesitated for a moment. "Yes, Forsyth: perhaps you could satisfy my curiosity. There is a particular young lady whom we have seen twice now on the streets of Cunningsborough. Her age, I should guess, is somewhere between twenty-five and thirty; height, about five foot three; with a pale complexion and red hair."

Forsyth frowned. "There are a few young ladies here who might fit that description, sir. Is there anything more particular about this one?"

Crowley said: "She has the face of one of Botticelli's angels, and a body that a man might give a kingdom to possess!"

"Ah!" The desk-clerk beamed. "All dressed in black, very simple yet elegant? That must have been Miss Reid, the Head-Mistress at the

Borough School. She is indeed a lady of great beauty, and a fine teacher."

"Do you speak from experience?" asked Holmes.

"Yes, sir: although naturally most of Miss Reid's time is spent with the girls, she also gives some lessons to the highest class of boys— those serving as pupil-teachers while studying in preparation for a College education on the mainland."

Holmes looked quizzically at him.

"Family circumstances have prevented me from following that path, sir; yet my mind has benefitted greatly from the stimulation which that lady's teaching has given me."

Crowley laughed. "I should think a class of strapping lads would have found Miss Reid quite stimulating in other ways, besides!"

"Indeed, sir: I think that, if the truth be told, we were all a little in love with her—quite hopelessly, of course! But that was a good thing, because it made us eager to impress her in the only way we could: by working hard and doing well in class."

"A most interesting innovation in educational methods," said Holmes, "although one which may have been anticipated in Alexandria, in the days of Hypatia. I look forward to our meeting with Miss Reid to-morrow—as does Mr. Crowley, I am sure."

* * *

It was late in the afternoon when Holmes knocked on Crowley's door.

"Just a moment!"

Soon the young man opened the door, with a smile and a courteous welcome on his lips. He was wearing the Hotel's slippers and dressing-gown over his own shirt and trousers. Behind him, a coal-fire burned brightly in the grate. The thick red curtains were drawn together, shutting out the wet and windy night. This room's *décor* was rather splendid in its old-fashioned way, with the heavy, dark furniture that had been so popular thirty or forty years earlier; although the wallpaper was a little more recent, and of good design—one of Morris's, Holmes thought. That great four-poster with its velvet curtains was a genuine antique, probably of the late seventeenth century: more impressive, although perhaps less comfortable, than the big brass bed on which Holmes had slept last night. Presumably the Hotel's name signified that some member of the Royal Family had once stayed here; if so, this room must have been the one in which that august personage had slept.

Two large wing-chairs stood invitingly on either side of the fireplace, and between them a small octagonal table on which lay an open cigarette-box, an ash-tray and a book: Gomme's *Ethnology in Folklore*, to judge from its striking combination of dark green cover and vermilion lettering. Holmes was pleased to see that the young man had been doing his research; and if the scent of the air did suggest that hasheesh had been smoked here, as well as tobacco, that was all right: Crowley had no doubt discovered the Herb's remarkable usefulness as a stimulant for the brain in certain types of intellectual work.

"Please take a seat" said Crowley, waving toward the chairs. Basing his deduction on the placement of objects on the table, Holmes took the chair that Crowley had not been using. Crowley waited until his guest was seated before seating himself.

81

"Would you like a cigarette, Mr. Holmes? Or would it interfere with your communicating to me the interesting information which I may justifiably hope that you have come to impart? For I am all agog to hear the news of your decipherment of Mr. Tollemache's last message; and I recall your Eastern *guru*'s prohibition on smoking while talking!"

"It is not an invariable practice of mine: simply one which I find useful on occasion." He and Crowley exchanged smiles. "Those black Russian cigarettes do look tempting; while I, too, am eager to tell you of my discoveries."

"May I take it that you have succeeded in drawing some meaning from those cryptic blots and splotches?" asked Crowley.

Holmes lit his cigarette with one of Bryant & May's Wax Vestas.

"Well," he said, savouring the taste of the Russian tobacco, "there are parts of the text of which I am certain; other parts at which I cannot guess; and some others where I see only a probable interpretation. Nevertheless, the gist of the message seems clear to me." He took the piece of blotting-paper from his pocket and leant forward to pass it over.

"See if you are convinced by my reading of these marks. Normally I should say, 'Hold it to the light', but on this occasion you may find it better to use a looking-glass, as the chamber is rather dim."

Crowley fetched a hand-mirror from the dressing-table. He sat, holding the blotting-paper in his left hand and the mirror in his right, studying the reflexion of the message as Holmes read from his own transcription of it.

"The first line, at upper right, is evidently *Trowley*, and the line beneath is the date—which is, unfortunately, illegible. But the facts of the case make it seem most probable that it was *Wednesday, 25ᵗʰ October, 1899*, and the marks are not inconsistent with such an interpretation.

"*My Darling Emily* comes next, of course; then what looks to me like *Success at last—or, perhaps, Catastrophe! But...* and there follow some words which may be *I am old*; then an ampersand, then more unintelligible words, another ampersand and a capital *I*; more obscurity, then, quite plainly, *gamble my remaining years against the scientific*; then several obscure words, then *to-night. I believe that I have—* something unintelligible—*a* something *Witch, who has shown me—* something, something—*was no ghastly Devil-Worship, but a joyful celebration of the Powers of Nature!*

"A new paragraph begins *Should I be wrong*, then lapses into obscurity, eventually continuing *but should I be right*—something, something—*Papa*—then several unintelligible words, then—*secrets of a Pre-Historic Religion!*

"The last paragraph is the most legible, but entirely of a personal nature, which makes it of little use to us in our investigation. The final sentence, with its pious wish *that I may write more to-morrow*, is interesting, however. And the signature looks like *Papa* again."

Crowley considered for a moment. "Your interpretation appears entirely convincing to me, Mr. Holmes."

"And, in your opinion, Mr. Crowley, what may we deduce from this?"

"Well." Crowley handed back the paper. Behind the curtains, rain beat against the windows. "I suppose we may conclude that Mr. Tollemache had at last made contact with a Witch who was willing to talk to him; that she had given him a favourable account of

83

Witchcraft, which he was inclined to believe; and that he expected to learn more at a meeting with her on Wednesday night. He knew that there was some risk attached to the meeting, but deemed it a risk worth taking for the sake of discovering the truth about this ancient religion."

"My conclusions exactly, young man—although I do not think that we may be so sure of the gender of Mr. Tollemache's informant; since, in his writings, like the old authors of the Renaissance, he often uses the word 'Witch' to designate men as well as women. It is most unfortunate that his message does not reveal the name of this person."

"I suppose that he might have promised not to do so, as part of the price that he paid for learning the secrets of Witchcraft."

"That is indeed the most likely explanation."

"I am very tempted," said Crowley, "to identify 'Atalanta' with the Witch."

"One should not jump to conclusions. But it may be as you say."

"Anyway, it seems that Miss Tollemache was right: there are indeed Witches on this Island, and they were responsible for her father's disappearance."

"That is certainly possible. On the other hand, this apparent Witch may have been an impostor, taking advantage of Mr. Tollemache's *idée fixe* for a selfish purpose—which could have been as commonplace as robbery, since the Reverend gentleman's wallet and purse have vanished with him. Perhaps somebody lied to him in order to lure him to the cliff-top, where they knocked him on the head and took his money, before throwing his body into the sea. The truth about many a notorious crime is just as dull and sordid as that." Holmes threw the fag-end of his cigarette into the fire, and enjoyed the little blaze of its brief combustion.

"I can conceive of other, more interesting, possibilities," said Crowley. "Let us grant that the apparent Witch was an impostor, and the meeting a ruse to lure the old gentleman to the cliff. We do not need to suppose the murderer to have been a common thief, and his motives pecuniary. There were others who would have wished to see Mr. Tollemache dead, for other reasons. As Sergeant Flett said, no Island would want the kind of reputation that the *Cinderella* book would have given to Trowley. The godly people of this place may have conspired to kill the Reverend gentleman, in order to prevent him from bringing shame on the Island.

"Think of it, Mr. Holmes—a conspiracy, not of the lower orders, but of the respectable! I can imagine that the Police themselves might have been instrumental in the elimination of the old gentleman, leading him from his house by dead of night and throwing him from the cliff; then trudging off dutifully to their Provost to report. That would account for all the footprint evidence, I believe."

"You are quite correct, Mr. Crowley: such an explanation is indeed compatible with the evidence that we have seen. But it is often the case that there are many possible interpretations of the same data. An imaginative mind will find no difficulty in making up complicated hypotheses to explain an event such as the assassination of the Empress Elizabeth, or the disappearance of Mr. Tollemache; but in the real world, as William of Occam realized long ago, the simplest explanation which fits all the facts is the one most likely to be true.

85

Not all the time, but on the whole, crime is a dull business. Dr. Watson's stories may have misled you about this—not so much by what they tell, as by what they leave out."

"Nevertheless, Mr. Holmes, you have come across some fairly strange things in the course of your career. A murder carried out by an Andamanese Pygmy with a blow-pipe, for Heaven's sake! Think of the bizarre case of the Red-Headed League—or that of the two feuding Mormons who fought a duel with poison-pills in the heart of London! You, if anyone, must know that sometimes life can be as strange as any fiction. Since the state that we are both in is certainly conducive to imaginative thinking, I propose that you and I together employ this intoxication to good purpose, by considering some of the more interesting, if less probable, solutions to this mystery."

"Very well: let us consider further your idea about a conspiracy of the _élite_ to assassinate Mr. Tollemache, in which the Police acted as foot-soldiers." Holmes paused for a moment or two, running the scenario through in his mind. "I see one serious objection. If the Provost were the man in charge of this conspiracy, one may readily understand how he might have found members of the Constabulary willing to obey him; but I find it hard to imagine any colleague of Sergeant Flett's cold-bloodedly throwing a helpless old gentleman from a cliff! If I were to take up your hypothesis, and tinker with it a little, I should hypothesize that the Policemen involved would not have been ordered to kill Mr. Tollemache, but merely to take him, as a prisoner under escort, to the house of their Provost."

"Perhaps he tried to make a break for it on the cliff-top; they struggled, and he fell into the sea. Is that what you're suggesting, sir?"

"Yes, that is certainly one possibility; but I see another, which is that Mr. Tollemache did *not* fall from there; that instead he struggled with the Policemen, and they overpowered him, before carrying him to the Provost's house, where we might suppose him to be still held captive. That hypothesis is equally consistent with the physical evidence; indeed, it would explain why the Policemen's footprints should have seemed a little clearer after the cessation of Mr. Tollemache's. If they were sharing the burden of his weight, their prints would have been somewhat deeper, and consequently easier to detect."

"How strongly does the physical evidence point to Mr. Tollemache being carried to the Provost's house?"

Holmes shook his head. "Given the state of the path after three days' weather and human traffic, certainty on the matter is impossible. The evidence does not conflict with such a hypothesis; neither does it prove it. Of course, I should like to believe that things happened as I have described, because then there would be some point to my being here: I might still be able to save the old gentleman's life."

"Would there be no point in bringing his murderers to justice, even if the gentleman were dead?"

"Perhaps. They say that hanging's a deterrent, and I suppose that it is, in that if we didn't punish murderers then more men would kill; but that's a rather abstract kind of benefit compared to the very real sorrow and pain that generally accompanies an execution. I would a thousand times rather be the rescuer of a living man than the avenger of a dead one."

"Admirable sentiments, Mr. Holmes! I can certainly appreciate why you might wish to believe that your client's father is still alive. But for what purpose might the Provost, or the other conspirators, wish to keep him a prisoner rather than simply kill him outright?"

"Ah, well, Mr. Crowley—there this hypothesis must become still more extravagant, I fear, since the only motivation that presently occurs to me is that suggested by Miss Tollemache: a ritual sacrifice on the night of Hallowe'en."

"Good heavens, Mr. Holmes! Are you suggesting that the Provost may be a Warlock?"

Holmes smiled. "It is conceivable that Mr. Grimson might be one and the same with the Witch whom Mr. Tollemache claims to have encountered: the person who showed him such surprising proofs that real Witchcraft had been an admirable thing. Who better than a grave Provost to convince Mr. Tollemache of that? For the sake of this rather extravagant hypothesis we must suppose that, on this Island, Witchcraft has not only survived, but infiltrated the Establishment, so that some of the leading men of society attend the Black Sabbath."

"I should guess," said Crowley, "that in such a case the Witch-Cult would be associated with the Masonic Lodge, or perhaps rather with a faction within the Lodge; and one might expect at least some of the Police Force, some of the Judges, and so on, to be members. Do you recall the Palladian Scandal in Paris, a few years ago? What was alleged, but not proven, in that case, is the kind of thing that I'm imagining here: a Diabolist Cult hiding inside the respectable Masonic Order."

"Yet the Masons are all men. Are there to be no female Witches in your hypothesis?"

"There are a surprising number of women eager for such carnal enjoyments as might be found at the Sabbat; and plenty of others so degraded as to do almost anything for money. I have no doubt that the relatively prosperous and powerful men of our hypothetical Cunningsborough coven would have found it easy to obtain female partners for their rituals. One need only recall the scandalous doings of Sir Francis Dashwood and his Hell-Fire Club, back in the decadent days of the Georges."

"You make a good point, Mr. Crowley. There were actually several Hell-Fire Clubs in various parts of Ireland and Scotland in the last century. If there had been such a Club on this Island, and also a surviving Witch-Cult such as Mr. Tollemache imagined, it is easy to imagine how the two might have come together and fused into a single organization. So, while some respectable people might wish to suppress Mr. Tollemache's book as an unjustified slur on the Island, other apparently respectable people might really be secret Warlocks, working to avoid the exposure of their secret society. Both kinds of people may have worked together to eliminate Mr. Tollemache, and to cover up the crime afterwards."

"It sounds very convincing to me, Mr. Holmes."

"As I say it to you now, it sounds very convincing to me, too. But that, as you must know, is usual when one is under the influence of hasheesh: the most imaginative theories come to one's mind, and they all seem quite credible; yet sometimes when one considers them in a sober state of mind, their flaws become apparent. I think it better not to commit myself to any one hypothesis at present. Perhaps our conversation with Mr. Brown and Dr. Strange to-night will enable us to confirm or to discount some of these speculations."

* * *

Crowley looked like a prince, albeit a prince of the 1880's, in his borrowed finery; but Mr. Brown and Dr. Strange were also very elegant in their evening-clothes. The Doctor was of about the same age as Holmes. He was a good-looking man, of Nordic type, with chin-length chestnut hair and neatly-cut beard. The resemblance seemed too close to be coincidental, Holmes thought: could this be a rather literal-minded example of the Imitation of Christ?

The two Island worthies sat on the sofa, Crowley and Holmes in the arm-chairs which stood on either side of a big coal fire. All were drinking Mr. Brown's fine Cognac.

"I understand that your School has achieved some remarkable results, Doctor," Holmes said.

"Yes, indeed: the last few years in particular have been an astonishing success. We have sent as many as seventeen pupils on to Colleges in a single year, if you can believe that, Mr. Holmes! My old *alma mater* awarded me my doctorate quite recently—not for a thesis, or anything of that sort, but simply in recognition of the superlative standard of the students that come from my School."

"To what do you attribute this success?"

"Well, I think the most important thing that I do as Head-Master is to be enthusiastic, and try to communicate my love of learning; I listen to everyone, and give encouragement where necessary, but I am always stern and inflexible in the face of disobedience."

"No doubt, Doctor. You must also have good Masters and Mistresses. We have been hearing praise for one of the latter in particular: your Miss Reid."

The Doctor's smile had a hint of exasperation. "She is, indeed, a very good School-Mistress."

"But sometimes a little trying?"

"It's her views, Mr. Holmes. She's very... advanced! To be fair, she doesn't force her opinions on anyone, and certainly not on the children; but now and then they'll ask her questions, and she'll say something that I end up having to apologize for."

"What kind of thing?"

"Something about Mr. Darwin's theories, or the age of the Earth, or the authorship of the Holy Scriptures, for example. Or else it's Women's Rights. Do you know this Gage woman—American—and her radical ideas about Female Emancipation?"

"I can't say that I do."

"Wild, crazy stuff, Mr. Holmes! Anyway, most of the time Miss Reid keeps all this under her hat; and she is certainly a good teacher. But what little she has let slip of her advanced opinions has been enough for some of the children to give her the opprobrious nick-name of *The Witch*."

"A-ha!" said Crowley.

"This is surely rather interesting in connexion with our present inquiry," said Holmes.

Mr. Brown and the Doctor laughed.

"Oh, no!" said the Doctor. "She isn't *really* a Witch, I can assure you! They just assume that anyone who isn't a Christian must be a

Witch; but Miss Reid has told me more than once that she believes in neither God nor the Devil. I'm sure that she'd have no time for any of that superstitious nonsense of sticking pins in dolls or tying the wind up in a cord, either: she's too much of a Rationalist to take such things seriously."

"She sounds like a most interesting person."

"I agree, Mr. Holmes," said their host. "I'm eagerly waiting for the lady to turn thirty, so that I can start to invite her to our little *soirées*. Only a couple of years to go!"

They smiled.

"How long has Miss Reid been with you, Doctor?" asked Holmes.

"Ever since she qualified, in '92; but, as Head-Mistress, only since the Jubilee Year, '97. Her predecessor left rather hastily to get married, as her *menarche* approached. I always think that being a School-Mistress these days is rather like being a Vestal Virgin in Ancient Rome: they sacrifice the best years of their lives *pro bono publico*."

"Do you expect Miss Reid to retire while still young, too?"

"I'd be surprised if she didn't: it's hard to imagine such a lady remaining a life-long spinster."

"No, indeed!" said Crowley.

"You have seen the lady?" asked the Doctor.

"Only in passing," said Holmes. "We have not spoken. I intend to interview her at the School, to-morrow. When would be a good time for that, by the way?"

"She'll certainly be free between one and two. Shall I tell her to expect you then?"

"That will be fine. We're seeing the Provost at ten."

"I think you'll find that interview less enjoyable," said Mr. Brown. "Provost Grimson is the kind of man that gives Calvinism a bad name—much like Johnnie Knox, or old Johnnie Calvin himself!"

This quip drew a little polite laughter from the two investigators; a smile and a quiet chuckle from the Doctor.

"We have been wondering..." said Crowley; then he looked at Holmes, who leaned forward keenly. "Do you think it possible, gentlemen, that your Provost's piety is merely a mask covering a darker secret: could he be a Warlock?"

This time the Doctor's laughter was unconstrained, and Mr. Brown's hardly less so.

"Well," said their host, "I suppose that *might* be the case; but, if so, it would be one of the most remarkable deceptions in history! I'm trying to think of a parallel."

He rubbed his chin, and smiled. "I know that in Edinburgh, two hundred years ago or more, there lived a old Puritan called Major Weir—a gentleman of seventy, whom everyone regarded as a pillar of rectitude, but who confessed on his death-bed that he'd been a life-long Witch, and had done all manner of shocking things, mostly of a sexual nature, and some of them with his own sister—and they burnt him alive for that! If Weir's confession were true, it might furnish a parallel to your supposition about the Provost; but I think it more likely that the old man's brain was so decayed that it could no longer distinguish fact from fantasy. The Major was confessing to things which he had not actually done, but had wanted to do; and he felt horribly guilty for having entertained such thoughts."

"His sister did corroborate the story, though," said Crowley. He had been doing his homework, thought Holmes, impressed by the boy's apparent confidence in his new-found knowledge. Crowley had attended only a minor Public School, but he had all the 'bounce' of an Old Etonian!

"Yes," said Mr. Brown, "but they were much of an age, and I suppose that she too was becoming confused about the difference between reality and fantasy—perhaps also the difference between what she remembered and what other people suggested to her. The confessions of these two confused old people can't be worth very much as evidence, can they?"

"There are cases in the trials of sane and healthy people who confessed to leading the same kind of double life, being outwardly a good Christian and secretly a Witch."

"Those confessions were generally extracted under torture, and so their evidential value is approximately *nil*."

"Isobel Gowdie was not tortured," said Crowley, in a reasonable tone. "She confessed spontaneously."

"Again, Mr. Crowley, I would think that a case more interesting to the psychologist than to the historian. From her confession, the woman was evidently deranged. I don't know much about this new science of Psychology, but I can just about imagine how some people, trapped in tedious, hopeless lives, might long so much for excitement and attention that they'd confess to crimes which they didn't commit, and invent the most lurid stories to back up their admissions. Such cases are known to-day, are they not, Mr. Holmes?"

"Indeed: they are so numerous as to be a nuisance to the Police, particularly in connexion with the more notorious crimes. You underestimate your own knowledge, sir. The historian and the psychologist both have the same subject-matter, Mankind; and to know Mankind is to understand Psychology."

"A graceful compliment, from a great connoisseur of the human spirit! I thank you, sir!" Mr. Brown raised his glass.

CHAPTER VI.
AMONG THE INFIDELS.

Holmes sipped Mr. Brown's fine Cognac. "It is certainly a weakness, in Mr. McKay's account of Scotch Witchcraft, that the evidence given in all Witches' confessions contains so much that is frankly incredible. Even those sources from which he draws his more credible stories, about nocturnal meetings, dancing and feasting, also contain many impossible things, such as levitation and metamorphosis. Do we see here a mixture of true memories with falsehoods invented by people wanting to appease their torturers—or is it all false throughout? I cannot tell. You have told me, Mr. Brown, that you are not much interested in the subject of Witchcraft. Yet it has played an important part of the history of this Island; and, as a local historian, you must have a view on it. So I put it to you: were there ever any real Witches in these parts?"

"There were certainly a few women, of the lowest class, who were known as Witches. Such women lived by selling charms and blessings—and also took payment for withholding their curses, which were considered to be extremely powerful." Mr. Brown thought for a moment. "They say it ran in families, in the female line; and so perhaps there was once some real tradition that was passed down from mothers to their daughters, making Witches of them."

"What do you think the content of this tradition might have been?"

"If there ever were anything, I'd guess some herbal lore, and perhaps something of what we might call mesmerism, or 'hocus-pocus'. Perhaps other things—who knows? Mr. Tollemache, of course, was convinced that they told a folk-tale about a fabulous period in the pre-history of this Island, called 'the Reign of the Crow'—and perhaps they did so, for all I know."

"Strange to hear the ninth century referred to as pre-history—but of course it is so, in these northern lands! You must know the new hypothesis about Witchcraft, sir: that it was the survival of an ancient pre-Aryan religion. What, I wonder, is your opinion on that?"

"It strikes me as entirely plausible, although the evidence in its favour seems a little thin. But I am a historian, and as such accustomed to marshalling regiments of facts in support of my own humble hypotheses. When one is dealing with pre-history, the evidence is naturally much sparser, and one is forced to rely more on speculation to fill in the gaps. But yes: I can easily believe that way back in the mists of pre-history, Aryans conquered non-Aryans and made serfs out of them, and that the serfs kept up the junketings of their Old Religion in secret places, just as the Negroes do in the West Indies to this day."

"When would that Aryan conquest have been, exactly? The books which I've been studying lately are very vague about dates."

"Well, that's quite interesting, Mr. Holmes. For most of Britain, it would have been at least as early as 500 B.C., and the coming of the Celts; but here it was as late as the Viking Conquest, around 800 A.D.—because before that time this was a Pictish Island, and all the latest research suggests that the Picts were a non-Aryan people."

"Aryan or not, these Islanders would have been Christians by the eighth century of our era, I suppose?"

"Officially—as certain tribes in Africa are to-day. The rulers and the headmen go to church, but the common folk still dance to the Ju-Ju drum! I should think it was like that here when the terrible blond men came from the sea to enslave them—and that would be an end to Christianity, I'm sure, although the old religion might well have carried on in secret. So, yes: if one were to assume that the Witch-Cult survived anywhere, this would be a likely place to find it."

"Did the Witch-women whom you mentioned have any un-Christian religious beliefs or practices?"

"If they did, they kept it to themselves. Under torture, of course, some of them confessed to all kinds of lurid things, sometimes involving nocturnal orgies attended by the Queen of Elfhame and her consort, Satan—but such evidence is obviously unreliable. I have no problem in believing that there was some kind of old Pagan Cult surviving here in very early times, and probably as late as the Reformation, since the Papist clergy were notoriously lax. But as soon as the burnings started in earnest, I think that folk would have dropped their Paganism like a hot potato. Why teach one's children something that might get them burnt alive? Who would think the dubious pleasures of the Sabbath worth the chance of a horrible death? We Islanders are not fools. I can understand how the traditions about healing would have been passed on, because of their practical utility, but I don't think that the Old Religion would have survived the coming of Calvinism. That's my judgment.

"But of course if there *were* a secret society, and I were not a member, I'd know nothing about it; and that's what I know: nothing. So perhaps Mr. Tollemache was right, and the Witches of Trowley are just very good at keeping secrets! I trust you to find out, Mr. Holmes—if anyone can do it, you're the man."

"I was just wondering," said the Doctor, looking from face to face, "about the connexion between nocturnal orgies and unorthodox medicine. Why should practitioners of a hedonistic mysticism have a side-line in healing the sick?"

"For the same reason that Holy Men do the same the whole world over, I suppose," said Holmes. "People think that their mystical practices give them unusual powers; and in this unhappy world there is always a demand for healing. Sometimes it even works, due to the power of faith. As for *not* cursing someone, nothing could be easier! It seems entirely natural to me that Witches would, as you charmingly put it, 'have a side-line' in such work."

There was general agreement.

"You mentioned earlier," said Holmes, "that Mr. Tollemache had met a number of people whom he suspected of involvement in the unholy Cult. I wonder if there was anyone to whom you could put a name?"

Mr. Brown thought. "No. The nearest I could come to identifying any of them would be the serving-girl who seemed to know something about the Crow's Daughter. I'm sure that he saw her working in the chip-shop at Storwick—the place with the pretty window that you see when you come off the ferry."

"Why, I know who that is!" exclaimed the Doctor. "Her name's Lizzie Grey. She was a bright student. We found her a place as a pupil-teacher for a few years, but as it turned out her family couldn't afford to let her go on to University. It's a common thing, sadly. She left school at seventeen—it must be three years ago, now. Or is it four? Yes, four: it was in '95. A shame. But she's painted the chip-shop window very nicely, I must say; and whenever I've seen her in there she's always seemed happy."

There was a gentle knocking on the door.

"Come!"

Mr. Brown's manservant, Kemāl, entered the room: a good-looking Levantine in his mid-thirties, dressed not unlike the gentlemen, but wearing a black tie rather than a white; and, instead of a white waistcoat, a scarlet cummerbund.

"Dinner is served, sirs." His accent was faint, but almost certainly Turkish.

They finished their drinks and followed him across the hallway; he opened the door of the dining-room and stood beside it while they went through.

Mr. Brown's dining-room was elegantly but rather austerely furnished in the Commonwealth style, with a sideboard on the right side of the room, a fireplace on the left, and a long table in the middle. A butler's trolley stood by the near end of the table, between the sideboard and the door.

The light in here came mainly from four oil-lamps, two on the sideboard and two on the mantelpiece. A choice silver candelabrum, probably early Georgian, stood in the centre of the table, bearing four lighted candles.

A linen cloth covered the table; four chairs stood around it. A Turkish rug lay on the polished floor. Dark oak panelling covered the walls to waist-height; between that and the picture-rail was a subtle wallpaper in two contrasting shades of green. There were two large paintings, in gilded frames: one above the fireplace, which appeared to represent the Birth of Venus; and the other above the sideboard, showing the Death of Socrates. A handsome bust of Hobbes stood upon the sideboard; on the mantelpiece one of Darwin.

Mr. Brown stood by the chair at the far end of the table, inviting Holmes to take the seat on his right-hand side. Kemāl pulled back the chair and placed it expertly as Holmes sat down. Then Crowley was seated, facing Holmes; then Dr. Strange, facing their host; and last of all Mr. Brown himself.

Plates and cutlery were already on the table, of course. Mr. Brown's crockery was Chinese blue-and-white ware. Covered vessels of silver stood near the ends of the table: a soup-tureen at Mr. Brown's end, and a fish-dish at the Doctor's. Kemāl, standing to the left of Mr. Brown, removed the lid of the tureen and held up a soup-bowl which Mr. Brown filled with the aid of a ladle. The first bowl came to Holmes; Kemāl served him from the left. The soup was *pottage Parmentier*: potatoes, leeks, chicken-stock, milk, cream and butter, blended into a delicious unity by the alchemy of a master-chef. The other guests were served in the order that they were seated: Crowley, Strange, Brown.

"This may be none of my business, sir," said Holmes, between mouthfuls, "but I can't help wondering how Kemāl here came to enter your service."

"Och, it's a very commonplace story, Mr. Holmes. He helped me out of a little difficulty in which I found myself once while travelling in Cyprus; and he had good reasons for wishing to leave that island himself. An enterprising young fellow, he put it to me that if I'd look after him, he could be a good and faithful servant; and so he has proved, over more than a dozen years now. I really don't know what I should do without him."

Kemāl beamed, but said nothing.

"*Servus tuus mussulmanus est?*" asked Holmes, wondering if he needed to watch what he said in front of the Turk.

"He's about as much of a Mohammedan as I am a Christian— aren't you, Kemāl?"

"Indeed, sir."

"There are free-thinkers in every land, you see, Mr. Holmes."

Holmes thought back over his travels. "Yes: I suppose there are; although in most countries they're obliged to keep their unbelief a closely-guarded secret, in order to avoid persecution—rather as, in our society, some men are obliged to conceal the truth about their sexual proclivities."

Crowley and the Doctor were listening with interest.

With a lively twinkle in his eye, Mr. Brown replied: "We Britons enjoy more liberty than the folk of any other nation; but not so much, I suspect, as our grand-children will do. The direction of progress is toward greater and greater toleration, in both of the matters that you

102

mention. It is easy to predict that, in a hundred years' time, neither penalty nor stigma will attach to either Atheism or Sodomy. The prejudice against both I consider a superstitious relic of the Age of Faith, when any kind of deviancy was likely to get a man burned at the stake."

There was general agreement. The Doctor said: "I have no problem with any of that, Mr. Brown, except that I consider the use of the word *Sodomy* to be inappropriate in this context. In the Bible the Sin of Sodom actually seems to be rape, which is a deed that I could never condone, as it violates the Law of Love; but an act of kindness and affection between two comrades, such as the late Mr. Whitman described so movingly, is quite a different matter. For such a thing I'd rather use the modern word, *Uranian*."

"What's the etymology of that, I wonder," mused Mr. Brown. "Something to do with Uranian Aphrodite, in the *Symposium*?"

"So one might suppose," said Crowley, "although at Cambridge I heard a somewhat coarser explanation: that to call a man a *Uranian* was to signify that he was interested in *Uranus!*"

"Oh, very good: very droll!" Mr. Brown spoke for the company, judging by the general laughter.

"That might be the true etymology," said Holmes. "When I was at University, the expression was just coming into use; and whenever one enquired into its meaning, that's the joke that one was told."

They hummed and hawed politely, and looked at him with interest. He could see that they were wondering about his College days. He should not have put the idea into their heads! It must have been the

103

influence of the strong Cognac that was making him careless. He looked down at his soup-bowl.

"Well," he said, "I know that in some of the best houses it's not considered quite polite to comment on the quality of one's dinner, but I have to say that was as good a bowl of soup as I have ever eaten. The man who made it is a true artist. Please give my compliments to the *Chef*, Kemāl!"

The other gentlemen endorsed this opinion. Kemāl seemed pleased. "I shall tell him, sirs!" He took their soup-bowls and spoons over to his wooden trolley, behind the Doctor, between the sideboard and the door; he put the bowls into a basket and the spoons into a drawer, and returned to the table with four clean plates. He stood to the left of the Doctor, from which position he uncovered the fish-dish, and then held a clean plate ready to receive a grilled sole with anchovy butter, served by the Doctor with a pair of silver fish-servers.

Again Holmes was served first. He took his fork in his right hand and a crust of bread in his left, to push the fish onto his fork. It was the old-fashioned way to eat this dish, and he liked it well enough. Here it was the only way, as Mr. Brown had no fish-knives on his table.

This André was a marvellous cook, no doubt of it! The excellence of the sole was such that everyone ate in silence for several minutes; and Holmes missed his chance to start a new topic.

Then Mr. Brown picked up the thread. "Since you have ventured to ask me about something which you feared might be none of your business, Mr. Holmes, I am emboldened to take a similar liberty with you. Could you settle a long-running dispute by telling us exactly *which* University you attended?"

He was ready for the question.

"The published accounts of me are deliberately vague about my early life and my family connexions, in order to ensure the security of certain people whom I wish above all things to protect. I'm afraid that there are some matters which I must refuse to discuss. If that makes me a poor guest, I apologize for it." He looked down and spread his hands. "*Ich kann nicht anders.*"

"I understand entirely, Mr. Holmes. Your answer tends to confirm a favourite hypothesis of my own: that if no 'Sherlock Holmes' is to be found on the rolls of any of our Universities, it is because such was not your name in your student days; that the improbable appellation is in fact an *alias*, adopted to put a safe distance between you and your family."

"As to that supposition, I shall make no comment—other than to say that you show considerable promise as a detective, Mr. Brown!"

That exchange had gone well, Holmes thought: no offence had been given, none taken, and no dangerous secrets had been revealed. Best of all, the subject had been gracefully brought to a close. He liked Mr. Brown.

When the Doctor had finished his fish, he said: "There is another question which the published accounts of you do not answer, Mr. Holmes: that of your religious beliefs. Our host believes you to be an Atheist, on the basis of your well-known admiration for the works of Winwood Reade; but in the stories of Dr. Watson there are a few passages in which you seem to express a belief in a caring Creator,

105

who gives rewards and punishments after death, and these incline me to see you as a fellow-Christian. Which is it, sir: are you a Christian or an Atheist?"

"If I must be classified as one or the other, sir, then I am an Atheist. But really I should want to qualify that. I don't think that God is nothing: in my considered opinion, He is a mythical character, whom Man has invented as the embodiment of all that which he most admires. In the days of Joshua, God was a great war-chief, smashing His enemies with irresistible force; as men grew wiser, so did their God, until now He embodies all the virtues necessary for the triumph of civilization over barbarism. He is, indeed, Goodness personified— just as He always has been, although men's ideas of what constitutes Goodness have changed greatly, over the centuries. The contemplation of a moral Ideal in such a personal form must tend to have an elevating effect upon those who worship Him; and thus Christianity *works*—in the sense that it makes men better."

"Hmm: an interesting idea! So you don't believe that God can actually *do* anything, such as intervene in the world to help His people?"

"No, Doctor, I do not. I have been present on many occasions when a little divine intervention might have prevented a great deal of human suffering: and never have I witnessed anything that I should class as miraculous."

"Might it not be that God acts through natural means?"

"Then what is one to say of all the occasions upon which natural phenomena work to the detriment of good people rather than to their benefit: the famous Lisbon Earthquake, for example, or the more

106

recent eruption of Krakatoa? Is God not controlling Nature at such times? Or are we to conclude that He is always in control, but sometimes enjoys chastising those whom He loves, as is suggested by some passages in the Old Testament? I have known husbands of that sort, and they did not seem like admirable men to me.

"But consider Occam's Razor, Doctor: is it not 'multiplying entities without necessity' to suppose Nature and God conjointly responsible for our varied fortunes here on Earth, when Nature alone, without God, is quite adequate to account for all the phenomena which we observe? My conclusion from a lifetime of experience is that Nature is undeniably real, whereas God is no more than a dream in men's heads. Admittedly, this dream has had great consequences in the world, both for good and for ill; but it seems to me that Man is starting to wake from his collective dreams and face reality."

"You foresee no long future for religion, Mr. Holmes?" asked their host, as Kemāl began to take their used plates and cutlery to his trolley.

"I think it obvious that, as scientific knowledge advances, religious beliefs must tend to disappear."

"You were right, Mr. Brown," said the Doctor: "our guest is undoubtedly of your party in this matter! For my part, I take Luther's view: that the existence of God cannot be proven, but must be believed as the primary act of Faith. Without my Faith I'd not see God's hand working in the world: like you, sir, I'd see only *Nature, red in tooth and claw*. So it should come as no surprise to me that a man of Science like yourself should be found among the infidels. But what about those apparently Christian remarks that you are reported to

107

have made? Did you really say those things, sir, or was Dr. Watson being a little... creative, for the sake of your reputation?"

Kemāl left the room with his trolley.

"Dr. Watson never lies—without good cause! In this case he is telling the plain truth: for a period of about five years before my apparent death in 1891, I did indeed talk like a Christian, for the good and sufficient reason that I then considered myself to be one."

"How could that be?" asked Mr. Brown.

"Mainly, I suppose, because of my deep distress about what Virgil calls the *lacrimæ rerum*." Holmes paused for a moment, and looked down before continuing. "I felt great sorrow in my heart for the suffering which I witnessed in my work as a detective, and in the world generally. I wanted desperately for there to be an after-life in which the blind would see, the lame would walk, and murdered innocents would play again, happy in the sunshine.

"I was also, in those days, a heavy user of cocaine: a drug which tends to blur the boundaries between things that are real and things that one might wish to be so. Nor had I then studied the Bible for myself: I mainly relied upon what modern writers told me about it. As you must know, sir, some of our recent theologians can make Christianity sound like quite a reasonable business!

"I thought it would be nice if there was a Heaven; about Hell I was less keen, but I imagined that, since God was reasonable and loving, the pain which he inflicted would be proportional to the offence, and so no one would be hurt very much for very long. After taking their punishment, the criminals could come into Heaven and join the party for all eternity, as far as I was concerned, and I felt sure that God

108

would be no less forgiving than I was. Like most modern Christians, I imagined God as having much the same tastes and attitudes as myself, and so I found him easy to worship!"

Gentlemanly laughter.

"You saw the world then as a battle-ground between the forces of Good and Evil," said Crowley. "The side of Good was destined to triumph, because God was its Captain. Now your Captain is dead, does the battle continue? Without God, how do you tell the difference between Good and Evil?"

"A good question!" exclaimed the Doctor.

"The battle continues, for me, Mr. Crowley; but now I see it as a battle between Civilized Man and the Beast. By the Beast I mean that ancient Ape who snarled, and flung filth, and settled his quarrels with 'tooth and claw': that deplorable Beast within us which we must subdue if we are to be worthy participants in our great civilization!"

They all liked that, he saw.

"That's pretty much what I mean by the Devil, too," said the Doctor.

Kemāl returned, his trolley laden with new dishes. First he set a covered meat-dish on the table before Mr. Brown. Standing to the left of his master, he removed the cover, and the smell of roast pork made the air delicious. He held a plate while Mr. Brown carved the joint.

Again the first plateful was brought to Holmes, but this he did not begin to eat straight away, since he knew that Kemāl would be bringing round vegetables to go with the meat. When everyone had his portion, Kemāl proffered a dish of *Dauphinoise* potatoes, then one of fried mushrooms, from both of which Holmes accepted a generous helping. As before, the food proved so delicious that conversation ground to a halt for several minutes, although expressions of enthusiasm punctuated the silence, creating a sense of shared experience among the diners.

"So," said their host, at length, "how did you come to lose your faith, Mr. Holmes?"

"It was a gradual process, sir; and it began in a Tibetan monastery, where a wise old Lama explained to me what the Gods of his people were: not literal realities, but creations of the human mind, symbols for religious Ideals. They have one Deity, for example, who symbolizes Wisdom; another who stands for Compassion. As I thought about what he had said, I realized that my God was of the same kind as the Gods of Tibet.

"He, too, was a personification, in this case of the Ideal of Goodness—which is, as Plato saw, a most comprehensive Ideal, containing within itself such lesser virtues as Wisdom and Compassion, for example. Re-thinking my theology in the light of this new understanding, I considered the person of Jesus: in him I fancied that I saw an Image of what Man might be if he perfectly incarnated that great Ideal. I even had some notion of fitting the Holy Spirit into my scheme, as a name by which Reason might be revered. At that stage of my journey I should still have called myself a Christian, although a most unorthodox one."

"And did you still believe in an after-life?" asked Crowley.

"Oh, I had a vague idea that there might be something of the kind: not literal harps and angels, of course, but something more refined and mystical, of which the harps and angels were but a symbol!" He chuckled, amused at his own past folly.

"The next part of my journey, however, took me to the lands of Islam, where I encountered men who took their religion absolutely literally: they really believed that they were living in the last days of the world, and that the Day of Judgment was about to come. I found much in the Soudan, especially, that reminded me of what I knew about the Holy Land in Biblical times; and I began to wonder whether the theology of Jesus might not have had more in common with that of the Khalifa than it had with mine.

"On my return to Europe, at the University in Montpellier, I undertook some serious study of the Bible in general, and the life of Christ in particular; and since then I have found it impossible to call myself a Christian—although I remain broadly in sympathy with the Christian project, as it is professed by progressive thinkers such as yourself, Doctor."

"But, Mr. Holmes—what did you discover concerning the life of Our Lord which made it impossible for you to believe in him?"

"I don't think that you really want to know that, Doctor."

"Yes, I do!"

"And I most certainly do," said Mr. Brown.

"As do I," said Crowley.

"Very well, then: I shall give you some account of the Gospel according to Sherlock Holmes. But let us save it until after dinner. I fancy it's the kind of thing which might go down more easily with a glass or two of good Port-wine."

There was general acquiescence.

111

"May I take the plates, sir?" asked Kemāl of his master.

"Yes, I think we're done with this course, aren't we, gentlemen?"

Kemāl took the soiled plates and cutlery to the trolley, and returned with fresh dishes. The new course was *confit* of duck, served with Puy lentils; the meat was so well cooked that it seemed to melt in the mouth, while among the lentils Holmes's palette could detect little granules of carrot and celery: another masterpiece from André! They did not take long to devour this, as the portions were small: it was a dish made not to satisfy hunger, but to delight the senses of men who were no longer hungry.

"I wonder how you can eat André's cooking every day without becoming as corpulent as the Prince of Wales," said Holmes.

Mr. Brown smiled. "Ah, well: I don't eat like this every day. Many a day I'll take nothing but toast and a little porridge: it's better for me, better for André, and better for my bank-balance! But once in a while I take great pleasure in dining well. A man appreciates a feast such as this all the more if he's not used to such fare."

"You are a wise man, sir."

Soon Kemāl took away their used plates and cutlery, and brought another covered dish to set before his amiable master. This dish turned out to contain a large cheese (apparently a Cheddar), which Mr. Brown carved and served just as he had done the meat.

Holmes was again the first to be served. Kemāl brought him a plate containing a wedge of the odoriferous comestible, and a sharp little knife with which to eat it. Mr. Brown did not care for raw celery, it seemed—and who could blame him?

When everyone was served, Mr. Brown said: "Are you fond of cheese, Mr. Holmes?"

"Why yes—although I recall that as a child I found it quite repellent. Strange how one can acquire a taste for decadence and corruption!"

Mr. Brown smiled. "This is our local Cheddar. It is a very... masculine cheese. I think that you will enjoy it. I should like to recommend a glass of my old Port with this, at some point. Just ask Kemāl when you're ready. You'll find that the tastes complement each other quite beautifully."

Holmes was already chewing the cheese. It was nutty and creamy in flavour, with a hint of fried onion; its texture slightly gritty, with tiny crystals of calcium lactate. How could all that add up to such an explosion of sensual pleasure in his mouth? It was a mystery, but a delightful one. At the end of that mouthful he raised his hand. "Kemāl? *Bir bardak Porto sharabi, lütfen.*"

Smiling, the Turk filled a glass from the decanter on the sideboard, and brought it over on a small silver tray, which he stood holding, by Holmes's left side. Holmes took a good swig of the port, and washed it around his mouth. Oh, yes: Mr. Brown was right! Both the wine and the cheese had very complicated flavours, and they fitted together as perfectly as two instruments in a Bach duet! He replaced the half-full glass on the tray and cut himself another gobbet of cheese. Wine on top of cheese had been good, but cheese on top of wine was good too; and then more wine. There were no words for such delight.

"You should definitely try that, Mr. Crowley!"

113

Kemāl performed the same service for Crowley, and then for the other gentlemen, and they concurred in their approval of the experience.

While they were finishing their cheese, Kemāl was busy taking the cutlery from the table to his trolley. When they were done, he took everything else, starting with the remains of the cheese, and then brushed the table-cloth over. He gave the gentlemen finger-bowls and napkins; when they had cleansed their fingers and lips, he took the bowls and napkins away again. Next he took the table-cloth and the green baize under-cloth, folding them neatly as he did so. The candelabrum was returned to its position at the centre of the table, and the handsome Levantine pushed his trolley to the kitchen, to fetch their final course.

This turned out to be *pot de crème*, made with the darkest of dark chocolate: a truly luxurious ending to a magnificent meal! Each gentleman had a glass of Port-wine, and more stood ready in the decanter. Kemāl stoked up the fire, then stood to attention.

"Will that be all, sir?"

"Yes, thank you, Kemāl."

He bowed and withdrew, leaving the gentlemen to their private conversation.

CHAPTER VII.

A VOICE FROM THE DARKNESS.

"Bravo, Mr. Brown!" said Crowley. "No Emperor on Earth can have dined better than the four of us to-night!"

They drank the health of their host.

"Can anyone tell me the vintage?" asked Mr. Brown.

"1870, if I'm not mistaken," said Holmes. "The Comet Vintage."

"You are correct, sir. It was a very good year—in many ways! And the company?"

"That's a harder question. Could it be Cockburn's?"

"Yes, indeed!"

There was gratifying admiration of Holmes's perspicacity.

"Now, then," said Mr. Brown: "cigars or cigarettes, gentlemen?"

They all chose the latter. In the proffered box there were three compartments. Holmes was pleased to see Sullivans in the first. Strange to think that these very cigarettes had been in the Burlington Arcade not long ago! Holmes's choice was, naturally, Turkish; Crowley took a Russian; and the Doctor, a Virginian. Mr. Brown's choice was a Havana cigar. He gave them each a porcelain ash-tray, and lit their cigarettes for them with a spill lit from a candle.

"There is still something that you could do to help me in my current investigation, gentlemen."

"Ask away, Mr Holmes—we shall certainly do our best."

"Well, then: perhaps you could just give me the gist of your conversation with Mr. Tollemache, when you and he were seated here last week?"

"He talked about his theories," said the Doctor. "In particular, about the historical reality which he supposed to lie behind the legends of the Reign of the Crow."

"What did he say?"

"He talked about something called the *Ur-Narrativ*—did he not, Mr. Brown?"

"Yes, Doctor, he did. He meant, of course, the original version of the story, from shortly after the time of the events. He considered the folk-tales in his collection as distorted versions of this *Ur-Narrativ*. He drew a parallel with Darwinian evolution, seeing different versions of a story arising through a process of random mutation and natural selection, just as happens in living things."

"How does that analogy work, exactly?" asked Crowley.

"Well, the random mutation is that the stories would change through people misremembering them; and the natural selection is that changes which the audiences didn't like would tend to disappear, whilst those which were popular would tend to persist."

"So," asked Holmes, "what kind of changes did he think would be most likely to come about, as a true story metamorphosed into a fairy-tale?"

"He thought that there would be an increasing element of the supernatural: real events would be re-imagined as miraculous, sometimes by a process of misunderstanding, taking metaphors for literal truths. In the same way other impossibilities in chronology, or in psychology, would naturally tend to arise. Characters would become impossibly good, impossibly evil, or impossibly stupid, for example. Basically Mr. Tollemache's approach to reconstructing the *Ur-Narrativ* was to reverse this process: to eliminate the impossible. Thus when we hear that little birds told the King something damning about his new bride, Mr. Tollemache would understand it that plotting courtiers, rather than wild-fowl, were meant.

"Where versions of an incident in the story differed, he would consider whether one of them was more likely to be true, or whether all were mutations of the truth; and, by comparing these mutated forms, deduce what true incident might have given rise to them, as a biologist might deduce the form of an ancestral species by comparing modern variants of it."

"A method which seems reasonable enough," said Holmes, "if one supposes that the original story was true. My own approach to the Gospels is very similar, in fact. What did you think of the results in this case?"

"As Mr. Tollemache reconstructed the original story," said their host, "it contained nothing incompatible with what we know about the Viking Age in Trowley. But then we know very little about that period from written evidence, and the archæological record is almost equally uninformative."

"What would you say that we *do* know, sir?" asked Holmes.

"Well—at the date favoured by Mr. Tollemache for the Reign of the Crow, around one thousand and sixty years ago, the Norsemen were in control of this Island, and had been so for about half a century. The native people, the Picts, were still here in great numbers,

117

but only as servants of their Norse masters. We don't know anything about the political arrangements of that distant time, but one may reasonably suppose that there was some kind of leader to keep order among all those quarrelsome Norsemen. Given the customs of the age, it's quite likely that the leader was called a King, and not improbable that he was a scion of some Scandinavian royal house. Probably one family had been in charge ever since the Viking Conquest of the Island; the founder of that dynasty having organized the Conquest in the first place."

"Like William the Conqueror, but on a smaller scale," said Crowley.

"Much the same," said Mr. Brown. "That's how things were done in those days. So, yes, there were probably Kings here, as Mr. Tollemache's hypothesis would require. The name of Cunningsborough itself, apparently signifying 'the King's fortress', suggests as much.

"Mr. Tollemache supposed that a Norse King of this isle, in circumstances of bereavement such as the stories describe, had married a woman of the Pictish race. She was not a native of this Island: she was a noblewoman from overseas, but of the same race as the downtrodden slaves here. Nothing implausible in that! Such mixed marriages have taken place in the real world. One thinks of Ahab and Jezebel—he being an Israelite King and she a Princess of the despised Slave-Race, the Canaanites. One may imagine the consternation in the Confederate States of America if their President Davis had suddenly married an African Princess, and demanded that she be treated with honour; all the more so if he'd encouraged her to practice Ju-Ju ceremonies, in which he'd taken an enthusiastic part! Well, that's how

118

it was in Israel, as we know, in the days of Jezebel; and Mr. Tollemache envisaged a similar situation here, with the King himself becoming a Warlock."

"Is it not a little remarkable," asked Crowley, "for two historical events to parallel each other so closely as that?"

"Remarkable, certainly, but by no means unique," said Mr. Brown. "Has it never occurred to you that a poetically vague description of the downfall of Charles I might, with appropriate changes to the proper nouns, be applied almost perfectly to the similar tragedy of Louis XVI? History is like that, young man: the same patterns recur in different times and places. Britain, to take a hackneyed example, is the New Rome, and many of our problems are analogous to those faced by the Romans.

"Let's face it, Mr. Crowley, Human Nature doesn't change: it's still by no means unknown for men to become enamoured with women of another race, even when that race is regarded as inferior; and sometimes a King may do as other men. And, given such a beginning, the story would unfold with tragic inevitability."

"One sees repeating patterns in my line of work, too," said Holmes. "I recall, for example, the case of a stock-broker's clerk in Birmingham which was uncannily similar to one of a pawn-broker in the City, a year or so later! You are right, sir: the human mind is much alike in all places and times, and so the same actions tend to recur, with similar consequences."

"So we may agree that Mr. Tollemache's hypothesis is plausible," said Mr. Brown. "What's lacking, as I told him, is evidence to support it. His response was that he was hoping to find such evidence here on

Trowley. A runic inscription mentioning the Witch-Queen would have been very welcome to him, of course, but he knew that such a thing was unlikely to turn up. The next-best thing would have been, not a physical object, but a tradition: a local version of the story, set on this Island, and less distorted in the telling than any of those collected abroad. He told us about his discovery of old documents referring to the Tale of the Witches and the Reign of the Crow, and how these made him certain that the Witches of this Island used to hold that story in particular reverence. Mr. Tollemache's hope was to encounter living members of the Cult, and to learn from them the Witches' version of the tale, which he expected to be very close to the *Ur-Narrativ*. When I last saw him, he had found no one willing to admit to knowing the story at all. And that was all that there was of any substance in our conversation last week."

"Thank you." Holmes smiled and turned to the Doctor. "You must hear a good deal of folklore from the children at your School, Doctor. I wonder if you've ever heard anything like the tale of the Crow's Daughter."

"No, I'm afraid not. The people here don't really tell stories as they do in other parts of Scotland. They don't sing many songs here, either, except psalms. I think the change of language from Norse to English on these Islands pretty much put an end to the old traditions. Anyway, I don't encourage the children to repeat such scraps of old nonsense as they might remember—my concern is rather with putting real knowledge into their heads! I gather that Miss Reid has some interest in folklore, so perhaps she might be of more assistance to you than I in this matter."

Holmes thought this very likely, but smiled affectionately at the well-meaning School-Master.

"Who's for another glass of Port?" asked Mr. Brown. Some people didn't drink again after they'd started smoking; Mr. Brown was someone who did. That was fine with Holmes; and with everyone else, it seemed. Their host filled Holmes's glass first, then handed the decanter to Crowley, who filled his own glass, then passed the decanter to the Doctor. When the Doctor's glass was filled, he gave the decanter to Holmes, who handed it over to their host. Only when Mr. Brown had filled his own glass and taken a sip from it did the others presume to drink.

Holmes had one final question: "Have you gentlemen ever heard anything about the former existence of a Hell-Fire Club, or anything of that sort, on this Island?"

The Doctor looked blank. Their host chuckled.

"No, Mr. Holmes. But of course if there were such a thing here, it would necessarily have been kept very dark; and so, once again, our ignorance proves nothing either way."

"Ah, well—I thank you gentlemen for your help."

"If there are no further questions, Mr. Holmes," said the Doctor, "perhaps you would be kind enough to favour us with your account of the life of Christ?"

* * *

The streets of Cunningsborough were very quiet as Holmes and Crowley walked back to their Hotel. Public houses could not open on a Sunday, and the weather was bad enough to keep most people indoors. Crowley held the Hotel's umbrella.

121

"I think the Doctor was a little shocked by what you said about Jesus."

"He certainly seemed dismayed by the revelation that the real Jesus' sympathies were so restricted; yet he seemed to cope well enough with my rational explanation of the miracles—and even with my proposal that St. Peter had deliberately counterfeited the Resurrection appearances of his dead Master. Was I mistaken in supposing that those ideas upset *you* a little, Mr. Crowley?"

"You were correct, sir: I should like to believe in miracles."

"You would certainly like to perform them. Isn't that the point of this Abra-Melin business?"

"In a word: Yes."

"And has anything that I've said to-night dissuaded you from a world-view in which such things are possible?"

"Well... on the one hand, I can see that what you said about Jesus, and about supernatural religion in general, makes a good deal of sense. On the other hand there are the teachings of my Order, which tell me that there is a God, and that he was incarnated as Christ for our Salvation—nay, more: that he is incarnate in every man. As I said yesterday, I have chosen to accept a Magical interpretation of reality until the results of the Operation of Abra-Melin either prove or disprove it, next year. My faith resembles that of the Doctor; but, unlike his, it is not unconditional. If the new century finds me disillusioned, I shall remember to-night and say: 'Mr. Holmes, you were right!' If the experiment works, then—and only then—shall I know for sure that you were wrong. For the moment I am agnostic, but by no means inclined to dispute your position, sir."

122

"Very well: I shan't persist."

They walked in silence for a little way; then Crowley said, in a more playful tone:

"Did you think that there was anything *queer* going on between Mr. Brown and his manservant—or Mr. Brown and the Doctor, for that matter?"

"I should consider it none of my business if there were—unless it had some bearing on our case, which it does not."

"Sorry! I meant no disrespect to any of those gentlemen. It's just that I find people so interesting."

Holmes smiled, and began to frame a comforting remark, when from an alley-way behind them he heard the unmistakable *sound of a pistol being cocked.*

"Halt there, gentlemen, and do not turn around. I have a pistol: if either of you should disobey, both of you will surely die." Good English, but spoken with the local intonation so reminiscent of Norwegian or Swedish; the speaker male, heavily-built, and about forty years of age.

"What is it that you want?" asked Holmes.

"It seems to me that you'd give a good deal to know what happened to old Mr. Tollemache."

"My business here is to find out."

"Well, I can tell you—but I want a tidy sum in return."

"How much?"

"Twenty pounds—in sovereigns."

Crowley gave a brief, derisive laugh. "Who carries so much chink?"

"You'll get it, Mr. Crowley, and bring it to the Bell Tavern, down on the sea-front at Storwick. Come between five and half-past, to-morrow night. The place has been closed for years, but you'll find the door unlocked, and there'll be all the light we'll need—which'll not be much. Go in and sit down, both of you, lay the cash on the table, and keep your hands there, where I can see them. I'll talk, but you'll not see my face. Do we have a deal?"

"Yes," said Holmes.

"Then you may start walking, gentlemen. I think it goes without saying that you would be most unwise to turn around. We shall meet again to-morrow."

They walked in silence for a while, then Crowley said:

"What do you make of that, sir?"

"I should prefer not to discuss it until we get back to the Hotel, Mr. Crowley."

"May I talk of other matters?"

"By all means."

"I was thinking of the footprints which we observed..."

"That, also, is a matter which I should rather not discuss here. We do not know who may be listening."

Crowley gave up on conversation then, and Holmes was left to his thoughts.

* * *

They sat in the chairs by Crowley's fireplace. The fire was a cheerful sight, since the maid had tended it during their absence. Holmes sipped a night-cap of the local whisky. Crowley asked:

"Do you intend that we should keep our appointment with the gunman?"

"I certainly do not! First thing in the morning I shall tell the whole story to Sergeant Flett, and let the Bobbies go there to arrest the man if they can."

"How disappointing!"

"This is not a 'penny dreadful', Mr. Crowley, and we are not invulnerable supermen. If we went to keep that appointment, it is quite likely that we should not return. Why should we take such a risk? For the chance of information, I suppose—but how reliable did that gunman seem? Most likely he knows nothing about the disappearance of Mr. Tollemache, and is merely seeking to enrich himself—at best, by incriminating some hated rival; at worst, by robbery and murder. He may, of course, have practiced a similar ruse on the Reverend gentleman. Anyway, I expect that the Police will get the truth out of the fellow. I should be happy to offer my services as interrogator, should old-fashioned methods fail."

"Yet the Police themselves may be responsible for the death of Mr. Tollemache," said Crowley. "They may even have sent this fellow to us to-night. Perhaps it's all part of a scheme by which the villains are hoping to cover up their guilt."

"In such a case, there would still be no harm in my telling Sergeant Flett about the gunman; and no point at all in our keeping that appointment at the Bell."

"No, I suppose not! Another cigarette, sir?"

Crowley proffered the box.

"I don't mind if I do: but this must be my last." He took one and lit it. "I think that you wished to say something about the footprints, Mr. Crowley?"

"You might consider this a flight of fancy, sir: but there is a good deal of folklore which suggests that agéd Witches could magically make themselves young again; or *vice versa*, that young Witches could appear in the guise of old hags. I keep thinking about that when I recall the footprints that looked like Mrs. Rendall's, but seemed to be those of a younger, nimbler woman."

"You're suggesting that Mrs. Rendall really is a Witch, and that she has the power to make herself young again?"

"Some auto-hypnotic process, perhaps..."

Holmes chuckled. "No, Mr. Crowley: I'm afraid that's quite impossible. A few of the Tibetan yogis claim similar powers of shape-shifting, but I never saw good evidence for such a thing; and it contradicts everything that I know about physiology. Perhaps some of the Witches were simply rather good at disguising themselves—did you ever think of that?"

"Well, then—do you think that Mrs. Rendall could be a young woman in disguise?" asked Crowley.

"Think of her sunken cheeks, her vacant mouth, and her withered, claw-like hands! Such things cannot be counterfeited. She must be really very old—at least seventy, I'd say."

"Another point about the footprints, then: because we cannot distinguish the prints of 'Atalanta' and Mrs. Rendall, how may we be sure which of them went into the grounds of Monksdale House?"

"From the evidence of the prints I am sure that 'Atalanta' went there; but I cannot be sure that Mrs. Rendall did not. Yet I cannot believe that good old woman to be a deceiver—far less an accomplice to murder."

"You see, Mr. Holmes, I can believe that. I can imagine a poor woman like Mrs. Rendall killing Mr. Tollemache for his money; and I can also imagine her, with her apparent detestation of Witchcraft, being part of a Calvinist conspiracy to suppress publication of Mr. Tollemache's book. I can even imagine that she might actually be a Witch, as that worthy gentleman came to suspect. Some people are good at pretending to be what they are not, as you must know better than most, Mr. Holmes."

"I have spent nearly two decades in studying how to read the human face. If my knowledge of this subject is worth anything, then Mrs. Rendall is exactly what she seems to be, and we may leave her out of our speculations."

"I defer to your greater experience, sir." Crowley puffed on his cigarette. "Are we any nearer to a solution of this mystery after to-night's conversations?"

"The most promising lead in our possession is that the Provost may somehow be involved in Mr. Tollemache's disappearance. On my visit to-morrow I shall take care to form an estimate of the man—and I shall also attempt to see as much of his house as is possible, looking out for any chambers in which a man might be held captive: a cellar to which I am denied access, for example."

"An admirable plan! And after that?"

"Well, we are meeting the fascinating Miss Reid at one, of course; and at some point I shall endeavour to interview Mr. Balfour at the Cathedral Archive. It might be rather interesting to check Mr. Tollemache's account of the documents that he found there, don't you think?"

"You are not convinced that his account was truthful?"

"I am inclined to believe him; but I am not certain."

"The writing of those old documents can be fiendishly hard to decipher."

"I have had some experience in that line."

"Oh, yes! You spent a few weeks at Cambridge, did you not, just before my time, studying ancient charters? I heard something about that when I got there, and rather kicked myself for having missed the chance to meet you then."

So Crowley had not heard of Holmes's return to the town in February of the Jubilee Year—which was good! His business then had been one which was best kept quiet.

"I liked Cambridge," said Holmes.

Crowley had such an expressive face that one could practically read his mind just by looking at him. Now he seemed to be wondering whether to ask if Holmes had been a student there, and deciding that the matter was none of his business. "So did I," he said; smiled, and sought another topic of conversation. He smiled again. "Shall we also be interviewing Miss Lizzie Grey?"

Holmes liked the way that Crowley called her 'Miss', apparently without ironical intent.

"Yes, I was coming to that: if you are agreeable, I should like you to see her to-morrow morning, while I am at Monksdale. I take it that you would have no objection to such a thing? No, I thought not; nor do I expect that Miss Grey will do so either."

"And what do you want me to do?"

"Arrange to spend an hour or two alone with her as soon as possible. The Hotel staff would no doubt let her in by the back-door, and keep quiet about it, for a consideration. Then you are to embrace her most heartily, Mr. Crowley, and find out what she knows about the Witches, the folk-tale, and the old scholar who came in search of them. You must know from experience how the intoxication of passion may serve to loosen a woman's tongue. It would be no great hardship to you to enflame the lovely Lizzie's cheeks with hot kisses, I suppose?"

"Oh, I think that I could probably manage it, out of a sense of duty," said Crowley, and they both laughed. Then the young man looked dubious. "But is it ethical to do so?"

"I have done much the same thing myself, in the course of an investigation, and consider my conduct entirely justified by the results. A man's life may be at stake. You are not being asked to hurt the girl. Did not a wise philosopher once say that in the mutual giving and receiving of pleasure there is nothing to which a reasonable man might object?"

"Thank you, Mr. Holmes—but if the girl *is* a Witch, then exposing the hidden Cult will certainly cause her distress, and may lead to graver consequences for her and those whom she loves."

"Being a Witch is no longer a crime under British Law; if Miss Grey should turn out to be also an accessory to Murder, she would surely deserve to be punished as such! But I find it hard to believe anything bad about that beautiful girl. Most likely she is not a Witch, but just knows something about the Cult, and goes in fear of them. Either way, we must find out if we are to help our client, and perhaps to prevent the murder of a venerable scholar."

"Yes, you are right, of course, sir: my moral duty is to seduce the girl!"

CHAPTER VIII.

DISTURBING REVELATIONS.

Sergeant Flett looked up and smiled, with a touch of embarrassment.

"Ah, Mr. Holmes!" He rose, and stood respectfully. "How smart you look in morning dress! Look, sir, I've been thinking: I'm sorry that things happened as they did yesterday. It seems to me that I over-reacted a little. Mr. Crowley is young, and young men often make mistakes; but he had good intentions, I can tell. I should not have chided him as I did."

"I have considered the matter too, Sergeant. I think that what really upset you was suddenly being treated like a servant, when we had been conversing together as equals. Am I right?"

"You're right, sir: that was it. At the time I thought that it was something to do with the dignity of the Queen's uniform, and the impartiality of Justice, or some such thing; but looking back I can see that it was as you say. I can see, too, that Mr. Crowley meant no harm. I owe him an apology—which I hope that you'll pass on to the young gentleman, sir."

"So we are friends again?" Holmes extended his hand, and the Sergeant leaned forward to shake it. "Always, Mr. Holmes," said Flett, and looked deep into Holmes's eyes. There was fraternity in their mutual gaze. After a long moment Flett sat down, and opened his day-book.

"So, sir: to your business!"

Holmes told Flett all that had happened with the gunman, on the previous night: of the threatening voice that spoke from the darkness, and of the pact that they had made with it; and the Sergeant made notes.

"I can certainly see why you don't want to keep that appointment, sir! Only a fool would walk into such an ambush!" He considered for a moment. "Three of us here have pistols: all ex-Army men like myself, who know how to shoot. I suppose the best thing would be for the three of us to go down to the Bell at the appointed time, and arrest anyone that we find there. From what you say, the man doesn't sound like a lunatic, so I don't suppose that he'd dare to fire on the Queen's uniform. But even if he started blazing away like a desperado in the Wild West, I reckon that I could beat him at that game. I've killed a lot of men in my time."

This was not bravado, Holmes could tell, but a simple statement of the truth. Holmes could see the proud young soldier still beneath the Sergeant's middle-aged exterior.

"Should you not consult your Superintendent to have this plan authorized?"

"Och aye; I'll tell him when he comes in. But he'll agree, I'm sure. What else is there to be done, in the circumstances?"

"A good point. Tell, me Sergeant, do you have any idea who our gunman might be?"

"Well, now: from what you say, he was a strongly-built local man of middling years, who spoke good English and was handy with a pistol. That narrows it down somewhat. A man of that age who spoke good

English would probably have learned it in the Navy or the Army. Let me think... It could be me, of course, sir!"

They shared a smile.

"When he spoke to me, he had more of Trowley in his voice than do you, Sergeant. But then I suppose that when you converse with your friends you have more of the Island in your speech, too."

"Och, yi're riht dare, sir. Wi' taak like dis."

"Well, he was not quite so local as that; but still within your range, of course—so, yes, I suppose it could have been you! But ruling out that hypothesis for the moment, Sergeant, purely on the grounds of my liking for you, who comes to your mind as the most probable suspect?"

"Well, sir, there's a fisherman called Adam Marwick. He was once a soldier, like me: a Sergeant, in fact, but cashiered for drunkenness. He still drinks too much, and likes to spend money on the ladies, so he'd have the motive; and I've heard he brought a service revolver home with him, so he'd have the means, too. No man else that I know of keeps a pistol here. But it's entirely possible that some other reprobate has just got a new toy from the Mainland. We'll not know for sure until we catch the man—which I trust we'll do this evening. Do you wish to accompany us, sir?"

"A tempting offer, but one which I must regretfully decline; my duty to my client entails that I do my best to stay alive, which means avoiding all unnecessary risks. But I should be most interested in talking to the man, if I could do so safely; so please take him alive if you can."

"I'll do my best for you, Mr. Holmes. We should have him here by seven o'clock, if all goes according to plan. You could talk to him then; or we could soften him up a bit for you first, if you like."

"No, thank you: I shall take him as I find him; I have my own method for getting the truth out of a man. If nothing comes of that, I might indeed ask you to do some little thing of the sort that you have found to be effective in such cases—with the proviso that you do not cause our prisoner any permanent injury. I should hate to have even a thug like Marwick crippled or blinded for life on my account."

"Well, I'm of your mind exactly, sir. Only a bungler maims a man when his intention is merely to hurt. I'm not one of those *sadists*, as they call them these days: I don't enjoy the business. But sometimes a Policeman needs to hurt a man; and I can do my duty well enough, should the need arise."

* * *

Monksdale House looked like a rather dull provincial Georgian building, thought Holmes, as his carriage approached it through the grey morning. As they drew closer, however, he began to detect signs suggesting that an eighteenth-century *façade*, with big sash windows, had been imposed on a much older building; and, when the dour old Butler had let him cross the threshold, the hypothesis was confirmed: both in its proportions and in its detail, this panelled hall suggested the fifteenth century rather than the eighteenth.

There were big stone lintels over the doors, a Gothic-arched fireplace to his right, and a trophy of antique weapons on the wall above it. Eight slender clubs, in shape and size not dissimilar to American baseball bats, were hung at a steep angle, four on either

134

side, to form a 'V' shape, at the centre of which, bolt upright, hung a remarkably primitive stone-headed mace. To Holmes's inquiry the Butler replied that it was the club of Grim (whose name he pronounced to rhyme with *cream*), the eponymous fore-father of the Grimson family.

"Is it of the Viking period?"

"Yes, sir: from Heathen times."

Holmes examined it as closely as he could, half-hoping to see a recent stain on the head. There was nothing. All the clubs had been very recently cleaned; but so had the rest of the hall, so that was not necessarily suspicious.

On the other wall, above the coat-hooks and hat-pegs, hung a rather *naïve* sixteenth-century tapestry, its style similar to those which he had once observed on a visit to Hardwick Hall, in Derbyshire. The hanging depicted the Massacre of the Prophets of Ba'al by Elijah and his followers, after the Contest at Carmel: as the blood of the Prophets flowed from their severed necks, rain was beginning to fall on the parched land.

After parting with his cloak, and taking his hat in his hand, Holmes was shown into a room on the right of the hall: Mr. Grimson's dark-panelled study, at the far end of which the Provost sat behind his big desk. A curious austerity prevailed in the furnishings and decoration here, to the extent that there were no patterns on anything: the carpet was as green and featureless as a billiard-table, and all the fittings were plain. The dark furniture was in the same Cromwellian style that Mr. Brown had in his dining-room: probably the work of the same local craftsman. Behind the Provost, and on the wall to his right, there stood large book-cases, their contents almost entirely consisting of law and theology, with the addition of a few standard works of reference, such as *Who's Who* and Cruden's *Concordance.*

Mr. Grimson himself was somewhat younger than Holmes had expected—no more than forty, with short flaxen hair and a long beard, like that of a Coptic Patriarch. Holmes now saw the full point of Mr. Brown's remark about John Calvin and John Knox, for the Provost certainly resembled the portraits of both those men, with his thin, intelligent face, long, straight nose, arched brows, and piercing eyes. He was dressed like Holmes, in single-breasted morning-coat and striped trousers, wing-collared shirt, and dark cravat: the uniform of a respectable, middle-aged gentleman. The Provost's tie-pin bore an interesting symbol, which looked to Holmes like the rune-stave on the old garden-door.

"Good morning, Mr. Grimson. I am Sherlock Holmes."

The Provost rose to shake his hand.

"I'm a busy man, as you can imagine, Mr. Holmes, but I can spare you a few minutes. Please take a chair. I gather that Miss Tollemache has engaged you to find her father; and that you are sympathetic to her wild ideas about Witchcraft and human sacrifice."

They both sat down.

"Miss Tollemache is my client, yes: but I have as yet formed no judgment as to the truth of her hypothesis. I am duty-bound to consider all possibilities. What, I wonder, is your opinion, sir? Might there be Witches on this Island still?"

Deep emotion flickered on the Provost's face. "My ancestors performed harsh surgery to eradicate the loathsome disease of

136

Witchcraft from this Island, Mr. Holmes. I believe that the operation was a complete success. When I observe developments on the Mainland, I sometimes doubt whether your ancestors were quite so thorough: so much of what passes for modern culture seems like nothing more nor less than rebellion against God!"

"What did you think of Mr. Tollemache's theories concerning the Northern *Cinderella* story?"

"If that old gentleman's notion of what happened here in pre-historic times was anything like the truth, I'd say that it was a shameful thing, quite unworthy of remembrance. A Witch-Queen ruling our Island—it's horrible to think about! In the case of a nation as in that of a man, some things are best forgotten, Mr. Holmes—don't you agree?"

The Provost's brief smile was reminiscent of the unctuous blackmailer whom the world knew as Charles Augustus Milverton. Was Mr. Grimson hinting that he knew some shameful secret about Holmes? No: surely that story had perished with Moriarty at the Reichenbach Falls! Holmes paused, looking expectantly at the Provost, waiting for another hint; but none came, only a calm, confident stare. Most likely, concluded Holmes, the Provost was just displaying a typically Calvinist cynicism about Human Nature, assuming that every man had skeletons in his closet. It was indeed a fair assumption, by and large.

"I take it that you did not approve of the Reverend gentleman's plan to publish his research?"

"I'd have had no objection if it had been an article in some scholarly journal; but you know the kind of books that Mr. Tollemache wrote, don't you?"

"He is generally considered to be one of the most eminent folklorists in the country."

"I'm not disputing that, Mr. Holmes: my point is that he wasn't really an academic. He was a popular author who wrote for a wide readership, many of them drawn from the lower orders of society. His book might well have created a popular interest in Trowley that would have resulted in our suffering an influx of vulgar tourists."

"Would that not be a good thing? Your fish-and-chip shops would do well out of it, and your hotels, for example. Their extra income would mostly be spent here, and so the Island as a whole would soon benefit from having more money in circulation."

"I should hate to see it," said the Provost. From his expression this was no idle word. "Such a thing would be certain to corrupt our youth. At present we are a relatively godly society; our few visitors are scholarly gentlemen who come to see the ancient monuments, and don't cause any trouble. Can you imagine what this Island would be like if it were regularly over-run by trippers from the Mainland? We should witness the triumph of vice, Mr. Holmes: drunkenness, gambling and prostitution would flourish, and virtue would come to be despised! Centuries of my ancestors' good work would be swept away on a tide of music-halls and mutoscopes!"

"When you heard of the disappearance of Mr. Tollemache, you must have thought that your prayers had been answered."

A Milvertonic smile played around the Provost's mouth.

"After my single meeting with that gentleman, on the day after his arrival, I did indeed pray that Mr. Tollemache would be unable to complete his ungodly work. I did not ask for the blast of wind that blew him from the midnight cliff; but I do believe that the Lord God controls the winds, and that He sent that one for His own good purposes."

"You wish for something and it happens," said Holmes. "In this case, a man dies. That sounds a lot like Witchcraft to me."

The Provost looked horrified by the suggestion. "I am a servant of the Lord, sir. That makes all the difference in the world: as great as the gulf which separates Heaven from Hell."

"That is indeed a most important distinction. Let us turn to more mundane matters. Pray tell me, sir: which members of the fair sex might have occasion to make use of the eastern gate of your property, and the foot-path leading thence to the coast?"

That rattled him. "What an extraordinary question! What connexion can there be between the disappearance of Mr. Tollemache, and the comings and goings of my Abigails!"

"Those would be your maidservants, I take it? How many of those ladies might use that gate?"

"All of them, I suppose: that would be seven, including the Housekeeper."

"It would be most useful to the progress of my investigation if I might speak with these ladies, and examine their footwear."

"Examine their—oh, you're thinking about footprints, I see! Very well, then: so long as you're brief: no more than five minutes with any of them. I don't want them to get behind in their work."

"Thank you very much, sir. And would those be the only ladies to make use of that portal?"

"I have two daughters. They sometimes go that way, on their walks, I believe." Mr. Grimson indicated a photograph on the wall, to Holmes's right. The girls who stood side by side in the picture were about twelve years of age, and absolutely identical. Their long, curly, blonde hair was partially concealed by their straw hats, which bore hat-bands with a diagonal stripe—perhaps the colours of their School. The twins were clad in dark, calf-length, sleeveless smocks, under which white blouses could be seen. Although there was nothing ugly about those round, innocent faces, they seemed a little uncanny. Perhaps, thought Holmes, it was just the strangeness of their perfect likeness: one of the girls on her own might simply have looked angelic, but two of them together were somehow disturbing.

"I presume that they are pupils of Miss Reid's, at the Borough School."

A look of distaste flitted across the Provost's face at the name of the Head-Mistress. "Yes."

"May I interview them there?"

"Good Heavens, Mr. Holmes—surely you don't suspect my little girls?"

"Of course not, sir. There is a possibility that during one of their walks they may have observed something which might be of use to me in my investigation—that is all. I am rather good at talking to children, and I promise not to distress them. Is this a recent photograph?"

"Yes. They are thirteen years of age."

"Their names?"

"Faith and Hope. But I cannot give you permission to speak to my girls, Mr. Holmes: I don't want them to be mixed up in this unpleasant business."

"Of course you have a perfect right to refuse, sir; but I beg you to reconsider."

"Absolutely not."

"Very well. Is there a Mrs. Grimson, may I ask?"

"I am a widower, sir."

"You have also lost a daughter, I deduce. Were your two losses related?"

Mr. Grimson nodded. "My wife and little Charity both died of typhoid fever, almost nine years ago, now."

"Please forgive me for touching on such a painful subject. Do I take it that no tradeswomen would be entering your property from an easterly direction?"

"No, they'd all use the town gate—the way that you came this morning. But what has any of this to do with the case of Mr. Tollemache?"

"Perhaps nothing: but I must leave no stone unturned if I am to solve this mystery."

"Well, I don't see what mystery there is to solve. A foolish old man went out for a midnight walk, and a gust of wind blew him into the sea!"

"There is much to be said for such a hypothesis, sir. Could you tell me how you first heard of these events?"

141

"A message from Sergeant Flett at the Police Station arrived soon after breakfast on Thursday morning. Then a little later Constables Scollie and Irvine came to report on the matter to me."

"Which way did they come?"

"Along the coast path, and through the eastern gate. It's the nearest way from the cottage."

"How did they unlock the door?"

"I knew that they were coming, and sent a servant to let them in."

"The Police have no key to that lock, then." Mr. Grimson shook his head. "Does anyone else, outside your household, possess such a thing?"

"Certainly not."

"And I take it that you were not expecting a visit from Mr. Tollemache at the time of his disappearance?"

The Provost seemed surprised. "Why, no, sir: I was not."

Holmes believed him. "Thank you for your time, sir: you have been most helpful." He rose, and shook the Provost's hand. "I wonder if I might ask one more favour of you, on my own account. Perhaps you know that I have a passion for mediæval architecture?" From his expression, Mr. Grimson felt the same. "This house of yours is quite fascinating to me. Do you know how old it is?"

"It is of various dates, Mr. Holmes. The *façade* is from the 1780's; this part from around 1450; the back-part from about a century earlier; and the cellar older still, with a round-arched vault that looks very similar to the crypt of the Cathedral. In the Middle Ages, this was a Papist monastery; my ancestors acquired it at the time of the Reformation, and we have made few alterations in the centuries since

142

then. To a lover of mediæval architecture, such as yourself, it must indeed be very interesting. You must certainly see the cellar—and indeed any other rooms that interest you. Drever shall give you a tour of the house after you have finished your enquiries."

"Do you mind my making a few sketches?"

"So long as they're not for publication, I see no problem. Only don't spend more than half an hour on your exploration, and please be respectful of our privacy."

"Of course; of course. Oh—just one final question, sir, to satisfy the curiosity of an amateur antiquarian: what is that symbol on your tie-pin? I have observed the same thing on one of your doors."

"It is the runic 'G', for 'Grim'; and also the emblem of an ancient fraternity founded by my distant ancestor, the Sons of Grim, which now exists as an exclusive Order within the local Masonic Lodge. All the Sons of Grim are Masons, but only nine of the Masons, at any one time, may be Sons of Grim."

"Does this Order have any particular purpose?"

"Simply to fight Evil, Mr. Holmes. Once the Sons of Grim were diligent in the eradication of Witchcraft; these days we have less dramatic work to do. But I'm afraid that I can't say much about it—there are oaths of secrecy involved."

"Of course."

* * *

Holmes and Crowley sat in the arm-chairs by the fire in Crowley's room. On the table between them a maid set down a tray bearing sandwiches and coffee. "Thank you," said Holmes. Crowley watched

143

the girl's departure with some interest. When the door closed, Holmes waited a few moments to ask:

"So, Mr. Crowley—how did you fare in Storwick?"

"Well, as you instructed me, I said nothing of Witchcraft, nor of our case; but I did communicate to the lovely Lizzie my sincere admiration of her female charms, and my desire for a closer acquaintance with them. She was certainly game—I can always tell! Nothing so vulgar as a price was mentioned, of course. She did, however, ask the time, which she used as a pretext to comment on the beauty of my watch, and how valuable it must be; and that led on to the subject of how I must be a millionaire (which I didn't deny). Then she said that if she were rich the thing about it that she'd like best would be being able to give presents to all the people that had been nice to her; and that gave me the opportunity to say that I enjoyed doing just that, and the nicer someone was to me the more I liked to give. We reached an unspoken understanding. She is coming here to-night, after the chip-shop closes, soon after ten. I squared the matter with young Forsyth before your return. Isn't it wonderful to be rich?"

Crowley helped himself to a sandwich. He seemed to be enjoying it.

"To be rich at the age of twenty-four must be bliss indeed. I congratulate you, Mr. Crowley."

Holmes took a sandwich, too. They were cold beef and mustard, with butter and good white bread: a classic combination.

"Was your morning equally successful, sir?" asked Crowley. "What discoveries have you been making?"

Holmes swallowed a mouthful. "Having seen the Provost for myself, I find it hard to believe that he is a secret Warlock: he seemed like an old-fashioned Calvinist to me. Of course that might be simply a very good pretence. His attitude to the publication of Mr. Tollemache's *Cinderella* book, however, inclines me to look rather favourably upon your earlier proposal, about the old gentleman being killed by a conspiracy of respectable people, in order to silence him. Indeed, Mr. Grimson told me of a secret fraternity which sounds like the perfect organization for such a conspiracy: the Sons of Grim."

"You no longer think, then, that Mr. Tollemache may be alive?"

"If he were being held anywhere, it would have to be at Monksdale; but I have looked the whole house over, from the cellar to the attic, and all the out-buildings, too; and I'm sure that he is nowhere on the premises. *Ergo*, he is dead."

"You suspect that the Sons of Grim killed him?"

"I am inclined to think so; and I suspect the Provost of some particular involvement."

"The footprint evidence might suggest as much. Are we any closer to discovering the identity of 'Atalanta', sir?"

Holmes chewed his sandwich for a while before replying.

"Like a character in a fairy-tale, I have examined the boots of many women this morning, and I have found that all Mr. Grimson's servants have feet much larger than those of 'Atalanta'; the footwear of his two daughters, however, seems to be of just the right size. I conclude that 'Atalanta' must be one of those girls—or perhaps more likely both of them! The girls are identical twins, and always dressed alike: their footprints would be indistinguishable."

"Do you suspect that they were involved in the murder of Mr. Tollemache?"

"I shudder to think of such a possibility."

"It seems quite plausible, though, sir, don't you think? The little girls go and tell some story designed to lure the old gentleman to the cliff; once there, a lurking thug dispatches him with a knock on the head from his bludgeon, while the twins run home without a backward glance: I can imagine that."

Holmes took a swig of coffee. It was just how he liked it, made in the true Viennese style: 'as sweet as love, as black as sin, and as hot as Hell!' He imagined Crowley's story happening in the real world. It seemed credible, up to a point; and then he saw a difficulty.

"It is true that the appeal of an innocent child is the hardest of all for a compassionate man to resist; but what kind of a father would make his daughters accomplices to murder? Unfortunately I have been unable to secure an interview with little Faith and Hope, and so I do not know what story they might tell. From speaking to Mr. Grimson's staff, I have gathered that the girls did definitely go for a walk on Wednesday: the Maid-of-All-Work said that their boots were particularly muddy the next morning, and the Laundry-Maid found two of their pinafores in the same condition when she did this morning's wash."

"Are young girls here in the habit of going for walks on their own, without a servant?"

Holmes nodded, chewing on his sandwich. "Yes: apparently so. It really is a safe enough place for them to do that kind of thing. The girls' Nurse thought that they had gone to see their friends at the nearby farmstead of Mickle Winning: another set of twins, would you believe, the Sinclair girls! She was vague about the timing of their visit, saying only that it must have been between tea-time and bed-time. Indeed, she was rather vague about most things. I suspect that the wretched woman is an ether-drinker: I know the signs. The path to Mickle Winning does indeed run by Mr. Tollemache's door, however, and so her story is in accordance with the evidence. Although I am forbidden to interview the girls, I hope to learn more about them when we speak with the charming Miss Reid."

* * *

The Borough School was an undistinguished example of the Gothic Revival, too plain to be distinguished as Early English or Perpendicular, and certainly not Decorated! But there was nothing ugly about it, and Holmes was well-disposed toward the building on account of its function. The Girls' School had its own front-door, much like that of a gentleman's house, with a letter-box and a bell, which Crowley rang. The sound of children at play could be heard in the distance. Soon an old Porter answered the door. His uniform was not unlike the Sergeant's, only black rather than blue.

"Gød day, gentlemen."

"We are Mr. Holmes and Mr. Crowley, come to speak with Miss Reid."

"Come dis way, sirs." His accent was heavy, but he seemed civil enough. The hallway was simply decorated, with black floor-boards and dado, walls painted mustard-yellow up to the picture-rail, and above that a white ceiling; all the doors were black, including the one on the left to which the porter led them. It bore a brass name-plate on which was engraved the word **HEAD-MISTRESS**.

The porter knocked, and a lovely woman's voice answered.

147

"Come in!"

They obeyed, and the Porter announced them. Behind her desk Miss Reid rose to her feet, hurriedly removing a pair of gold-rimmed *pince-nez*, which left little dents in the sides of her aquiline nose. She was wearing a long black skirt and a closely-tailored white blouse with thin, vertical, blue stripes; a cameo brooch fastened it at her throat. Beneath her clothing, her corset was evidently of the old-fashioned kind that pulled the waist in and pushed the bosom up. It suited her figure very well, Holmes thought. As to her face, it was even more beautiful than he had remembered it: quite dazzlingly so, in fact! Her eyes were green. She smiled at him. He could see her begin to offer a hand; but she restrained herself, and put her hands together in a Hindoo *namaste*. Had she been in the East? Mr. Brown had not mentioned it. More likely she had spent time with Indians in this country—in her student days, presumably. Her diploma came, he noticed, from University College, London, where there were many Indian students.

"Ah, Mr. Holmes! I am very pleased to meet you!" Her speech was that of a well-educated Englishwoman, with only the faintest undertone of the local accent.

"A pleasure for me, too, madam." He bowed also.

"And you must be Mr. Crowley!"

Holmes was unreasonably irked to see the Head-Mistress smiling at his handsome young companion.

"Pleasure is too mild a word, dear lady!" Crowley made a rather theatrical bow, with a flourish of his hand like that of some Regency fop; it appeared to please her.

148

"Thank you, Mr. Johnston," she said. "I don't see why you shouldn't leave us alone for a few minutes."

The Porter was unperturbed. "I cannae, Miss. Yi' ken da regulations."

She sighed, but did not argue. "Please be seated, gentlemen. What can I do for you?"

The gentlemen sat on a pair of elegant bent-wood chairs, while the Porter went to warm his old hands at the fire.

"As you have no doubt heard," said Holmes, "I am investigating the disappearance of the Reverend Mr. Melchior Tollemache. I understand that you had a conversation with him last week; and so I wonder if you could tell me what passed between the two of you on that occasion."

The lovely School-Mistress cast a resentful glance at the Porter's back. Holmes had the distinct impression that she did not feel able to speak freely in the old man's presence.

"It was exactly a week ago, Mr. Holmes; he sat where you are sitting now, and told me of his research into the story of the Crow's Daughter. I found it most interesting, and wished him good luck in his quest; but I regret that I was unable to help him."

"You know nothing, then, of any surviving society of Witches on this Island?"

She shook her head.

"Nothing at all, I am sorry to say." Was she simply nervous, or was she lying? He could not tell.

"That is most disappointing. And of the fairy-tale?"

"No, I'd heard nothing of that, either."

149

Again, he was not entirely convinced; but she was clearly disinclined to say more. He changed the subject. "I believe that the Provost's twin daughters, Faith and Hope, are among your charges?"

She smiled ruefully. "They are indeed—until the summer." Clearly she was looking forward to the day when the girls left School.

"You do not like them?"

"It would be extremely unprofessional of me to dislike any of my pupils," she said, with the faintest hint of irony. "The problem is rather that *they* do not like *me*. It's not their fault, of course: all their lives they've had their little heads filled with their father's prejudices, and to him I must seem like the embodiment of everything which he most dislikes about the modern world. When the girls grow up enough to start thinking for themselves, they may look back on these days and see me in a more favourable light: perhaps we might even be friends. But at the moment they're dead set on being my enemies. They are the ones who started calling me *the Witch*—a nick-name now widely used among the children."

"Not universally?"

"No: many of them do like me, and won't use it."

"How else do the Grimson girls make your life difficult?"

"In the usual ways that children torment their teachers, Mr. Holmes: by disrupting my lessons, throwing things at me when my back is turned, leaving tacks on my chair—that kind of thing! Once when I went into the stationery cupboard the door was closed and locked behind me, so that I had to bang and call to be released."

"Oh, nasty!" said Crowley.

"Yes," she said, "and that's not the worst trick that they've played on me. Usually they manage to do it in such a way that they can't be found out, but sometimes they slip up, and I am able to punish them—not that it seems to do much good."

"How do you punish them?" asked Holmes. "With the tawse?"

"Och, no! I'll not do that! I don't want to teach the children that violence can ever be acceptable behaviour. There was a tawse here when I came, but I threw it away."

She was radical indeed, thought Holmes.

"Then what disciplinary methods do you employ when your pupils misbehave?"

"Generally I just give them a stern telling-off, and make them apologize for what they've done. In the case of graver offences, I make them stay after School and sit quietly for an hour with me: they hate that!"

"Foolish girls!" said Crowley. "I could happily sit and look at you all day!"

She smiled at the compliment. Holmes saw a practical difficulty.

"Are parents not alarmed when children fail to return home at their customary hour?"

"Should a girl offend on one school-day, she'll be detained on the next. Her parents, or her guardians, will expect her to be late on that day."

"An ingenious system—but, I gather, not entirely effective."

"Well, Mr. Holmes, it works well enough with most of the girls. Among the current crop of pupils, only the Grimson sisters and their friends the Sinclairs have ever required more than a single detention."

151

"Ah, yes, the Sinclair girls. What can you tell me of them?"

"They are twins, like the Grimsons, which is, I suppose, the reason for their intense friendship; but the Sinclairs are mousy little creatures, completely in thrall to the Grimson girls."

"You wouldn't know if the Provost's daughters had visited their Sinclair friends at home last week, I suppose?"

"They don't confide such things in me, I'm afraid."

"Would it be possible for me to speak to them?"

She started to say *Yes*, but the Porter cleared his throat. She exchanged a glance with the old man over Holmes's shoulder.

"No," she said. "I'm afraid that you'd need their father's permission for that."

"Well, then," said Holmes, "there seems to be no reason for us to keep you any longer from your work. You must be very busy."

"Yes, Mr. Holmes. I am sorry that I could be of so little help in your enquiry. Please let me give you something to remember me by." She reached into her drawer and took out a cheaply-printed pamphlet, which she handed to him:

THE CASE
FOR
WOMEN'S
SUFFRAGE
BY
A LADY
OF U. C. L.

"You may find the outward form of it unappealing, but I believe that the contents will be of great interest to you."

"May I have one, too?" asked Crowley.

"Alas, I have no other to give; but Mr. Holmes will doubtless share his gift with you. Farewell, gentlemen; I hope that we may meet again!"

* * *

"Where to, sir?" asked the coachman.

"Mickle Winning, please. Stop just before we get to the gate," said Holmes.

As he and Crowley were driven to the farmhouse, Holmes leafed through the suffragist pamphlet; and discovered, as he more than half-expected, a hand-written note, which he read with some excitement.

CHAPTER IX.

THE OLDEST GAME IN THE WORLD.

"What does it say?" asked Crowley.

"It is most extraordinary. She asks that I go to visit her at home this evening."

"A-ha!" Crowley smiled knowingly.

"For reasons entirely of a professional nature, to do with the disappearance of Mr. Tollemache."

"I see."

"She has information which she will reveal only to me, in private: information that she dared not give to the Police for fear of a dreadful conspiracy going back more than a thousand years."

"Do you think that she means the Witch-Cult, or the Sons of Grim?"

"The latter, I should imagine. She seems to be a rational person; and the results of our investigation suggest that the Witch-Cult is no longer in existence on this Island, while the fraternity is undoubtedly real—and quite probably up to no good. But she may surprise me."

"Does she say any more?"

"Only to give me directions to the house, and to impress upon me the importance of my not being observed by anyone on my way there."

"I am not invited, then?"

"Regrettably not. Anyway, you have your appointment with Miss Grey."

"That's not until after ten. What time are you seeing Miss Reid?"

"Eight."

"Well, I suppose that our appointments might overlap—if you're lucky!"

Holmes was embarrassed. "Please do not speak so of a lady."

"The Colonel's lady and Judy O'Grady/ Are sisters under the skin," quoted Crowley, merrily. Then he looked at Holmes and grew graver. "Your pardon, sir—I go too far sometimes."

"Granted," said Holmes, a little grudgingly.

"But seriously, sir: don't you think that it's rather inconsistent to refuse the appointment at the Bell and accept this one? Might not this be another trap?"

"Miss Reid inspires more confidence than our unknown gunman. She is an outstanding practitioner of a noble profession; everything that one hears about her indicates that she is both highly intelligent and keen for justice."

"She is also very beautiful."

"Agreed—but that is not a factor in my decision."

Crowley smiled.

Soon the driver pulled up outside Mickle Winning, and the gentlemen stepped out. They had been at this point on the path the day before, with Mrs. Rendall. Her footprints (or, perhaps, those of the Provost's daughters) could be seen here and there on the mud; but, at the entrance to the farm, heavy traffic had obliterated them.

Inside the gate, the yard was cobbled, and showed every sign of having been recently swept; so there was no footprint evidence there, either. The farm-house was a long, low, vernacular building. Knocking on the door summoned an old Butler.

"Good afternoon. I am Mr. Sherlock Holmes, from London. I should like to speak with the master of the house."

"I'll see if he's at hame, sir. Bide ye here." The servant closed the door. After a few minutes, it was opened again, and they were confronted by a stout, middle-aged man with a large moustache— clearly a gentleman by his dress. His runic tie-pin proclaimed him a member of the sinister fraternity.

"Mr. Sinclair, I presume?"

"Yes, Mr. Holmes."

Holmes offered his hand, which Sinclair did not take.

"My colleague, Mr. Aleister Crowley."

Crowley did not offer his hand, and Sinclair merely grunted.

"Might we come in, sir?" asked Holmes. "It's a little chilly out here."

"May I ask your business?"

"I am making enquiries related to the disappearance of the Reverend Mr. Melchior Tollemache."

"Then there is no necessity for you to come in, for I have nothing to tell you."

"Just a few simple questions, sir –"

"If a Policeman asks me questions, I am obliged to answer him— but who are you, Mr. Holmes? Merely a nosey-parker from London. I

156

see no reason to speak to you—nor to suffer your continued intrusion on my property. Please leave now, sir; and take your Bosie with you."

Holmes winced in sympathy with his young friend.

"I fear that I must have unwittingly offended you, Mr. Sinclair—for only grave offence could explain such incivility on the part of one who has every appearance of being a ..."

But before Holmes could finish his sentence, the door was closed in his face.

* * *

The carriage rolled towards Cunningsborough.

"Why are we going to the Hotel first, Mr. Holmes?"

"I see no reason for you to accompany me on my visit to the Archive, Mr. Crowley. I shall wish to bathe at five o'clock, and you would oblige me by giving the Hotel some notice of my intentions. You might also tell them to lay out my tweeds. I think a 'high tea' at six would suit both of us admirably, don't you?"

"Right-ho, sir. What would you like me to do between now and then?"

"I suggest that you visit a public house and engage some of the locals in conversation. Don't be too overt, Mr. Crowley: begin by speaking of other matters, to establish a *rapport*, and then casually drop in a few questions about the things that interest us. You may well be met with stony silence, as was the Reverend gentleman, on occasion; but observe facial expressions, too, and give me your report when we meet again at table."

"I too was intending to bathe at five—will that be all right?"

"With the Hotel, do you mean? I'm sure that they will rise to the challenge."

"No—I meant that it would cut down my time for interviewing locals."

"Don't worry about it. You must be clean for your assignation, after all."

Crowley thought before speaking. "You know, sir, when we rode in from Storwick, I formed an impression of you as something of a puritan in matters venereal; and so I am still a little surprised by your apparent approval of my forthcoming *liaison* with Miss Grey. Did I misread you on that former carriage-ride?"

Holmes leaned back and steepled his fingers. "Personally, I find the thought of sexual congress quite unattractive, but I recognize that my temperament is somewhat unusual. I have no objection to other people enjoying themselves. My fear was that you might be the sort of cad who leads poor girls on with the prospect of marriage, and then deserts them, never caring in what condition they are left. Remember, sir, I'd only just met you. I've seen a great deal of that kind of behaviour from young men with money—or rather, I've seen its sad consequences! But what's going on between you and Miss Grey is rather different. You are both free adults making an informed choice to perform an action which may reasonably be expected to increase your mutual happiness, and to bring no harm to anyone. In the course of a long life, I have learnt that people find their satisfaction in various ways; so long as no one is hurt or coerced, I have no problem with any of them. *One Law for the Lion...* eh, Mr. Crowley?"

* * *

158

To reach the Cathedral Archive, one passed through the cloisters, and then through a charming Norman doorway. The Archive was a large room with an elaborate plastered ceiling, apparently dating from Tudor times—although in these parts, Holmes reflected, one should probably say *Stuart*, since that dynasty had already been the ruling House in the sixteenth century. Of the same date was the oak panelling, and the wide, low-arched fireplace whose breast was built out from the wall. Book-cases stood on three sides of the room, and a complex array of pigeon-holes, holding scrolls, on the fourth. There were three large Georgian sash-windows in the wall facing him; before each window stood a desk. Two were currently unattended, but the nearest one was occupied by a man in a shabby suit, writing with a quill-pen in a large book like a ledger, apparently transcribing part of an old register. He span round on his swivel-chair to face Holmes, revealing a long face, with large, intelligent eyes and a shaggy moustache; his short, unruly, dark-brown hair was parted in the middle.

"Mr. Balfour?" asked Holmes, rather expecting the answer *No*.

"No, sir: Mr. Balfour is out to lunch; although he should be back very soon. I am his secretary, John Spencer."

He rose to offer his hand.

"My name is Holmes—Sherlock Holmes." They shook hands. "I have been engaged to investigate the disappearance of the Reverend Mr. Melchior Tollemache. You must have met him on his visit here, ten days ago."

"No, sir: I was indisposed on that day. I have heard that he made some notes from the documents. Mr. Balfour said that the old

159

gentleman had a theory about the story of Cinderella having really happened here, on Trowley—which seems rather ridiculous to me! White mice and pumpkins, indeed! Sad how a once-great mind may slip into folly, is it not, sir? And even sadder when that madness leads to death."

"In what way do you consider that Mr. Tollemache's 'madness', as you call it, led to his demise?"

"Well, we don't know what drove him to the cliff-edge in the middle of the night, but the chances are that he thought he was following some clue or other—something to do with Witches, or the tale of Cinderella. He wouldn't have been on the Island at all if it wasn't for his wild theories, and so, however this little tragedy happened, they were the ultimate cause of it."

"Well, that's certainly one way of looking at it," said Holmes. "Anyway, don't let me keep you from your work." Seeing that Spencer's expression indicated no inclination to resume his task, Holmes asked: "What are you doing, by the way?"

"Part of the work of the Archivist is to inspect the documents, and to remove any which show signs of infestation."

"By book-worms, you mean?"

"Yes. It is quite a problem here."

"What happens to the documents which are removed?"

"Sometimes we are able to conserve them, by cutting parts away; and sometimes we have no choice but to commit them to the flames. Of course in such cases Mr. Balfour always ensures that a fair copy is made of any information which may be of importance to future generations. Some passages in this register have been marked for me to transcribe."

"I see," said Holmes. "It seems a great pity that any information should be lost."

"Oh, most of these records are of no interest to any living soul." Spencer waved dismissively at the old book from which he was transcribing. "Who cares that on a certain day, centuries ago, a servant-girl went missing, or that a farmer had some turnips stolen from his field? But things of historical significance, like the signing of a petition to the King, deserve to be noted; and that's what I'm doing now."

"Well, while you're getting on with that, perhaps I could be looking at the documents which Mr. Tollemache consulted on the occasion of his visit here. They are the local books of Church Discipline from the late sixteenth and early seventeenth centuries, and a letter written by Bishop Thomas in 1449."

"Yes, I know; and, sadly, I am unable to oblige you. All of those documents have been removed and burned. They were riddled with worms."

"The letter, too? Surely that was written on parchment."

"It had a bad case of mould, I believe."

"Is there any chance that these documents have not yet been committed to the flames?"

"None. I saw them burned myself, at the end of last week."

"Did you transcribe anything from them?"

"A little."

"Anything about the Tale of the Witches, or the Reign of the Crow?"

"No, sir."

"Did you see any such references in the documents?"

"No, Mr. Holmes; but then I wasn't looking. It's such hard work to decipher this old hand-writing that I generally don't read any more than the passages which I am instructed to transcribe."

Just then the door opened, to admit a large gentleman with short fair hair and beard: the very image of a Viking warrior, grown stout and somewhat florid in his middle years.

"Ah, Mr. Balfour! May I present our distinguished visitor, Mr. Sherlock Holmes?"

Holmes noted the gentleman's tie-pin, and its now-familiar runic motif. Mr. Balfour shook his hand without enthusiasm.

"I can guess what brings you here, sir, and I can assure you that you're wasting your time."

"At least you were present on the occasion of Mr. Tollemache's visit—as Mr. Spencer was not. I should be most interested in hearing your recollections of him. Any scrap of information, no matter how trivial, may be useful to me in my investigation."

"I hardly spoke to the man. He introduced himself to me, and gave me a brief account of his project; I gave him permission to use the archive. He searched the shelves and selected several volumes, which he took to the desk over yonder, where he copied parts of the documents into his note-book."

"Ah yes—the note-book! What did it look like, exactly?"

"Quite small: 'Kings', I should say." That was eight inches by six-and-a-half. "It was bound in black leather, with a fancy brass clasp."

"I don't suppose that you read any of it, did you?"

"No. I didn't get close to the man—in any sense."

"Would you say that your encounter was a hostile one?"

"We were not rude to each other, but I made it plain that I thought his project ridiculous, and that created a certain coldness between us."

"Was this the first that you had heard about 'The Crow's Daughter'?"

Mr. Balfour hesitated. "Yes," he said.

Holmes did not believe him.

"Mr. Spencer tells me that all of the documents which Mr. Tollemache consulted have since been burnt. I must say that it seems rather extraordinary that you should have found them all to be infected at the same time."

"Hardly, sir: it's perfectly natural. You see that little notice over yonder?" Balfour pointed to the wall above the far desk. "Perhaps it's too far away for you to read. It asks readers not to replace books on the shelves after reading them. We've found too many gentlemen to be careless in the matter. As requested, Mr. Tollemache left the documents which he had consulted on the desk; and when I went to put them back I discovered their worm-eaten condition."

"Were they badly affected, then?"

"Riddled, sir."

Holmes turned to the secretary. "Were they in worse condition than the volume on which you are working now, Mr. Spencer?"

"Oh, I should say so," said Spencer, without much conviction.

163

Holmes looked Mr. Balfour in the eye. "What was the problem with the Bishop's letter, exactly?"

"It was largely covered in an unpleasant black mould. I burned it immediately, along with a couple of other scrolls which I found to be infected. Such a thing cannot be allowed to spread. Doesn't the Holy Scripture say that it's better for one man to die than for the whole nation to perish?"

"Caiaphas said that, to justify the execution of Jesus, as I recall, sir. One ought to take these things in context. I must say that this destruction of irreplaceable historical evidence is rather distressing to me. While it is evidently impractical for Mr. Spencer to transcribe all the documents in their entirety, I wonder whether it might be possible to photograph them instead."

"Possible, yes: but prohibitively expensive. I have a very limited budget here."

"On behalf of future generations, may I ask you to consider raising the money for a camera and dark-room equipment, and training Mr. Spencer in their use? I am sure that there are many local scholars and other gentlemen who would subscribe to such a venture: my friend Mr. Brown, for one. It is a shame to lose so much of your Island's collective memory."

"I will give your suggestion the consideration which it deserves, sir. Now, is there anything else that I can do for you?"

Holmes felt free to shock Mr. Balfour with his final question: "Has the case of Mr. Tollemache been discussed in the meetings of the Sons of Grim?"

In the space of a second, Mr. Balfour's face showed first recognition, then anger, then coldness.

"You must know that my oath forbids me from discussing the business of my fraternity with any outsider."

"Of course; my apologies. You have been most informative, Mr. Balfour. Now, with your permission, I shall conduct a little research of my own. Where might I look for other Books of Church Discipline?"

* * *

High tea at the Royal began with pork sausages and mashed potato: a classic combination given an exotic twist by the addition of Heinz Baked Beans, a delicacy from the New World. The tastes and textures combined very well, Holmes thought. Drinking tea with such food seemed more natural than drinking wine; and the Hotel's tea was very good.

"So, Mr. Holmes, did you find anything interesting?"

"I found no other references to the Tale of the Witches, or the Reign of the Crow. Of course that doesn't mean that Mr. Tollemache was lying about his own discoveries; but it does mean that now the only proof of their existence may be the brief account of them which he gave in his letter. Not even the transcriptions which he made in his note-book have survived. I doubt whether any other scholar will be inclined to pursue the same line of inquiry, given the lack of evidence."

"All very nice for the Provost!"

"Yes, indeed." Holmes chewed the sausage. "I did, however, manage to purchase, for an exorbitant price, the register from which

Mr. Spencer is transcribing. I shall attempt a chemical treatment of the worms."

"Do you expect to find references to the forbidden tale in there?"

"Frankly, no. I don't think that Mr. Balfour would have agreed to let the book go if there were anything of that sort in it. But I was a little intrigued by the case of the missing turnips."

Crowley laughed. "Perhaps Dr. Watson can make a story out of it!"

"Somehow I don't think that would be quite in his line. How was your afternoon, Mr. Crowley?"

"I passed a couple of pleasant hours in the lowest public house that I could find. I learnt how to play what I am assured is the oldest game in the world: they call it 'Mill'. Do you know it, sir?"

"Yes, I used to enjoy playing it when I was a boy—although we called it 'Nine Men's Morris' in my part of the country. I would expect you to be good at it."

"Yes, I was. And of course it gave me the chance to converse with a variety of other players."

"Did you learn anything of interest in the course of your conversations?"

"The men to whom I spoke were in agreement about most things: none of them had heard of the story of the Crow's Daughter, and most of them agreed that, although there had, in centuries past, been many Witches on Trowley, there were none here now. One young fellow, of a skeptical bent, thought that there had never been any real Witches at all. The fishermen were the ones most reluctant to speak of Witchcraft, saying that it was 'ill luck' to do so. Older men in particular seemed to find the subject positively distasteful. From their

166

facial expressions I should guess that they know some dirty secret—something of a sexual nature—about what happened at Witch-meetings."

"And the Sons of Grim?"

"Most of my informants had heard of them, and appeared to regard them as a powerful force in local politics; but nobody wished to discuss the possibility of a link between the fraternity and the disappearance of Mr. Tollemache. It's best for a man to keep his 'neb oot' of such things, I was told."

"So far everything tends to confirm the conclusions which we have been forming to-day."

Crowley paused dramatically. "There was one surprising thing. A young barmaid to whom I chatted for a while actually *blushed* when I asked about the story of the Crow's Daughter."

"Hmm. I wonder: could she have been reacting to something else? Were you touching her, for example?"

Crowley chuckled, and shook his head. "I didn't think that she was game for any of that—although I might have been wrong. She was a hard one to read. But I just mentioned the story, and she blushed. Then she said that she'd never heard of it; but I didn't believe her."

"With reason, Mr. Crowley. Let us not forget, however, that she may have heard about the tale from the Reverend Mr. Tollemache, or from someone to whom that gentleman had spoken, rather than at her mother's knee. Nevertheless, it is curious that all those who give some indication of knowing about the story are female."

"Yes: first Lizzie, then Miss —"

"*Pas devant.*" Holmes glanced at the waiter.

167

Crowley smiled. "Quite right, sir."

When they had finished the first course, the waiter took their plates away.

"What's for pudding?" Holmes asked.

"Treacle tart with custard, sir."

They both wanted that. The waiter returned from the kitchen with their pudding already served in two dishes, and a jug of Bird's custard. He took the teapot away and replaced it with another.

This was a pleasant meal, but nonetheless a very humble one. Up and down the country, labourers and factory-workers were sitting down at their kitchen tables eating good, simple food like this. Happy the land, thought Holmes, in which even the lower classes could hope to dine so well!

"Do you wish me to accompany you to the Police Station?" asked Crowley, when they had polished off the tart.

"Not really. I should prefer to speak to the fellow on my own. Do you have plans for the next few hours?"

"After the excitements of the day, I think that I had best conserve my strength. My evening shall be spent sitting by the fireside, smoking hasheesh and reading about Witchcraft!"

* * *

It was starting to rain again as Holmes approached the Police Station. The Cathedral clock was just chiming seven. Inside the building, Sergeant Flett rose to greet him.

"Did you catch the fellow?"

"Yes, sir!"

"Good man! Was anyone hurt?"

168

"Not a bit, sir. He hadn't even loaded his gun; and he threw it down as soon as we challenged him."

"Was it the man that you suspected?"

"Adam Marwick, indeed, sir."

"Right then—perhaps I could have a word with him."

The Sergeant led him into a drab little room, lit by an overhead oil-lamp. It was cold, with no fire in the grate. Marwick sat on a simple wooden chair, with his hands cuffed behind his back. He was an impressive figure, built like a circus strong-man, with a shaven head, and a big moustache of an unnatural blackness. His face would have been handsome, were it not for an old wound which had deprived him of part of the tip of his nose, and sliced off the right nostril, leaving a deep scar on his cheek.

"I think, Sergeant," said Holmes, "that you might remove the handcuffs."

"Are you sure, sir?"

"Yes, thank you: I can take care of myself." After Flett had released Marwick's hands, Holmes said: "I should be obliged for a few minutes alone with the prisoner."

Flett looked a little disappointed, but said only: "Very well, sir. I'll be right outside if you need me."

When the door was shut, Holmes offered Marwick a smoke.

"Hmm. A Turkish fag!" said Marwick, and sniffed Holmes's Sullivan. "It's a good 'un, though. I'd sooner ha'e a Woodbine, but this'll do!"

Holmes lit both cigarettes with one match, throwing it into the dead fireplace afterwards.

"So you are the rogue who threatened me with a pistol," said Holmes.

"Aye, that was me, sir. But the gun wasn't loaded."

"Does that make it any better?"

"I should say that it did! You were never in any real danger from me."

"What was your plan?"

"To make a lot of money without working!"

Holmes smiled. "In detail, though: what were you planning to do when we came to the Bell and laid our money on the table?"

"I was going to spin you a yarn about how I'd heard old Mr. Tollemache talking to a Norway seaman, and making an appointment to meet him on the cliffs. I had a real name and a real ship for you to chase across the ocean. Of course it would have been a wild-goose chase, for I never heard any such talk; but it would have got you out of the way long enough for me to make off with your sovereigns."

"Did anyone put you up to this?"

"No sir; it was all my own idea—and a pretty plan it was, I thought. But you were too clever for me; you've kept your money, and I'm bound for prison, I suppose."

"If you tell me the truth, things will go easier for you."

"That *is* the truth, sir!"

Holmes took a long drag on his Sullivan. "Where did you get the scar?"

"Abu Klea."

"Ah, in the Soudan! You were an honourable servant of the Empire once: a Sergeant, I'm told. How did you fall from that to this?"

"My fall—if you wish to call it so—came in the course of that campaign, sir. The Soudan was the place where I lost my illusions about life."

"How do you mean?"

"Well, I was a pious wee laddie when I went out there. I thought that we Christians had a God-given right to take over other people's countries, just as the Israelites did in the Bible; and that, like them, we were always victorious because the Lord was on our side. I didn't need to see much of real combat before I understood the way of things: that victory comes to the best-trained men with the most up-to-date weapons, and God has no part in it. Those Fuzzy-Wuzzies were calling on God to help them just the same as we were. *Allah hu Akbar*, they kept screaming, as they charged toward us, but Allah proved no match for our guns."

Marwick threw his cigarette-stub into the fireplace. "While I was out in those parts I asked a lot of questions, and found out as much as I could about the Mohammedan religion. It seemed very interesting to me, because on the one hand it was so obviously a pack of lies, made up by men for all-too-human reasons; and on the other it was so like Christianity! After I'd talked about this to one of the officers, he gave me a battered copy of *The Martyrdom of Man*."

"What did you think of it?"

"It was a bit too wordy for me, sir—too much fancy writing. But it led me on to read Mr. Darwin's books, and I found that they made a lot of sense. By this time I'd been transferred to the Commissariat, on account of my wound, and I had plenty of time for thinking. It seemed to me then, as it seems to me now, that there's no God, and

171

no great purpose to the world; that we're just animals fighting for grub, and all this talk of morality and patriotism is nothing but lies designed to make us act in ways that suit our leaders. Men write fine poems about the conquests of Kings—but what's that really but robbery with violence? What's our famous Empire really but a great protection-racket, in which the blacks give us their goods for fear of being shot? Since I twigged that I've looked out for no one but myself. If the interests of the British Empire should coincide with those of Adam Marwick, well and good; if not, then to Hell with it!"

Holmes was appalled by this cynicism—although such thoughts had occurred to him, too, in his darker moments. After a moment he responded, calmly:

"You oppose yourself to the civilization that bore you, but I question whether these things are separable, even in principle. As the Apostle says: *What hast thou that thou didst not receive?* You did not make your boots, nor your watch, Mr. Marwick—neither did you make the English language in which all your thoughts are framed, nor the books that have shaped those thoughts. Without our Island Nation and its ancient culture, there would be no Adam Marwick!

"And that Empire which you disparage as a 'protection-racket' is, despite its faults, the most powerful engine that Mankind has yet invented for spreading the benefits of civilization throughout the world. Can you not see that it is in all men's interests to live in a civilized society, rather than in conditions of savagery? Her Majesty's law prevents you from taking a weaker man's property, which is, admittedly, a restriction on your liberty—but it also protects you from being robbed or murdered by another, stronger man, without which

172

protection your liberty is worthless. All the amenities and comforts which we enjoy, and which the savages of the Dark Continent do not—from gas-light to lending-libraries, from the music of Handel to Fry's Chocolate—are made possible by our adherence to law and morality. We work together, we compromise, we pay our debts; we do not kill one other, nor threaten one other with weapons: in short, we act like civilized people, and the result is a better life for all of us."

Marwick looked thoughtful. Then he retorted: "Have you seen much of the East End, Mr. Holmes? Not too many amenities and comforts there! And parts of Edinburgh and Glasgow are just as bad. It seems to me that this civilization of yours is a fine thing for the upper classes—but what has it done for the poor?"

"Well, you can't deny that the lot of the working man is slowly improving. In our life-times we have seen, for example, the extension of the franchise, the provision of universal education, and the many Acts of Parliament which have gradually reduced working-hours and improved working-conditions. Many thinkers are currently engaged in devising schemes for the elimination of poverty. Some form of Socialism is generally agreed to be the way forward. For my part, I should not, with the followers of Dr. Marx, wish to see the present order of things entirely overthrown; yet I consider that some Socialist policies are sensible enough, and might usefully be adopted by Her Majesty's Government. Let us by all means tax the rich in order to help the poor; and let us hope that more people live happier lives as a result! If you are so concerned about these issues, Mr. Marwick, I wonder why you do not join the I.L.P., or some other reforming organization. It seems to me that your eloquence would make you useful as a speaker, and perhaps even as a Member of Parliament."

Marwick thought for a moment. "Like Keir Hardie!"

"Yes: you see, the thing can be done. It is easy to sit back and decry injustice, Mr. Marwick. Any poltroon can do as much. But it takes a real man to stand up and take action to right the wrongs of the world. I wonder...."

"If I wasn't bound for gaol, I think that I might indeed embark upon such a course of action. Your words have made me see things in a new light, sir."

Holmes judged that Marwick was sincere.

"Well, I shall see what I can do about that. You will have to give up the gun, though. And please write to me from time to time, letting me know how things work out for you. Do you know my address?"

CHAPTER X.

THE CULT OF HEL.

Holmes's way lay to the north. Because of the rain, the streets of Cunningsborough were almost deserted, and there was no one at all on the road that he followed northward out of town, with the sea to his left and the land to his right. A little quarter-moon was the only source of illumination, and that was often obscured by clouds, so that he could see very little. There were a few modest, middle-class villas, fairly widely-spaced, dotted along the coast. At what seemed the very edge of human habitation stood a small, two-storey house, of plain Neo-Classical style, with the name **ROSE COTTAGE** in brass letters on its gate. This was the place. He walked up the stone-flagged path. Miss Reid's letter had asked him to imitate the beginning of Beethoven's Fifth Symphony when he knocked, and now he did so, feeling a little like a character in a melodrama. But he could understand why a lady might wish to know who was knocking on her door; and the tune that she had chosen was certainly a good one for the purpose.

The door was opened by a maid dressed in black, with white apron and cap: a pretty young woman with black hair, pale skin, and bold features, of which the most striking was her rather large, shapely mouth, which now turned upward in a smile. Contrary to the practice of servant-girls, this one was actually looking him in the eye.

"Please come in, sir!" She held the door open and stood by it as he entered. It seemed in the spirit of this egalitarian establishment for him to hang up his own hat and cloak. The maid liked that: he could tell from her smile as she handed him a towel. He dried his face, and checked his reflexion in the mirror. The man who looked back was about ten years older than he felt himself to be, but otherwise presentable enough.

"The Mistress is through here." The maid opened the door on the left of the corridor. The room was lit by candles, with a coal-fire burning in the grate; a mingled smell of cannabis and patchouli hung in the air. The *décor* in here was *Art Nouveau*, but not exclusively so, for there were some Oriental pieces too, looking quite in keeping with the rest. The colour-scheme was mostly red—a deep, dark red, like venous blood—then there was white, and black, and gold. His hostess was certainly a woman of taste—and, seemingly, of some wealth. But his attention was mainly focused not on the lady's possessions but on herself.

She rose from a high-backed arm-chair to the right of the fireplace: magnificent in an emerald-green evening-dress, which displayed both the beauty of her figure and the alabaster perfection of her arms, shoulders and bosom. Her jewellery was of the same fashionable style as her *décor*—and, rather shockingly, her eye-lids were visibly painted gold. She was, as the saying went, 'dressed to kill'. He wondered if Crowley might have been right about her amorous intentions towards him. More likely this provincial beauty simply wanted to look her best for her meeting with a famous man. Women were like that, he found:

176

even female clients, like Miss Tollemache, generally dressed in their smartest clothes when they called on him.

"Ah, Mr. Holmes!" Miss Reid smiled, and gave her right hand to be kissed. "I am delighted to meet you properly at last."

"As am I to meet you, Miss Reid."

She turned to the maid. "Thank you, Tanith. You may take the rest of the evening off; I can look after my guest." Miss Reid sat down.

Tanith lingered momentarily at the bookshelf.

"Do you want something to read?"

"Just a French dictionary, please, miss. I'm still wrestling with *Juliette*."

Holmes could recall only one novel of that title: rather a surprising one for a maidservant to be reading. "What do you think of it?"

She had the dictionary, and looked pleased. "I like the philosophical discussions, sir. They often make me laugh out loud! Sometimes he's right and sometimes he's wrong, but he always makes me think! As to the rest of it, well: some bits are funny, but most of it"—she groaned slightly. "Let's just say it's not my cup of tea. There are some pictures that I don't want in my head—*merci beaucoup, monsieur le marquis!*" Her French accent was surprisingly good.

"Indeed," said Holmes, donnishly, "de Sade is one of the few authors whose works might actually have benefited from the attentions of Dr. Bowdler!" He had once heard Wilde say that, and it had gone down well; it did so here, too, for they all laughed together. This was plainly a very advanced household.

"Well..." said Miss Reid.

"Yes," said Tanith. "Good night, Mr. Holmes! It was nice to meet you."

"The same to you, Tanith! I do not know if we shall meet again, but I am sure that I shall never forget you."

She liked that, he could see.

"I hope that we shall see a great deal more of each other, sir." She gave him a saucy smile, and was gone.

"Did her parents really name her after a Carthaginian Goddess?" asked Holmes.

"No: They called her 'Abigail'—but she didn't like it. It must be a particularly galling name if one actually *is* a maidservant, I suppose. So for the last seven years she's been Tanith—to me and her other friends, at least."

"Well, it rather suits her. She's not my idea of an Abigail." He seated himself in a low arm-chair, free to concentrate on the beautiful woman who sat opposite him. Her chair was of simple but elegant construction: either one of Mackintosh's or a good imitation. Above and behind the lady's head was a great oval held aloft between the two uprights of the back. A round hole had been cut in the middle of it, like the pupil of an eye, giving it the hypnotic power of a primitive totem. Seated on this throne, in her *Art Nouveau* jewellery, Miss Reid looked like a poet's vision of the Fairy Queen.

"It is a great honour to be received in such a lovely room, by so charming a lady," he said.

"You're kind to say so."

"Not at all, Miss Reid: simply honest." They smiled at one another. He looked around, and fixed his gaze on the picture which hung over

178

the fireplace. It was a large, hand-coloured photograph: an image of his hostess apparently posed upon a stage, dressed for some Shakespearean 'breeches part'—probably Rosalind in *As You Like* It, judging by the forest setting. She was sitting at the foot of a painted oak-tree, head to the right, with her legs stretched out before her to the left. What made the picture so striking was the way that those splendid limbs were displayed, in vermilion tights, vivid against the dark background: the right leg flat on the ground, the other flexed and raised. She was wearing a black doublet over a white shirt; her boots were pale tan, almost golden, and her auburn hair hung loose, like a lion's mane, over her shoulders. It was a most artistic image—but to a man of Holmes's vintage it was bound to appear disturbingly erotic, almost as shocking as actual nudity. Yet, he considered, the shape of Miss Reid's legs was undeniably pleasing: like the line of an ogee arch, or a logarithmic spiral—beautiful and fascinating! He searched for something innocuous to say about the picture. "You have been on the stage, I see."

"Yes: when I was a student. It helped me to pay my way through College."

He could imagine large audiences of enthusiastic young men for plays in which she wore such costumes. "You must have been a great success as Rosalind."

"Viola, actually. But it does look as if it should be Rosalind, doesn't it? One doesn't usually picture Viola in a forest. Anyway, thank you, yes: I enjoyed it tremendously. I even considered doing it for a living—but it's a very uncertain life, especially for a woman."

179

"That's true. And so you became a School-Mistress for the sake of financial security?"

"Basically, yes. But I also wanted to make the world a better place, if that doesn't sound too prissy, and I thought that I could do that more effectively in the classroom than in the theatre. My work is hard, but on the whole it's satisfying. Sometimes I do wish that I could perform again, though. It sounds childish, but I really liked being applauded!"

"I know what you mean. I had similar experiences in my student days, and once considered the stage as a career; but I think that I do more good as a detective." They smiled again.

"Oh—by the way, Mr. Holmes, does it have to be 'Mr. Holmes'? You are welcome to call me 'Louisa' if you'd like to!"

"You are most gracious, Miss Reid; but I am so unaccustomed to being called 'Sherlock' that the name would startle me out of my train of thought whenever you used it. Perhaps, when we have known each other rather longer, I might feel ready for such intimacy, but for the moment I consider it more *professional* that we remain upon our present terms."

Oh, that was cold, he thought, seeing her reaction; but it had to be said.

"Of course," she said, brightening, "you are a detective engaged in an investigation. I suppose it's rather like being a Policeman on duty, isn't it? Well, I hope that, unlike such a visitor, you will at least allow yourself a glass of wine, and perhaps a smoke of some fine hasheesh."

She indicated a long, low table between them, on which stood an ornate water-pipe of northern Indian workmanship.

180

"I will take a little, but not much, of both, thank you, Miss Reid. I must keep my memory intact, and my mind alert, if I am to do my duty to my client in this matter."

She looked pleased. "Quite so. A little hasheesh energizes the intellect, but a larger dose may stupefy it. One must smoke carefully to achieve the desired effect."

"You seem quite the expert. I must own myself surprised to find a hasheesh-smoker on Trowley. Did you acquire this habit as a student?"

"Yes, indeed. Some of my friends at College were Indian, and they taught the rest of us how to enjoy the drug. I still have my supplies sent up from the same pharmacy where I used to buy it in those days."

"Would that be Lowe's, in Stafford Street?"

"The very same. You are indeed a wizard, Mr. Holmes!"

"The deduction was quite elementary: Lowe's is the best shop in London for the purpose; and you are an intelligent woman who spent two years in that city, quite recently."

"You realized that the pamphlet was my work, then?"

"There was that—but also I observed the certificate on your office wall."

She laughed, charmingly. "Did you read the pamphlet, Mr. Holmes?"

"Yes, of course."

"And what did you think?"

"You write beautifully, and with passion—but to do justice to the substance of your argument would take many hours; and I am here on other business, which must, I fear, take priority over such a political discussion, interesting as that might be. You have information relating to the fate of the Reverend Mr. Tollemache, I believe."

"Indeed. Forgive me, sir; I am a little nervous. Some of the things that I have to tell you are of an extremely personal nature, and potentially embarrassing for me. I need another smoke and a little alcohol inside me before I can begin to speak freely. Which would you like, Mr. Holmes? I have Port or Sherry."

"Port, please."

She crossed to the sideboard, brought back a salver bearing a decanter and two chalice-shaped glasses, all of the *Art Nouveau* style, and set it on the table next to the hookah. She poured.

"Your health, sir!"

"And yours, madam!"

Cockburn's again, he thought, as he tasted it, probably the '96. It was not a Comet Vintage, but it was very good.

The hasheesh was from Bengal, judging by its characteristic odour. Miss Reid took a few draws from the pipe, and passed the mouthpiece to him. As the smoke bubbled through the rose-water, he could hear the sea breaking rhythmically on the rocky shore outside. The hasheesh-intoxication began to make itself felt, like a warm radiance spreading through his body and his brain. Holmes reflected that Miss Reid had excellent taste in drugs, as in all other things.

"Let me tell you something about myself," she said, leaning back in her chair, visibly more relaxed now. "I am from here. My father was a local man, a solicitor's clerk; my mother was a girl from the north, who was working here as a maid. She never used to say much about where she'd come from, or her family. Every now and again she'd let something slip, and I gathered that she had been brought up in a house of women: a grandmother, a mother, and two sisters—or half-sisters, or stepsisters. She called them all these names at different times. She gave me the impression that she didn't like any of them very much, but she never said why. Something bad had happened, I supposed.

"Mother was a devout Christian, and did her best to raise me the same way. Father, however, was skeptical about such things; and, though he never argued with Mother, he would teach me in private to think critically about what I was being taught. The result was that I played the *rôle* of a Christian to please her, but inwardly I was a complete agnostic.

"When I was thirteen, Mother was taken ill. Nobody would ever tell me what was wrong with her. Now I suppose that it was a mental illness, and that she had been confined in the local Asylum. Anyway, Father knew that she was going to be away from home for many weeks. He couldn't afford to hire a full-time Nanny; and, as the school holidays were approaching, he thought it best to send me to stay with my grand-mother and my aunts in the north.

"So off I went, with some trepidation. I was rather scared that the same bad thing that Mother wouldn't talk about—whatever it was—was going to be done to me. On arrival I found that my great-grandmother had died; my grandmother seemed very old, and spoke little, although she seemed happy enough. My aunts were two handsome women in early middle age. They lived in a cottage by the sea, with a little land on which they grew kale and potatoes. From time to time people would call on them, and there would be conversations which I was not allowed to overhear. I wondered at first whether my aunts might not be... 'gay'; yet so many of their callers were female that I soon discarded that hypothesis. My relatives seemed a little wary of me at first; but when, by subtle questioning, they had established that I did not share my mother's religious beliefs, they became much friendlier. It was then that they revealed to me a startling fact, Mr. Holmes: my family were Witches."

"Meaning what, exactly? That they cast spells, and sold herbal remedies?"

"Yes, they did such things; but that was only a small part of their Witchcraft—and not, to them, the most important. They told me that their spells were no more than performances designed to instil confidence in their clients; and that, more often than not, their potions worked only because people had faith in them. They did have some real knowledge of herbal medicine, however; and they knew a technique very similar to hypnosis, which they often found useful in their healing-work. That was as much of their Witchcraft as any outsider might know."

"What more was there?"

"During the summer that I spent with them, they shared with me a number of old tales and songs, a few rituals, and what I can only describe as a philosophy of life. They told me that Witchcraft was the Old Religion which had come down from the beginning of the world."

"The Old Religion, eh?" He recalled that Leland's Italian informants had used the same phrase: *la Vecchia Religione.* "Most interesting! What did they worship, exactly?"

"She whom the modern world calls Mother Nature, and whom the ancient world called Isis, Diana, Astarte, or a thousand other lovely names. The Witches honoured no transcendent Deity, but only Nature, who gives rise to all things and, in time, destroys them."

"Your relatives did not, presumably, use these Classical names?"

"They told me that the Goddess had ten thousand names, but the one that had come down to us from our ancestors was Hel. Often they called her just 'the Goddess'. In some of their rituals they used a name which they said was Pictish—but that was never to be spoken, except to other Witches."

"Yet you have heard it." Their eyes met and lingered on each other for a long moment.

She smiled. "Indeed, Mr. Holmes, you have found out my secret. That summer they converted me to the oldest of this planet's religions: I am a Witch."

To hear those words spoken at the end of the nineteenth century was astonishing, in much the same way that it would have been if Miss Reid had announced 'I am a Vampire' or 'I am a Mermaid'! Yet there she sat on her *Art Nouveau* throne, looking calm and sincere. Was she an impostor, like Mr. Leland's Maddalena, or a fantasist, like Isobel Gowdie? He could not think so. Perhaps she was indeed a Witch—whatever that meant, exactly. A worshipper of Nature, he supposed.

"It seems," he said, "an odd religion for a School-Mistress."

"Why so?"

"Is it not a teacher's task to civilize her pupils? And is not Nature the enemy of civilization?"

"I don't see it that way." She thought for a moment. "To me civilizations are natural productions, like flowers or stars. If there is no God—as I am sure that you and I are agreed—then Nature alone must be ultimately responsible for everything that we do. She has given us hearts that crave comfort and refinement, and we satisfy those cravings by creating civilizations, just as termites build their mounds, or beavers raise their dams, to satisfy the desires that she has implanted in them."

Holmes had never thought of it in those terms. Although he had long ceased to believe that God had given the Commandments to Moses at Mount Sinai, he had continued to think as if civilization and morality had been handed down to Man from some other-than-natural source. In Miss Reid's world-view there was no such dualism. He was impressed by the boldness of her thought, but a little disconcerted by some of its implications.

She took a smoke and passed the mouthpiece to him. Against his earlier resolve, he took another draw on the pipe.

"Morality," he said. "Good and evil. How does that work, exactly, if one worships Nature?"

"Well, Mr. Holmes," she said, and paused for a moment before continuing, "when I look into the heart which the Goddess has given me, I find that my primary urge is to be happy; and that, insofar as is possible, I'd like others to be happy, too."

"Why should you desire the happiness of anyone except yourself? Is that something natural—or is it something that you were taught?"

"Well, a little of both, of course" she said; "but I think it's basically a natural thing. Like most people, I feel sad when I see others suffering. That's part of it. Then again it's an obvious fact of life that unhappy folk are more likely to make *me* unhappy, by trying to hurt me or rob me, than they would be if they were content." She crossed her legs, revealing a high-heeled shoe which, although dainty, was at least a size bigger than that of 'Atalanta'.

"So," she continued, "the natural consequence of desiring my own happiness is that I want there to be more happiness in the world around me; and as a consequence of that, I do things which I think will increase the general happiness, and I abstain from actions that tend to produce suffering—either in myself or in others. But isn't that how all healthy-minded people behave anyway, irrespective of their religious beliefs or their philosophical opinions?"

"I suppose it is." He considered her logic, and found it flawless. "I think that your analysis is quite correct, Miss Reid."

"It's really nice to hear you say so! Many an educated man has his mind set on such a lofty plane that he finds it hard to see something that's so simple and obvious: something that doesn't require a complicated explanation using lots of technical terms like the 'Categorical Imperative'! But it seems to me that the answers to the Great Questions of Philosophy are often very straightforward indeed. I mean:

"'Does the world exist?' 'Yes—here it is!'" She pointed to it, all around.

"'Does God exist?' 'No, we made him up!'

187

"'What does it mean to call something *good*?' 'It means that you like it!' And so on."

They laughed together. He was impressed by her impudent intellect.

"Would you like some Turkish delight?" she asked.

He pondered. "Yes, I think that I should."

She returned from the sideboard with a plate on which there were not only four pieces of the pink sweetmeat, but also four chocolate truffles.

"The cakes are very nice, Mr. Holmes—but be warned, they do contain more hasheesh, so leave them alone unless you wish to become a good deal more intoxicated than you are already."

The Turkish delight was worthy of its name. She left the plate on the table, within easy reach if he wanted more.

"Let me clarify something," he said. "You talk about Nature as a Goddess—but you don't actually believe that there is a divine *person* whose will directs the course of the winds or the growth of the crops, do you?"

"Not literally, no. It's a figure of speech."

"And was that also the belief of your relatives?"

"Do you know, Mr. Holmes, it's not something that we ever discussed. At thirteen, I don't think that I would have been capable of framing the question, and I don't know whether their education would have fitted them to answer it. All I can say is that nothing which they taught me conflicts with such an interpretation."

"Why do you call Nature a mother rather than a father? Indeed, why personify Nature at all?"

188

"The short answer is because that's what Witches do: it's our tradition, that's been handed down to us from the earliest times. A longer answer might be that such a personification comes very naturally to the human mind, because we emerge from Nature, like a child from its mother's womb: she makes us out of herself, and nurtures us; then after a few years she takes us back into herself again, and the illusion of our separate existence is dissolved."

She ate a piece of Turkish delight, thoughtfully. "When I was at U.C.L., one of my fellow-students was a Hindoo, who told me a story about a holy man called Ramakrishna. It seems this man was a great devotee of Kali, and longed to have a vision of her whom he served. Then one day she appeared, to him, like a giantess standing in the sacred river. At first she had the form of a beautiful young woman. He watched as she gave birth to an infant, suckled it and played with it. Then she assumed the aspect of a frightful she-devil, and in that terrifying form proceeded to devour her child. Ramakrishna looked on in silent reverence, recognizing that the creative and the destructive faces of the Goddess were equally holy. When I heard that story I knew beyond doubt that the Goddess of the Hindoos was the same as the Goddess of the Witches.

"We are her children: she has borne us, and nurtured us; now she is playing with us. Let us enjoy her favours while they last, for soon enough she will rend and devour us. Yet how wonderful to have received the gift of life at all, even for a few years, on this beautiful planet, where we may enjoy so many pleasures! To worship the Goddess is to celebrate that gift."

189

Holmes took her point. "Nietzsche says somewhere that Buddhism is saying 'No' to life. Witchcraft, if I have understood you aright, is the opposite of that."

"Exactly so, Mr. Holmes! I really think that's the essence of it. Witchcraft is saying 'Yes' to life! Even more so than Nietzsche, because he actually said 'No' to quite a lot of life: he was often more concerned with rising above it heroically than he was with enjoying it! Witches, however, seek out pleasures of every kind, and strive to make them exquisite. Pleasures of the mind, and pleasures of the flesh." She had quite a sultry look as she said that.

He took out his cigarette-case. "Do you mind if I smoke?"

"Och, Sullivans! Could I have one, please?"

He lit both cigarettes. The familiar taste of the smoke was a comfort to him amid this welter of novel ideas. He tried to get his thoughts on track.

"So, part of your inheritance as the last Witch of Trowley was a collection of stories."

"Yes, indeed."

"Was one of them a version of the tale which Mr. Tollemache called 'The Crow's Daughter'?"

"Yes, that was the most important of them all; but we called it 'The Reign of the Crow', which seems like a better title to me, as it's not all about the Queen's daughter, important though she was."

"When Mr. Tollemache came to you in search of the original version of the story you must have considered telling him your tale."

"I very much wished to do so. But obviously I couldn't—not in front of Mr. Johnston. He would have gone straight to the Provost

190

and told him all about it. So I did the same on the occasion of Mr. Tollemache's visit as I did for you, this morning. When Dr. Strange informed me that the Reverend gentleman was intending to call on me at the School, I wrote him a note, and hid it inside a pamphlet which I gave to him at the end of our interview. He came here that night—exactly a week ago; he sat where you are sitting now, and listened whilst I told the old, forbidden tale."

Holmes reconsidered his interpretation of Mr. Tollemache's last letter. Miss Reid must have been the Witch to whom the Reverend gentleman had referred; and, if their meeting had taken place a week ago, then the date of the message must have been not *Wednesday, 25th October,* but *Monday, 23rd October.* He visualized the blots in question (a mental feat which the cannabis-intoxication made easier) and concluded that the latter interpretation was entirely plausible. But he saw a difficulty in Miss Reid's story.

"Mr. Tollemache was a Christian priest. Were you not a little apprehensive that he might be hostile to you, as a Witch? If he revealed your secret to the world the consequences would have been just as bad for you as if Mr. Johnston had done so."

"Yes, I know; and if I hadn't liked Mr. Tollemache when I met him I wouldn't have given him the pamphlet. But in my letter I set him a test, anyway: I asked him to read Karl Pearson's lecture, *Woman as Witch,* in the Public Library. I was present at the Somerville Club when Professor Pearson gave that lecture, in 1891; and I thought that it was the best account of real Witchcraft that I'd ever heard. So if Mr. Tollemache were to come round here full of outrage at the horrible Witch-Cult that he'd been reading about, I would have known not to tell him anything about my being a member of that Cult. I might have still told him the story, though, because it would have been nice to set the record straight about 'The Crow' and her daughter, after all these years; but I would have made something up about how I knew it. Probably I'd have said that I heard it from a pupil, whose name I couldn't reveal for reasons of professional confidentiality." She smiled, winningly.

"Was that Karl Pearson, the Gresham Professor of Geometry?"

"Indeed, Mr. Holmes, that is his current position; but his interests are very wide-ranging. Much of his academic work has been concerned with folklore and anthropology; he is also a statistician, a philosopher, and the author of some very rational arguments for Socialism. If you have not read any of his work, I would highly recommend it—especially that lecture, *Woman as Witch*. Many an author has written on the subject of Witchcraft, but none has come closer to the truth."

"Where may I find it?"

"It is the first chapter in the second volume of his collection, *The Chances of Death*. There is a copy in the Library, as I said. You will need to tell Miss Deck that I sent you; she keeps it under the counter."

"I shall endeavour to read it at my earliest opportunity. How did Mr. Tollemache react to your test?"

She smiled. "Oh, he was lovely! He said that it confirmed what he'd been thinking for a long time: that the Old Religion of the Goddess had not been an evil thing, and that the Church had been wrong to persecute it. In fact he thought that Christianity could learn a lot from the Witches about reverence for Nature, and for the body. So he was about as sympathetic to Witchcraft as a man could be and still remain a Christian; and, naturally, I told him everything I knew. We talked late into the night."

"I should be most interested to hear the substance of your talk. But first let me ask you what you know of Mr. Tollemache's intentions on leaving your house. Was he planning to continue his quest here, or had his evening with you quite satisfied him?"

"Och, Mr. Holmes, it was more than enough for him! He said that he'd need a day or two to think it over. He was sure that the things that I had told him were true; but he didn't know if he could publish them without ruining his reputation, as seems to have happened to Mr. Leland, with the scandal over *Aradia*. He also faced a more personal dilemma, as he was uncertain whether he would be able to continue in his office as a minister of the English Church. Hearing the story had made him look at the Bible in a new way."

"During his visit, did he smoke hasheesh with you?"

"Yes; and he knew how to, although he'd not done it for years. It made the experience more special for him, I think. When I told him the story, he said that he could see the people and the setting very vividly in his mind, as if he were remembering those events."

An unsettling possibility occurred to Holmes: if the balance of Mr. Tollemache's mind had been disturbed by a combination of hasheesh-intoxication and Miss Reid's forbidden story, perhaps the old gentleman really had taken his own life! Could a thousand-year-old folk-tale have the power to drive a man to his death? It was a fancy worthy of Eastern legend.

"What do you suppose has become of Mr. Tollemache?" he asked.

193

"I fear that he is dead, and I suspect that he was murdered."

"Do you discount the possibility of suicide?"

"Yes. When he left here, he was happy."

"Happy—at the prospect of renouncing his living?"

"Nothing so drastic was in prospect, Mr. Holmes. He was thinking of becoming a Unitarian."

They shared a brief smile. It made sense: the Unitarians were tolerant enough to accommodate a theologian as liberal as Mr. Tollemache; and his modest fame would no doubt have earned him a comfortable living as one of their ministers.

"So your favoured explanation is murder—by whom, do you think?"

"Have you heard of a fraternity called the Sons of Grim?"

"A little," said Holmes, "but I should be most interested to hear what you have to say about them."

"Well, they are a secret order, like the Masons, but more exclusive. There are only nine of them at any time, but those are always nine of the richest and most powerful men on the Island. This Grim whom they honour was an important man in the Reign of the Crow. He was the leader of the faction opposed to the Witch-Queen. In his life-time, Grim killed many Witches, and the Sons of Grim have followed his example ever since. My grandmother told me that, even since the law changed, and folk like us could no longer be burned at the stake, the fraternity had still arranged for some of us to meet with an untimely death. They used to waylay suspected Witches, club them to death, and throw their bodies into the sea."

"They sound something like the Ku Klux Klan in America, or the Vehmgericht in Germany," he said.

"Yes, that's just how they were. Our Provost is the current head of the order, and I know that he was very much opposed to Mr. Tollemache's intention to publish his research on the story. The inference seems obvious."

"Those are certainly grounds for suspicion, although as yet I have found no definite proof that would connect the fraternity with Mr. Tollemache's disappearance."

"I'm not surprised—they're good at covering their tracks."

"Do you consider yourself to be in any danger from them?"

"I don't think so. That my family were Witches was a well-kept secret: their clients liked them too much to inform on them. And of course I'm very careful what I say about it, and to whom."

"Dr. Strange does not know, I think."

She laughed. "No; he's a nice man, but I can't imagine that he'd want me working at the School if he knew that I was a Witch."

A thought occurred to Holmes. "Do you consider it possible that the Sons of Grim were reading Mr. Tollemache's letters?"

"Yes," she said, "I consider it not only possible, but highly likely; and I told him as much in my note, because I was worried about being found out. But when he came here he said that he'd written nothing about me except for a single letter to his daughter, which he'd written that day but hadn't posted yet—and even in that he hadn't indentified me by name; merely said that he'd met someone whom he believed to be a Witch, and who claimed to know the story. He promised that

195

he'd burn the letter when he returned to his lodging-place—so I think that I can be in no danger on that account."

"Well, then: I should very much like to hear the remarkable story that so many people have been so anxious to suppress for so long."

All the Turkish delight was gone. He bit into one of the truffles, and found it delicious.

CHAPTER XI.

THE REIGN OF THE CROW.

"So," Miss Reid began, "this happened in the time of the Norsemen, more than a thousand years ago. The King of this Island in those days was an able ruler by the name of Mani."

The 'a' was broad, as in 'father'.

"Mani was in his mid-forties: a handsome man with a much-loved wife. But he didn't have a son to succeed him: only a daughter, whose name I never learnt from my aunts. According to Mr. Tollemache, in one version from Iceland it was *Mjadveig*—which makes sense, because the Norsemen frequently used the alliterative principle in choosing names for their children."

The first syllable of the Princess's name was like 'mad', but with the initial consonant-cluster of 'mew'; the second sounded like 'vague': *M'yAD-vayg*.

"At the start of the story, the Princess was fifteen years old; ripe for marriage, according to the custom of that age, and very desirable, since it was understood that, in the absence of a male heir, whoever won her hand would inherit the Kingdom. She was pretty, too, and she must have enjoyed being at the centre of so much attention.

"Then the Queen died, in suspicious circumstances. She took ill suddenly, and was dead within an hour—which sounds like the effects of poison rather than disease. No one else was taken ill around that time; and the day she died was the day after she'd announced, to an astonished court, that she was again pregnant. So my aunts said that no one could know for sure what happened, but our belief was that the Princess had poisoned her."

"It is rather horrible," said Holmes, "to suppose a young girl so depraved as to murder her own mother."

"Well," said Miss Reid, "all that we know of the Princess suggests that she was a shallow, vain child, obsessed with her own popularity. I know from daily experience how selfish some adolescent girls can be. I agree that she probably didn't mean to *kill* her mother; but she might well have tried to terminate the pregnancy, so removing the threat of a male heir. My aunts knew something of these matters, and they told me that an overdose of such a drug was likely to prove fatal not only to the unborn child but also to the mother. I can imagine the Princess obtaining a supply of such a substance from a faithful retainer, and then slipping some of it into her mother's food. She was a child, after all; she probably thought that if a little was good, a lot would be better."

"Yes," he said. He could imagine that, too. In fact, he could see it happening quite vividly in his mind's eye. "What a tragedy for all concerned!"

"Yes," said Miss Reid, "I don't know how so young a girl could deal with the guilt of having done something like that. It must have twisted her up inside. And her subsequent behaviour was rather what one might expect from such a tortured soul."

"Did the King suspect anything?"

"One might think so, for his reaction was rather more extreme than one might expect: he was plunged into a deep melancholy. He took to his bed, and stayed there, refusing to attend to any affairs of state. At last things got so bad that the King's Chief Counsellor decided that something had to be done. He considered that a new wife would the best remedy for the King's condition; and so two Ambassadors were sent out on a mission to find a suitable bride. I suppose that they must have been heading to Scandinavia, to do the rounds of the royal courts there; but before they'd gone far a thick mist came down, and the sailors lost their bearings. They let their ship drift with the current, looking out for any sign of land. This went on for several days: one of my aunts said 'nine days and nine nights', but I suspect that just means 'a long time', rather like 'forty days' in the Bible. Anyway, after that the fog cleared, and they found themselves close to a little island. It was late in the afternoon, so they decided to land and make camp for the night.

"While the sailors were preparing a meal, the Ambassadors went to have a look around. They probably considered the island too small and remote to support inhabitants. But they hadn't gone very far before they discovered that they were wrong: approaching a little cove, they heard the sound of a harp being played, down on the beach; and so delightful was the sound that they went down towards it, without fear. They found a spectacle to match the music. By the light of the setting sun, they beheld two women of extraordinary loveliness: one of mature years, clad all in black; the other a maiden, wearing a scarlet tunic. The older woman was playing the harp, and the younger was dancing; and what with the women, and the music, and the dance, the Ambassadors' minds were quite overwhelmed with the beauty of it all."

Holmes had a picture in his head, and was curious to know how closely it matched up to Miss Reid's. "Do you have any more precise description of these women?"

"My aunts told me only that they were quite small, and had straight black hair, which the mother wore long, and the daughter, short."

"How short is short?"

"Well," she said, seemingly pleased by his interest in this question, "there is evidence in the story that it wasn't cropped close to her head at this stage, because later on she was said to cut it even shorter, like a slave's. At this stage I've always imagined her to have a haircut like that which one sometimes sees on young girls in France: the '*Jeanne d'Arc*', as they call it. You know"—she gestured with her right hand— "cut off level with the chin at the sides and the back, with a straight fringe over the forehead."

That was the very same image that had come into Holmes's mind. Mr. Tollemache had described his experience of hearing the story as being like remembering something rather than imagining it, and Holmes knew what he meant. It felt as if there were some deep collective memory on which the hasheesh-intoxicated mind could draw, and these pictures came from there. Or was he merely reading Miss Reid's mind, unconsciously, from clues in her gestures and facial expressions? Either way, it was an interesting experience.

"Do you have any idea about her face?" he asked.

"I imagine her to have had pale skin, a short, slightly turned-up nose, and big blue eyes."

"That's just how I imagined her, too. What about her mother?"

"To my inner eye her face looks almost identical: a little older, of course, but still just as beautiful."

"With brown eyes?"

She smiled. "Yes."

"Is this telepathy?"

"I don't know," she said. "All I know is, that it's something that can happen when one tells a sacred story; and the hasheesh facilitates it, I'm sure. Whatever it is, it's nothing bad. Just lie back and enjoy it, as one of the pleasures of my hearthside, Mr. Holmes: an inner picture-show more interesting than the kinematograph!"

She resumed her tale. "Now, these women had names, and those names are holy to us, for reasons that you will discover in the course of this story. The mother was called *Nemani*, which meant 'peace' in the language of the Picts."

Stress was on the first syllable, with secondary stress on the third, and all the vowels were short: it sounded rather like 'anemone' without the initial 'a-'.

"And the daughter's full name was *Turabel*, which meant 'beloved' in Pictish; but people generally called her Tura."

The 'u', which bore the main stress, was broad, as in 'too'; the other vowels were short.

"Mr. Tollemache was delighted to learn this, by the way. He said that the folktales of the Hebrides sometimes referred to Trowley as *Inis Tura*, 'the Island of Tura', even though no one there remembers who Tura was."

"Did you not know that?"

"No, it was the first that I'd heard of it."

That was a fact suggestive of the tale's authenticity. "*Nemani* and *Turabel*," said Holmes, checking the pronunciation. Miss Reid's expression told him that he was correct. No Pictish female names were known to the scholars of the nineteenth century, and so he possessed no standard with which to compare these charming appellations. They were, at least, not obviously counterfeit. He was interested to learn that 'Turabel' meant 'beloved'.

"Do you know what the verb 'to love' was in Pictish?" he asked.

"No, I'm afraid not. I know some chants in Pictish, but I don't know what they mean—oh, and I know the names of the festivals, which I think must contain the words for the four seasons— but that's all. If I had to guess, I'd say that 'love' would be 'tura', and 'bel' would be an inflexional ending, like '-ed' or '-en' in English."

"That seems a reasonable hypothesis, Miss Reid. So, who were these lovely women—and what were they doing on that remote island?"

"Such was the Ambassadors' first question, after their greetings; and they were told that Nemani had once been Queen of a little Pictish Kingdom, which had been over-run by Vikings. The normal practice of such invaders would have been to make her the concubine of their Chief; but, as she was with child, they had set her adrift, with a few possessions, in a boat which, although seaworthy, lacked both sail and oars. Yet she had prayed to the Goddess, and the currents of the sea had brought her safe to this island, where her child was born; and in that wild place the two of them had lived, quite alone, for eighteen years. No ships save three had ever come their way, driven by the wildest of storms—and all had been wrecked on the rocks to the north, so that none of their men had survived. Turabel had grown up without ever seeing the face of a living man."

"It all seems oddly reminiscent of Prospero and Miranda in *The Tempest*," said Holmes.

"Yes; and there are other Shakespearean parallels later on. I can only think that Shakespeare must have heard a version of this story, and made use of it for his own purposes. Mr. Tollemache said that most of these details were present in the Icelandic versions of the story which he'd collected; and we know that there was trade between Britain and Iceland in Queen Elizabeth's time. I can imagine the Bard buying drinks for Icelandic sailors in some London tavern, and being repaid by them with a tale or two."

"Hmm, yes: that seems quite feasible."

"Of course, Nemani didn't have the fantastic powers of Shakespeare's Prospero, but she was a powerful Witch. She and Tura took the Ambassadors into their cave; and, when those gentlemen emerged in the morning, they were convinced that they'd found the perfect woman for their King. So they returned with the women to their ship, and put to sea. As their position was quite unknown, they sailed due east until they reached the coast of Norway; navigating from there, they soon found their way back to Mani's realm. The day that they landed here was the Vernal Equinox, which many thought to be a good omen.

"Nemani practised her arts on the King so skilfully that he very soon recovered, and was eager to marry her; but she said that she would agree only if he would free her people from bondage. She must have been very certain of the strength of his passion, to make such a difficult condition, don't you think?

"Now, if slavery were to be abolished, the only way of doing it would be to pay large amounts of silver and gold to the great men of the Island, in compensation for the slaves that they'd be obliged to let go; and funds were running rather low in King Mani's exchequer. But this was no great problem, as Nemani had brought with her a number of large chests full of gold and silver coins, which seemed likely to contain more than enough for the purpose."

"What was the source of the lady's great wealth?"

"By her own account, she'd found it in a cave on the island, left there by some pirate who never returned for his ill-gotten gains. Nemani said that she was happy to spend it all in so good a cause; for nothing could be dearer to her than that of the freedom of her people. So Mani called a parliament, and, with his customary political dexterity, he managed to persuade his nobles that having a functioning King was worth the inconvenience of giving up their slaves. Actually, not much was going to change, he said: their former slaves would still be doing their old jobs, or others would, only they would now be paid wages for doing so; and the former slave-owners would be excellently compensated for this expense by being given a considerable quantity of gold or silver in return for every slave whom they had freed. The nobles must have liked Mani, or perhaps they just liked the prospect of abundant treasure; anyway, they passed the law, and the slaves were all set free. Then the parliament turned into a joyous marriage-feast, as Mani and Nemani became man and wife."

"I now understand something of the significance of 'the Reign of the Crow' to mediæval serfs," Holmes said." It must have been like 'the year of Jubilo' in the minstrel song: the time of liberation!"

"It was a time of liberation in other ways, too" she said: "Sexually, politically, and socially—as you shall hear. But the greatest liberation of all was that, for the first time in centuries, the Old Religion could be practiced openly on this Island. The Queen was a practicing Witch, of course, and the King soon became one; the Cult of Hel enjoyed quite a *vogue* among young people of the upper class. Mani and Nemani did not outlaw the worship of Odin, Thor, and the other Norse Gods; but they certainly did what they could to encourage the resurgence of Witchcraft. If one is attempting to transform a society, I suppose that changing the religion must be a good way to begin.

"Turabel naturally became the object of popular interest. She was very beautiful and charming; many young men desired her, and many young women wished to be like her. Some girls even went so far as to imitate her distinctive haircut, and the fashion of her clothes, which their fathers tended to consider immodest. She was a dancer, you see, and she used to wear her skirts very short, rather as ballet-girls do now."

"The other Princess, Mjadveig, must have been vexed to have such a decorative rival."

"So her behaviour would suggest. The story goes that Tura tried to strike up a friendship with her; but that when the girls were alone together the Norse Princess attempted to kill her Pictish stepsister, by bashing her on the head and tipping her head-first into a barrel of ale. The sounds of the struggle brought guards to the bower, and Tura's life was saved—but only just, for she remained unconscious for several days. The Princess refused to admit any guilt in the matter, saying that her stepsister had slipped and fallen. When Tura regained consciousness, she told another story, and the King believed her, although some of his courtiers did not. The Princess received quite a lenient sentence, in the circumstances: she was exiled to the King's fortress on the more northerly isle of Yetland; there's a place called Cunningsborough there, too, and I suppose that it might have been the place where she was kept. She was to stay there until she admitted her crime, and made a public apology to her victim."

"Did she do so?"

"No, she did not; and to her admirers that was proof of both her innocence and her devotion to truth. They must have seen her as a figure rather like Cordelia in *Lear*. But the Witches' version of the story was that she was too proud to admit that she'd done anything wrong; and so she stayed in exile, when she might have been welcomed back at court. I don't think that it was really too unpleasant for her up on Yetland: she had visitors, and lived in some luxury. But of course she must have missed being at the centre of things."

"What of Tura? Did she suffer any lasting injury from the Princess's attack?"

"Nothing physical, fortunately; but she did become quite frightened and withdrawn for a while. She requested some time alone—which obviously wasn't possible, since she was a Princess, and had to be guarded day and night. But Mani did the best he could: he sent her, with eight bodyguards, to a little fortified hall on the coast, about a day's walk from here. For a few weeks she lived there, without

206

visitors; and as the days passed she began to come out of her shell a little, and started to interact with her guards.

"Meanwhile the King and Queen were facing other problems. To meet the terms which the nobles had demanded for the liberation of the slaves, the royal couple had been obliged to part with almost all their wealth, and they couldn't expect to receive more taxes until after the harvest. The normal expedient in these circumstances would have been for the King to send out ships on a Viking expedition, but the Queen had taught him to abhor such things."

"They did not outlaw the practice, then?"

"No. The King of this Island had some power to control what his subjects did in his realm; but he could have no way of preventing them from doing what they liked out in the world. I suppose he was hoping that the spread of the Old Religion would change men's hearts, and make them lose their liking for such things."

"Was that a realistic expectation?"

"Absolutely: practicing Witchcraft can certainly do that. As it happened, the King and Queen wouldn't have enough time to change all the hearts on the Island; but they were going about their task sensibly enough, and quite effectively.

"However, one of Mani's predictions was proving wrong: a great many former slaves were showing no desire to remain in their former stations. These people tended to come here, to the King's fortress, in the hope of largesse from the Queen—although she had little enough to give away, as we know. There was work here, of course, but not enough for all those who were coming. Something had to be done, and Nemani had a bold idea about what it should be.

207

"She wanted to re-create the kind of Midsummer festival that her people had enjoyed in former times: a large-scale event, out of doors, where folk would come to trade, to socialize, to listen to music, to dance, and to worship the Goddess. The location she chose for this festival was an old stone circle: the Ring of Brogan. But to put the site in order for visitors, to erect fences, and buildings, and so on, would require the labour of a good many people; and Nemani's idea was to put the unemployed former slaves to work on the project."

"As conscript labourers, or as paid workers?"

"The latter, of course. She had not freed them from private slavery only to make them slaves of the state."

"Well, then, the obvious question must be: how were the King and Queen to pay their workers, or even to feed them, when funds were so short?"

"Nemani had an ingenious strategy. Instead of asking the great men of the Island to help out, she went to their wives. In a series of private conversations, she explained her project and asked these ladies to support it, thus making the project into a women's thing—like many a modern charity, in fact. I don't suppose that any wife in those days would have agreed without asking her husband; but women can be quite persuasive, and there was a good case to be made for taking part in the Queen's great enterprise. The arguments ranged from simple kindness, on the one hand, to a desire to curry favour at court, on the other; but the most potent was the purely rational one: that it made sense to offer the freed slaves an alternative to beggary, prostitution, and theft. Many high-born ladies participated in the scheme; some of them used to visit the festival-site, and took an active part in the work there. It must have been enjoyable for them to see that they were engaged in an enterprise of some consequence in the world, making something rather wonderful come about."

"A clever scheme indeed! But what did Nemani think would happen after the festival?"

"By that time she was hoping to have a good deal of her treasure back. Her plan was to charge the traders for having stalls at the festival, and to demand a large entrance-fee from the sons and daughters of the ruling class; all the music and entertainment being provided free by Pictish volunteers. In this manner, the Queen hoped to amass wealth sufficient to solve her people's problems; enough, for example, to purchase farms for them, or set them up in businesses, just as they wished.

"While all this was going on, in early May, Turabel returned to court, quite transformed. From her daily intercourse with her bodyguards she had acquired something of the manner of a tough young warrior; and she could no longer, strictly speaking, be called a maiden—quite the contrary, in fact! I suppose that you've read what classical authors say about the sex-lives of the Picts; it was all true, apparently! They were... extremely liberated." Miss Reid seemed more amused than embarrassed by this delicate subject. "Tura in particular was the kind of girl who gets called a 'man-eater' these days. I don't blame her: she was young, and such feelings are natural."

"It is natural to feel the sexual impulse; but to act upon it has certain dangers for a young woman."

"Do you mean pregnancy, Mr. Holmes? In Pictish society, that wasn't a problem, since people rarely married: children were always brought up by the mother's family, usually without a father; and so there was no stigma attached to bearing a fatherless child. But if a lassie didn't want to have a baby, for any reason, the Witches would have known how to prevent such a thing, just as my aunts did; and the resurgence of Witchcraft in the Reign of the Crow must have meant that more women had access to such potions.

"Apparently, the Witches of those days had other potions, too. Some of them were made for pleasure, and some for contemplation. Tura was particularly fond of one that sounds, from its effects, to have been rather like the Indian *bhang*. My aunts said that one could make something similar, but not so good, from common hemp. I suppose the trade-routes from here to North Africa or India must have been good, back in the Viking Age; or perhaps the weather was just much warmer than it is now.

"I told you earlier that Tura cropped her hair, so it's worth mentioning that this was the time when she did so. It was a gesture of solidarity with the freed slaves, who were sometimes mocked for having short hair; and it was copied by both girls and boys of the upper classes.

"She had always danced, played, and sung, on the island of her birth; and she continued to do so here, delighted to have an audience for her work at last. At King Mani's feasts, she put on regular performances for his guests. You can imagine how controversial that must have been. All of this served to create an intense popular interest in the girl. Many young people wanted to see her; and, when it was announced that she would be performing at the summer festival, a good attendance was guaranteed."

210

"So may I take it that the festival was a success?"

"It ran for three days, and seemed a great success for the first two. The weather was fine, and uncommonly hot; young men and women had fun together in the sunshine. Tura gave four shows, two in the night and two in the day; and all were enthusiastically received.

"But on the last day, something awful happened. The story that the Witches tell is that she was dragged into a tent and violated; and, in self-defence, she stabbed her attacker to death. He was the eldest son of a rich Priest of Odin, a man called Grim. It seems that Grim must have secretly identified himself with the God whom he worshipped, because he'd given this son of his the name of Odin's son, Balder. Anyway, you can imagine that Grim interpreted the events of his son's death rather differently; he said that Balder had been lured into Tura's embrace, where she had stabbed him to death, quite callously, at the height of their passion, just for the pleasure of watching him die."

"What was Grim's evidence for this version of events?"

"Nothing but his own fancy, as far as I know; though as he was a priest he probably said that his God had revealed it to him. The problem was that, to many of the more conservative Norsemen, it must have sounded quite credible. There were sinister rumours about Nemani and Tura: that they had eaten human flesh whilst on their island, and that they continued to do so during their time here, having sexual relations with men and afterwards killing them for the pot."

"Presumably these rumours were baseless."

"Well, actually, I think that there might have been some basis to the first part: on an island which had no large mammals, the flesh of drowned sailors would have been a valuable source of nourishment;

211

and the Picts had no taboo against cannibalism. According to classical authors, they used quite regularly to eat the flesh of their own dead relatives, just as Witches were said to do in more recent times. But I can't believe that Nemani and Tura ever *killed* anyone in order to eat him! They were civilized people, Mr. Holmes."

"Yes: such was my impression."

"Anyway, this accusation of eating human flesh was how Nemani came to be known as the Crow—that and her dressing in black, I suppose. But she took the name up, and used it of herself, saying that she loved crows, because they were beautiful and intelligent birds who managed to survive, and to keep their young alive, even in the most difficult of circumstances.

"But, as you must know, Mr. Holmes, whether an accusation is true is of less importance than whether it is believed; and there were plenty of people here who believed the worst of Nemani and Tura. When Grim went so far as to demand that Tura be prosecuted for murder, it might have seemed inevitable that the innate conservatism of the nobles would lead to her conviction, quite irrespective of the evidence."

CHAPTER XII.

THE CROW'S DAUGHTER.

"You seem to imply that events turned out rather differently."

"So they did—thanks in large part to the extraordinary performance of Tura herself. She was tried in the King's hall, by a jury that consisted of all the noblemen who cared to attend; she dressed in male clothing, as was her frequent practice, and she spoke to the men as equals, appealing to their feelings of common humanity. When she told them her story, they believed her. The custom at that time was that a girl who'd been violated should commit suicide, as a matter of honour; but Tura asked the lords what course they would have followed, in her situation. Surely, she said, they would have done just the same as she: killed the rapist and carried on with their lives! So persuasive and so likeable was she that, by a small majority, the nobles found her not guilty. Of course that was a vote of confidence in Mani, too. You can imagine the rejoicing in the palace that night!

"But Grim's thirst for revenge was not satisfied. He heard news of a little coven that was meeting in his domain. These were young people who'd been at the summer festival and had learned about Witchcraft there; they were having a nocturnal meeting at a stone circle—my aunts said that it was the one called 'Haltadance', in the North of this Island. Anyway, Grim and his war-band went there at dawn and slaughtered all the young Witches. He said that Odin had commanded him, in a vision, to purify the Island of their contagion."

"I presume that wasn't legal, even if they were in his domain."

"No, it wasn't; the parents of these young people called on the King for justice, and he summoned Grim for trial. But Grim said that he'd seen what passed for justice in the King's hall, and he refused to come. The King was forced to go with his own war-band and try to arrest him. There was a siege of Grim's compound, which lasted several days; but when the troops at last broke in, they found that Grim was no longer there, and neither were half his men. Mani supposed that the rebel priest was planning some further atrocity; and the most likely place for it seemed to be the festival-site, where many of the former slaves were still living—including a girl called Ren, formerly Grim's house-slave, who'd given evidence about the character of Balder during the trial.

"Mani's hypothesis proved correct; but unfortunately he arrived too late to prevent a fearful massacre, in which poor Ren had been singled out for a particularly slow and painful death. Soon after this, however, Grim was tracked down and brought to the King's fortress for trial."

"Well, at least this trial must have been straightforward, since there could be no doubt of his guilt."

"Grim was a nobleman, and entitled to trial by a jury of his peers. He was also an eloquent speaker, who presented himself as an upholder of traditional values, with which most of the nobles were in sympathy. The people that he'd been killing were a mixture of freed slaves and Norse youngsters who must have seemed, to many of the older generation, like traitors to their race. By this time, the nobles had

214

seen how their Island was changing, under the influence of Nemani and Tura; many of them didn't like it one bit, and rather approved of Grim's efforts to turn the clock back.

"There was a legal argument, too: since the King owed his status to the supposed fact that he was a direct descendent of Odin, Grim said that by turning away from the worship of Odin, and even allowing a temple of that God to be burned, during the siege, Mani had forfeited his right to rule; and that this right would not be restored until he put both Nemani and Tura aside, restored the slaves to a condition of bondage, and cleansed the land of Witches. *If he does these things*, said Grim, *he will be a true King again, and I will obey him; until then he has no authority over me or any of you.*

"Mani used all the eloquence at his command to persuade the nobles to find Grim guilty; but it clearly wasn't easy. When the votes were counted, there were an equal number on either side. In such a situation, the King had the casting vote; Mani, however, declined to use it there and then, saying that he needed time to consider his decision. Of course he didn't want to set Grim free, but neither did he want to risk starting a rebellion and a civil war. I suppose he hoped that, with the passage of time, tempers would cool. It was late in July, and the grain-harvest was approaching; he knew that his lords would want to be at home for that. So the assembly broke up, and Grim stayed in prison. We hear that Nemani and Tura visited him there, and tried to change his heart; but to no avail.

"Then something rather surprising happened. The story goes that, on the eve of the first of August, when the harvest was due to start, Tura got up to dance in Mani's hall, in front of his guests. *This is for*

215

Ren, she said, quietly; and, to the accompaniment of her musicians, she proceeded to do the most amazing dance that anyone had ever seen."

Holmes had a vivid mental picture of the scene. Tura's hair was styled in a manner that he had never seen in the real world: stiffened with grease and teased upward into many little spikes. Her eyes were painted black with kohl, like those of an Arab girl; and her tanned, athletic body was quite superb.

"At the conclusion of the dance, Mani was so moved that he had tears in his eyes, and offered to give Tura anything that she wanted in return for her performance—even if it were half his Kingdom! Of course, this is the story of Salome, from the New Testament, isn't it?—and it goes on the same way, too, with Tura asking for Grim's head on a charger! I recognized it at once; but my aunts had never heard of Salome, or of John the Baptist; they never went to the kirk, nor heard the Bible read. All they knew was that these things happened in Cunningsborough, in the Reign of the Crow, according to our tradition."

"Salome," said Holmes, "or Herodias, as she was known in those days, was a popular figure with mediæval Witches. I wonder if they might not have introduced this episode as a kind of tribute to her."

"I've wondered about that, too; but since the episode fits so well into its context, and with what we know about Tura's being a dancer, I think that it must have really happened. Certainly Grim was beheaded, and public opinion held Tura responsible."

"Then I suppose the most probable explanation would be that Mani, Tura, and Nemani deliberately re-enacted the events of the Gospel story. Most people on Trowley would not have known it; but

216

Nemani would, since she must have been raised in a Christian society. One can see why they might have decided to perform this *charade*: it would put an end to Grim, and deflect public indignation from Mani to Tura. He comes out of it looking like an honourable man who made a rash promise, while she seems like the villainess of the piece."

"Unless, of course, one thinks that Grim's fate was well-deserved," she said. "I suppose that most of Tura's admirers would have been of that opinion."

"As am I, Miss Reid, of course. I was merely considering how it would appear to the nobles; and I can see why the King might have thought thee stratagem justified if it kept him on the throne. Did it in fact do so?"

"There was no uprising, certainly," she said. "It must have helped that harvest-time was upon them, and everyone was busy with that. Tura took an active part, working in the fields alongside common folk. The harvest was a good one—the best that anyone could remember, in fact—and some took this as a divine endorsement of the new *régim*. Tura's behaviour in the harvest-field had won her some new admirers, too. Obviously the situation was difficult, but Nemani must have thought that her project of transforming the Island still had a good chance of success.

"What happened next would put paid to that dream—although it must have seemed like a good thing at the time. A handsome young King named Helgi came to visit. My aunts knew only that he came from Norway—of course in the ninth century that country was not unified, but they'd never heard over which of the Norwegian Kingdoms this young man had ruled. When I discussed the matter with Mr. Tollemache, I was interested to learn that he favoured Haalogaland, in the north; partly on account of the King's name (since many of the early monarchs of that land had borne it), and partly because he considered that there might be some remembrance of Tura in the legendary history of the place, as I shall tell you in due course. Anyway, Helgi soon made it plain that he loved her, and wished to take her for his wife."

"How did she feel about that?"

"She was interested in the offer; but she didn't feel ready to commit herself to a lifetime of fidelity to one man—which is what marriage meant to the Picts. Instead, she suggested that they do something that my aunts called 'hand-fasting', which involved a promise to be faithful to each another for a year and a day, and to stay together for that time, come what may. After that, she said, she might consider the notion of marriage."

"What a sensible girl!" he exclaimed. "And what a sensible custom, too! Was Helgi expected, as a condition of this arrangement, to abolish slavery in his realm?"

"Only if she actually married him: not for their hand-fasting. He said, however, that he would endeavour to change public opinion on the subject, in preparation for an eventual change in the law."

"I can see why she went," Holmes said. "It would have seemed like a clean slate for her: a chance to start again, avoiding the mistakes that had marred her time on this Island."

"Just so, Mr. Holmes. It must have seemed like a good plan to Mani, too. I'm sure that he loved Tura, but he knew that many of his subjects felt quite differently. His Kingdom would be easier to govern

218

if she were out of it—even if only for a year and a day! Then there was the matter of her bride-price; for Helgi had rather generously offered to pay a handsome sum just for the privilege of hand-fasting with her."

"So off they sailed, I suppose, to that cold Kingdom in Norway."

"Yes, Mr. Holmes. As she had arrived on our Island at the time of one of the equinoxes, many thought it significant that she departed on the day of the other, exactly half a year later."

Holmes found that very significant, too, although he could not exactly say why. Then he thought of Persephone, and understood— with an inward twinge of dread.

"What happened to Turabel there, in Helgi's land?"

"For a long while, we heard nothing. Public attention was taken up with the terrible news from Yetland: how the King's fortress had fallen to unknown invaders, the garrison had all been slain, and— worst news of all for Mani!—the Princess, his daughter, had been slain too, and so fearfully hacked about that she could only be recognized by her clothes and her jewellery! It was noted that these events had coincided with the hours that King Helgi's ship would have been in the vicinity, had he chosen to call at Yetland on his way back to Norway. You can imagine how those who disliked Tura would have been quick to see her hand in this atrocity; how it was rumoured that the Crow's Daughter had at last taken revenge on her detested rival."

"Were no bodies of these invaders left at the scene of the crime?"

"No: that was the strange thing. One could hardly imagine that the invaders would have suffered no casualties in such an attack; but there were no bodies to be found except for those of King Mani's folk; and

219

none of them were armed. All their weapons had been taken away. This was another argument for Tura having been involved: the rumour was that she'd used her authority as a Princess of the Realm to make the soldiers open the gates, and then to give up their weapons; after which her besotted new husband ordered his men to slaughter them, while she took a bloody vengeance on the Princess."

"Hardly her style, I should think!"

"Well, whoever did it, and for whatever reason, it certainly happened; and, while it made the King and Queen very unpopular in some quarters, it also meant that Mani's position on the throne was more secure. Up until that time, those who'd wanted to replace him as ruler had always spoken of the possibility of making Mjadveig Queen, with some wise nobleman as Regent until she married; now there was no obvious successor to Mani until he and his Queen produced more children. So some folk blamed Mani for the massacre, too—as if any sane man would have had such things done to his own daughter!

"Anyway, autumn turned to winter, and Mani was still on his throne. Early in November there came Ambassadors from Helgi's land, with the news that Helgi and Tura had decided to marry, and that she had chosen the day of the Winter Solstice as the most appropriate time for the ceremony. It was surprising that she'd made her decision so quickly; but the timing of the wedding made sense, not only because of the general symbolism of that day, but for the particular reason that it was Tura's own birthday. Travelling in the winter was generally hard, and often impossible, but the King and Queen said that they would make every effort to attend the wedding-feast.

"As it happened, the weather in late December was good; Mani and Nemani sailed away to Norway for their daughter's wedding. What they found there was rather disappointing: the slaves had not been freed, and the Norse folk seemed not to have been changed by Tura's influence, as they had been here. Indeed, Turabel seemed generally unpopular in Helgi's realm. Mani and Nemani were not allowed to speak to her, or even to see her face, until after the wedding: she had to remain veiled and silent till then. It seems that this was an old custom of the Norsemen—one that Mr. Tollemache said was corroborated by certain passages in a poem called *Thrymskvída*."

"How, I wonder, did the Witches of Trowley know what happened in Helgi's land?"

"From the testimony of folk that went with Mani, I suppose. All this happened more than a thousand years ago, one must remember, and the details of who said what have long been forgotten; but the information that we have about this episode seems to be the kind of thing that Mani's retainers would have known.

"Anyway, the next day was the day of the wedding-feast, and it was a very different event from the wedding that Nemani had imagined for her daughter. Far from being the centre of attention, Tura sat there like a dummy, completely covered in white veils; she neither ate nor drank, and spoke never a word. There were some ceremonies, but these seemed tedious to Nemani. The food was good, though: it appeared to consist mostly of pork, but the meat was cooked and served in many different ways, and all of them were delicious. Mani wasn't eating, because he wasn't feeling well: some kind of stomach-bug, I think. It probably made him rather dull company, too. Anyway, after a long time, the ceremonies seemed to be over.

"A big gong was struck, and the bride slowly unveiled her face and head. She was Mjadveig.

"Nemani rose to her feet and cried out: *Where is my daughter?*

"Mjadveig smiled. *Did you like the meat?*

"She pointed at the Page who stood behind the King and Queen, holding a charger on which lay Tura's severed head.

"*That sow's flesh is what you've been eating! And we ground her bones to make your bread!*

"Cruel laughter echoed around the hall. Nemani fainted."

"What a shocking thing! I've heard this part of the story before, Miss Reid; but it's more upsetting when one knows something about the people involved. As one who has himself returned from the dead, however, I am curious to know what explanation was given for Mjadveig's apparent resurrection."

"Like you, Mr. Holmes, she had never really been dead at all: the girl who died in Yetland was someone else. What Helgi told Mani, at that terrible Yule banquet, was this: when they were returning from this Island to his Kingdom, Tura had asked him to land on the coast of Yetland, and wait for her while she attended to some business; a couple of hours later she re-appeared, with a strangely meek and silent Norse serving-maid, and they continued their journey back to Norway. Tura fell ill on the voyage, and had to be nursed by this maid for more than a week after her arrival in his realm. After her illness, she had seemed stupid and depressed, taking pleasure only in eating; as a consequence of which, she soon grew fat. It's said that she suffered from chronic flatulence, too. She did not prove popular in Helgi's land; and many asked why their King had chosen to marry this dull and unattractive girl."

"What reason did he give for his choice?"

"Ah, that was quite interesting—if only because it obviously wasn't the truth. He told his people that, as he'd walked on the beach one day, thinking of matrimony, he'd prayed to Odin to guide his choice in the matter. Then a raven had flown overhead, and let fall a beautiful, high-heeled, gold-embroidered shoe; and Helgi had felt sure that the raven was Odin's messenger, telling him to marry the girl whose shoe this was. From the quality of the shoe, one could tell that it had been made for a Princess; and from the style of the embroidery, it was thought to have come from this Island. So Helgi had come here, hoping to discover his destined bride.

"Queen Nemani, he said, had told him that the shoe belonged to her daughter Tura, who'd lost it recently while out walking. Mother and daughter had gone into Tura's bower, from which the girl had emerged wearing the shoe, with one very like it on her other foot; and Helgi had never seen her without it from that day on.

"On the last night in October, in Helgi's great hall, he quarrelled with Tura. He asked her angrily why she'd never danced in his realm, as she used to in Mani's; and he commanded her to demonstrate her talents for his guests. She was reluctant to dance; but did so, very awkwardly, until she fell, losing her right shoe as she did so. It was obvious to all the onlookers that her foot had been mutilated, the little toe having being neatly cut off, and the stump partially healed over. Helgi exclaimed that she had cheated him, and was not his destined bride after all. The other shoe that she was wearing did not even match this one, he said; but on the foot of Tura's maid he suddenly spotted a perfect match for it. While Tura sprawled on the floor, sobbing, her servant tried on the true bride's shoe; and in doing so she miraculously recovered her lost memory.

"She was, she said, the Princess Mjadveig; her wicked stepsister had put her under a spell, but now that enchantment was broken. Helgi commanded that Tura be taken to a dungeon and tormented for her wickedness. Mjadveig, meanwhile, was restored to her dignity as a Princess and a future Queen. All of this was, of course, kept secret from those outside the court."

"So Tura was tormented from Hallowe'en to the Winter Solstice!" he said. "That's horrible!"

"Yes: there are some things that it's best not to imagine. I don't know what they did to her, and I don't want to. On the other hand, I'd very much like to know the truth that lies behind Helgi's fairy-tale about the shoe. What's your opinion on that, Mr. Holmes?"

"Hmm," said Holmes, leaning back and steepling his fingers. "I think we may take it that that the massacre on Yetland was carried out by Helgi's men—but not for the sake of Tura. It seems most likely to me that Helgi had never seriously intended to make her his wife: that his interest was rather in Mjadveig, and that he was merely using Tura as a means of taking the King's fortress. The gates were opened, and the soldiers disarmed, on her orders, we may suppose; but the purpose was Helgi's."

"Do you think that she would willingly have been complicit in such an action?"

"I imagine that Helgi could be quite persuasive," he said. "In Tura's case, for example, he might have threatened to mutilate her feet if she did not co-operate: a terrible threat to a dancer! Perhaps that was when her toe was cut off, and the lie about the shoe was concocted later to explain it. There is a passage in Herodotus which might have served as the inspiration for that—about a beautiful maiden's sandal being carried by a falcon to a King of Egypt, who sought the maiden out and married her. Her name was Rhodopis, I think. There might have been some scholar at Helgi's court who knew Greek."

"Or perhaps someone who knew the oriental Cinderella story, in which the shoe plays a similar part—that was Mr. Tollemache's suggestion." She smiled. "You and he think along similar lines. What I can't understand is why Helgi would have wanted Mjadveig when he could have had Tura!"

"I suppose for the very practical reason that marrying Mani's daughter would have given him a claim to the throne of this Island; while Tura was not of the royal bloodline, and could have brought with her no dowry but her personal charms."

"And what do you make of the report about Tura being stupid and flatulent in Helgi's realm?"

"It suggests to me that the villains were keeping the poor girl drugged."

"Yes: I thought that, too," she said. "But why, do you suppose, did they keep her in that state for so long?"

"The young King's plan from the beginning must have been to lure Mani and Nemani into his trap, and to take over their Kingdom, most dramatically. I suspect that he might have been using the time

225

between the Autumnal Equinox and the Winter Solstice to negotiate, by proxy, with the magnates of this Island, ensuring their support for his new *régime*. The cruelty of his actions with regard to Tura, however, suggests the influence of the vengeful Mjadveig. I am fully expecting to hear that some horrible method of execution was carried out on Nemani, Miss Reid; but I can hardly believe that the Princess would have been complicit in the murder of her own father. Are my suppositions correct?"

"Not entirely, Mr. Holmes, for both Mani and his Queen survived that terrible Yule. He offered to swear allegiance to Helgi and govern this Island in his name, sending taxes to him and carrying out his orders. Helgi and Mjadveig were to be the Island's King and Queen, while Mani would be reduced to the status of an Earl. His only condition was that Nemani's life be spared. Rather surprisingly, Helgi agreed—but with two conditions of his own. The first was that Mani should be emasculated, so that he could not produce a rival heir; and the other, that Helgi should have the choice of where Nemani was kept."

"Not in his dungeon, I hope!"

"No, I don't suppose that Mani would have agreed to that; but he did, reluctantly, agree to what Helgi actually proposed: that she was to be returned to the remote island where she'd first been found. She was to be left there, quite alone, with no supplies other than two great barrels of food: the one containing flour, mixed with Tura's ground-up bones, and the other holding her salted flesh, mixed with pieces of salt pork."

"Oh, that was cruel indeed!" he said—"but Mani must have considered that it was a better fate than death for his beloved wife."

"Yes; and I think that he was right. Anyway, he submitted to the knife, and came back here as the Earl of this Island, not as its King; and for nearly ten years he played a double game, seeming to carry out the new King's orders while secretly helping many of our people. When he died, one of the sons of Grim was appointed Earl in his stead."

"How did the Witches of this Island react to these terrible events?"

"Many of those who'd become Witches when it was fashionable to do so, in the Reign of the Crow, abandoned the religion after Tura's death—quite understandably, of course! Those who remained Witches had somehow to make sense of the tragedy. Already, in Tura's lifetime, folk had tended to speak of her and Nemani as being embodiments of the Goddess, just as in India to-day any particularly holy or talented person is likely to be considered as an *avatar* of a Deity. Now that the girl's life was over, those of a thoughtful disposition could not help but see a pattern in it. She was born at Midwinter; she came here on the Vernal Equinox; at Midsummer she enjoyed her greatest triumph; on the Autumnal Equinox she left us; at Midwinter she died, and was taken back into the belly from which she had first come. If Nemani, 'the Crow', who always dressed in black, seems like a symbol for the dark womb of Nature, from which all things come and to which they must return; then Turabel, 'the Crow's Daughter', who habitually wore red, seems like a symbol of Nature made manifest: of all creatures that come into being, flourish awhile,

227

suffer and are destroyed. The two figures together make up a perfect ikon of the Witches' Goddess.

"That was, in essence, the theology which my ancestors developed to make sense of the Reign of the Crow. They considered that the whole thing had been a kind of epiphany, a sacred showing-forth, in which the Goddess revealed to us what she was like, in human terms. I told you earlier that the names of Nemani and Tura are holy to us; now you can see why that is so."

"They are to you rather as Jesus is to the Christians," he said.

"Yes, that's a good analogy. And it seems that Witches elsewhere, beyond this Island, had the same attitude. I suppose that you have heard the uncouth appellation 'Nic-Nevin', used of the Witches' Goddess in Scotland? Well, Mr. Tollemache told me that, if the name 'Nemani' had been taken into the Gaelic language a thousand years ago, regular sound-changes would have turned it into something that sounds like 'Nevin'— *n-e-m-h-a-i-n*, he spelled it. And the prefix 'Nic-' is often used to mean 'daughter of', so that 'Nic-Nevin' appears to signify 'daughter of Nemani'!

"In Haalogaland, too, he told me, the last Pagan ruler, Earl Haakon, is known to have been devoted to a local Goddess called Thora Hölgabrud, or 'Thora, Helgi's Bride'. She had her own temple, with a life-size image; the Earl used to stand there and worship her. She was said to be his 'wife'—whatever that means. When the Christian King Olaf conquered Haalogaland, he had the image taken out, stripped naked, and dragged about in that state for the people to laugh at; then struck with a club and burnt on a pyre. While the image was being dragged about the King asked repeatedly: 'Does anyone want to marry this bitch?'"

"A curiously sadistic way of disposing of a statue," said Holmes.

"Yes, indeed! When Mr. Tollemache told me the story I couldn't help imagining these things being done to the body of a living woman, a Priestess who represented the Goddess in ceremonies; but from what he told me later I think that it was only a statue. I certainly hope so. Probably they were just doing what they would have liked to do to Tura, had she been there. Anyway, one can see how the Norsemen might have corrupted her name into the more familiar 'Thora'.

"There is more a little more to tell. Mr. Tollemache had discovered a Haalogaland folk-tradition which said that Thora had been a foreign Princess married to the local King, Helgi; but that his brother, Hedin, had fallen in love with her. When Helgi had tired of her and had her tortured to death, Hedin had ordered a life-sized image of her to be made, and a temple built in which he might worship her. She became emblematic of all the victims of Helgi's cruelty, and those who were opposed to their King's tyrannical rule flocked to her worship. For a hundred years or so her Cult grew and flourished, before it was embraced by that land's last Pagan ruler. To be frank, Mr. Tollemache thought that this story might have been an invention of the poet who sent it to him; but it has the ring of truth to me."

"Yes; it is indeed a fascinating story, Miss Reid!"

CHAPTER XIII.
WITCHCRAFT: ANCIENT & MODERN.

Miss Reid arose to put more coal on the fire, and to light another of her patchouli-scented joss-sticks.

"What was life like for your people in the years that followed Mani's death?"

She resumed her seat. "It was increasingly difficult. Slavery was reintroduced; and, since every former slave-owner had already received compensation for the slaves that he'd lost, Helgi decreed the former slaves to be the property of whoever could capture them. There were distressing incidents, as you can imagine, and many of my people were returned to bondage. Others ran away to the wild places of the Island, where they eked out a meagre existence by hunting, gathering, and stealing from farms. These wild folk were known as 'Trolls'—a word which the passage of time has corrupted to 'Trows' in the Island speech. Originally, I believe, the term was simply a synonym for 'Witches'; but it came to be used only to denote those runaway slaves, who lived and died in the wilderness centuries ago."

"I had thought the Trows to be an imaginary people, like the Pixies of Cornwall."

"They were real enough once. I have some Trow-blood, on my mother's side."

"You imply that there were other Witches who did not take to the wilderness."

"Yes: there were Norse folk who kept up the Old Religion in secret, or at least tolerated it, and some Picts worked for such people. So in a few places the Cult was kept up, and there were big parties for the seasonal festivals. Often, my aunts said, the local Trows would come and join in."

"What were these festivals?"

"There was one for Midwinter, called Tol-Berit." Stress fell on the first and final syllable; all the vowels were short. "Another for Midsummer: Tol-Keren." The same stress-pattern—which was also observed in the names that followed. "The Equinoxes were Tol-Nadak, in the spring, and Tol-Akoi, in the fall. In between these holy days were four others, whose names began with 'Dor': Dor-Keren on May Eve, Dor-Akoi at Lammas, and so on."

"Then to-morrow night must surely be Dor-Berit."

"It is indeed." There was a hint of some mysterious meaning in her smile.

"What form would these celebrations have taken? Were there special ceremonies for each one?"

"Not really: it was much the same each time. The Witches would make a fire, and sing and dance around it. One woman, usually the most beautiful, was chosen as the Queen of the Night, who would be the central figure in the ensuing ritual. She would leave the circle for a while, and return to stand by the fire, wearing a long black cloak with a hood that covered her face."

Holmes thought of the famous statue of Saitic Isis, veiled and mysterious, with the inscription *I am all that has ever been, all that is, and all that shall ever be; and no mortal man has ever seen beneath my veil.*

"They would dance and sing about her for a while; then she would throw back her hood and open her cloak, to reveal her naked beauty, and they would all worship her as an epiphany of the Goddess. Usually she made a speech in that character, giving counsel to her people; and that would often have some appropriateness to the season. They might address her or ask her questions, and she would reply in character as the Goddess. Then a lamb, or some small beast, would be sacrificed to her, and the meat put to seethe in a cauldron. The Witches all paid ritual homage to the Goddess, by kissing the mouth of her womb; then they would dance and sing some more, removing most of their clothes as the night wore on."

"What were their songs like?"

"Here's one:

> *"Eri riuf dol,*
> *Üri uri tol,*
> *Glestë potë nol."*

She repeated it three times. The tune was pentatonic, and sounded very old.

"Is that Pictish?" he asked.

"I think so. I've no idea what it means, though."

It seemed somehow familiar to Holmes. Had not there been found a few Anglo-Saxon rings inscribed, in runic characters, with a similar form of words? The word 'Kingsmoor' came to mind. He should look it up. It was exciting to think that this little poem might be a fragment of the pre-Celtic speech of Britain. Perhaps the strange, archaic melody was also non-Aryan in origin.

"You are a good singer."

"Yes, I know; but it's still nice to be told! Anyway, that's the kind of thing they sang, but some of their songs were more complicated. Sometimes the Queen of the Night would sing the verses of a song, and the other Witches would sing the chorus. There was drumming, and other simple instrumental music; and plenty of drinking, of course. The effect of all this was to produce an exalted state of consciousness. After they had danced enough they would feast on the stewed lamb, and other delicacies; and then they would pair off for the last stage of the proceedings. The idea of these festivals was for the participants to enjoy themselves as much as possible, in order to give pleasure to the Goddess."

He thought of some of the self-mortifying Christians and Buddhists that he had known: people apparently convinced that their God delighted in human suffering. "This is quite the opposite of asceticism."

"Yes, but it has a similar goal. It is not simple hedonism, but an act of worship."

"I have heard of an Indian rite called the *Chakrapooja*," he said. "This sounds very similar to that."

"You are quite correct, of course. From my Indian friends in London I heard much of the Tantrics and their ways, including that ceremony. The likeness is very evident; and must, I suppose, go back

233

to a common origin in very early times. Witches and Tantrics worship the same Goddess, with very similar rites. The Indians, however, like to sacrifice a black he-goat instead of a lamb. I suspect that was the original practice; but there are no goats, of any colour, on this Island!"

"One hears a great deal in Continental Witch-trials about the black goat of the Sabbath. The theory of the Inquisitors was that he was an incarnation of Satan; one more recent Austrian scholar has suggested that he was perhaps the embodiment of a pagan Goat-God, like Dionysus. But from what you tell me it seems that the beast was probably there not to be worshipped, but to be eaten."

"Yes: we didn't worship Dionysus, or any other God—only a Goddess. If the goat represented anything, it was the ego of the worshipper."

"What exactly do you mean by *ego*?"

"The sense of being a self separate from the Universe. In worship one surrenders that, to find a greater selfhood which is not exclusive."

"Which is cosmic, in fact, if I have understood you correctly."

"Just so, Mr. Holmes. The aim of the ritual is to induce a state which one might call Cosmic Consciousness."

He was more intoxicated than he had intended to be; but he felt good. He could understand the Witch-religion, as Miss Reid explained it— and it was not at all what he had expected it to be. How surprising, to learn that the infamous Black Sabbath had been no more than a pleasant way to achieve Enlightenment!

"Would you care for another cigarette?" he asked, after a moment of silence.

"Yes, I think that I should."

He lit their Sullivans.

"You mentioned earlier that you might know the names of the seasons in Pictish. From what you have told me, I deduce that you take them to be: 'Berit' for winter, 'Nadak' for spring, 'Keren' for summer, and 'Akoi' for autumn."

"It seems a reasonable hypothesis," she said. "Also that 'Dor' has something to do with the beginning of a season, and 'Tol' with its mid-point—but really I don't know. They might mean something else entirely." She smiled most charmingly.

It was hard to judge the authenticity of Miss Reid's Pictish, given the almost complete lack of surviving information about the language. Researchers were agreed that it had been non-Aryan, and so quite unlike the Germanic or the Celtic languages; and these words were certainly very different from their supposed equivalents in Celtic or Germanic! 'Dor' seemed rather reminiscent of 'door', he thought; but that could well be a coincidence. All of these words might be genuine Pictish, for aught that Holmes could tell—or they might all be counterfeit. But he was inclined to believe her.

"I suppose that the Witch-Cult was persecuted by the Sons of Grim," he said.

"Yes, and by others, too. Sometimes a meeting was raided, and the participants put to death—those that couldn't run away fast enough, that is. But in those early days our enemies were more concerned with exterminating the Trows. My aunts knew some terrible stories about men, women, and children being hunted down and slaughtered like two-legged vermin. It was only when all the Trows were dead and gone that the focus shifted to us. This was the Reformation-time, and all of Europe was mad for burning Witches. Men like Calvin and Knox really thought that if they killed enough of us, Jesus would come back and bring in the Kingdom of God. It's a dangerous delusion, and it just about put an end to Witchcraft here—and elsewhere, too, as far as I can see."

"But your family continued the old traditions, in their northern retreat. Where was that, exactly?"

"I'd rather not tell you that, Mr. Holmes. There would be no point in your going there, for all my relatives are dead now. They died in the typhoid epidemic of 1891—as did my mother. If you went asking questions in the north, no one would tell you anything; and you'd only stir up suspicions that could harm me."

"Harm you—how?"

"You may be certain that the Sons of Grim are keeping an eye on your activities. If you start enquiring about Witchcraft in my family, they'll make the connexion to me, and I may go the same way as Mr. Tollemache."

"I take your point. But do they not suspect you already? Your nick-name is 'the Witch', after all."

"The little girls might call me that, but I hardly think that their parents can take it seriously. To the Provost, I am a bad example of what happens when women are educated on the Mainland: he knows that I am an Atheist and a Feminist, but I'm sure that he would think it absurd that I was actually a practicing Witch."

"So you are not just a believer, but a *practicing* Witch. Are you a healer, like your aunts?"

236

"No, I don't do that—partly because it would attract suspicion, and partly because I don't think that it's necessary now that we have modern, scientific medicine. Young Doctor Snoddie is much better at treating most things than my aunts were. In the olden days, Witches became healers partly because they wanted to help people, and partly because it earned them gifts and goodwill. I help people in other ways, most notably in my work as a teacher; and I earn a comfortable living from that. I have done the thing that's like hypnosis sometimes, but more for psychological reasons than medical ones; and I've made a few potions for my friends, but that's all."

"So what form *does* your practice take?"

"My aunts showed me some patterns which could be drawn in honour of the Goddess, and to represent her. They used to draw these and chant, as a way of worship. For years that was my only practice. In London I learned about the rituals which solitary Tantrics perform in adoration of the Goddess, and I resolved to do something similar. But those Indian rituals are really complicated, and they involve making offerings of things like ghee and hibiscus petals, as well as chanting lots of prayers and mantras in Sanskrit! It didn't seem fitting for a Trowley lass to be doing such things. So I took the ritual right back to basics, and re-made it to fit my own tradition. For example: I worship at an altar, before a geometrical pattern which represents the Goddess, yet the pattern that I use is not an Indian *yantra*, but one which I learned from my aunts; and, though I sing *Jai Mata Kali* there, I also sing *Eri riuf dol*, and other chants of this Island."

"What is the ritual part of your worship?"

"Well, anyone watching me might conclude that I'm performing a kind of Black Mass, for I burn incense, bow and pray; I offer a cup of wine, and I take communion from it; after which I stand in meditation for a long time, staring at the pattern. Sometimes I sing; sometimes I sit before the altar, holding my wand, and go on imaginative voyages through time and space."

"Mr. Crowley has told me about a similar practice among White Magicians: 'Travelling in the Spirit Vision', it is called by the members of his Order."

"Och, he must be in the Hermetic Order of the Golden Dawn, then! A girl that I knew at the Club was a member of that; it was costing her more than a hundred pounds a year!"

That was a great deal of money: more than Miss Reid's annual income, he supposed. Membership of the Somerville Club would have cost her but five shillings a year. "I take it that you think she was overcharged."

"Yes: what they were teaching her mostly seemed like rubbish, to be honest: lots of stuff about alchemy, the Jewish Kabbalah, and such old nonsense as that—but the 'Travelling in the Spirit Vision' thing was an exception, because that's something that actually works. My aunts had a similar practice, and I think that it must be an ancient one, to judge from all the stories that have been told about Witches flying through the air. I find that it works particularly well for me after I've performed an act of ritual worship."

"Do you actually believe that your spirit leaves your body in these experiences?"

"No—I'm a Materialist, Mr. Holmes. I think it's a sort of dreaming. But there is a deep part of the mind that knows much more than our consciousness; and in this sort of dreaming the consciousness simply watches while the deep mind controls the dream. One can learn much from these experiences, although it is mostly of what one might call a 'spiritual' kind."

"...if one were not a Materialist."

"Quite so." She returned his smile. "So many of the words for such things come from the cult of the Sky-God, that it's often hard for a worshipper of the Earth-Mother to express herself!"

"Have you ever considered reviving the old rituals of the Black Sabbath?"

For a long moment she just looked at him. "Well, actually, Mr. Holmes, I have. When I first heard Professor Pearson's lecture, I discussed it with a number of the other women at the Club, and I found that a few of them liked the idea of such a thing. Later I talked to those women alone, and suggested that we get together with some male friends to revive the old practice; but somehow it never happened. I suppose the thought of the disgrace that would follow discovery was enough to put them off."

She studied his face, evidently judging his reaction before continuing. "Since my return to this Island, however, I have found some friends who are more amenable to the idea. For the last few years, the seasonal festivals have again been celebrated in the old way, with what you call the 'Black Sabbath'. We don't do the sacrifice any more, but that doesn't matter, because the whole thing's an offering."

239

Well, that was a startling admission: somewhere on this Island, a Witches' coven was holding regular meetings of the sort witnessed by Burns's Tam O'Shanter; and at the centre of proceedings was the lissom figure of the School's Head-Mistress! Who were the others? He could hardly expect her to tell him. Still, it seemed a fair assumption that Tanith was a member of the Coven; he wondered if Lizzie Grey might be another. There was also a philological point of interest.

"What do *you* call it, Miss Reid?"

"The Game of Hel, or just the Game."

"Where do you hold your Games—surely not in a stone circle, these days?"

"I have trusted you with so much already, Mr. Holmes, that I don't see why I shouldn't trust you with this: we worship here." She pointed downward. "My cellar has been converted into a chapel of the Dark Goddess. It's all painted black, with hypnotic patterns done in red, white and gold on the walls. At one end there's a little chancel, where my altar stands; in the centre, a stove with a chimney; and, around the walls, low tables and couches. Everything's black: black sheets, black walls, black furniture. There's a fancy circle painted on the floor to mark the boundary of our dancing-space, where a ring of candles burn. If the Provost's men could see the room, they would think it a Black Magic Temple, with a circle for calling up the Devil."

"May I take a look?"

"Entry to the temple is on business only, I'm afraid. But I hope that you will indeed enter it, to-morrow night."

"I am invited to the Black Sabbath?"

"If you want to put it like that, yes."

240

"Hmm. I don't think so."

"Och, I think you'd love it! You like looking at beautiful bodies, don't you? There will be many such there, including mine—which I can see that you admire. Would you not like to see this form made glorious by the Presence of the Goddess?"

"It is glorious already; but yes, I should like that. My difficulty would come nearer the end of the party. I have attempted to engage in venereal congress, and... shall we just say that it proved to be not at all my sort of thing?"

The clock ticked several times before Miss Reid replied, calmly:

"I wonder if you might have mistaken your vocation in these matters. Have you made the experiment with men, as well as with women?"

"Indeed I have. The results were unsatisfactory in more than one respect, since they included the abrupt termination of my academic career."

"You have been very frank with me, Mr. Holmes."

"As you with me: no more. I think that you deserve it. I know that you are good at keeping secrets, and I shall expect you to keep this one."

"I will take it to my grave."

He believed her. "So there seems little point in my attending your Game, does there?"

"Och, I wouldn't say that. Not everybody stays until the end: a few usually leave after the feast. You could leave then, if you wanted to— but you might find that you want to stay. The potion which we drink before-hand could well arouse your amorous propensities. It's the one

241

that the Tantrics drink before their *Chakrapooja*; they call it 'the giver of victory'. Or perhaps the ceremony itself might affect you in such a way that you'd want to stay for the end; and, if so, I should be very glad indeed." She gave him a look the meaning of which could not be mistaken.

"I shall seriously consider your invitation." Mr. Crowley would love this, he thought. "May I bring my young friend?"

"I am leaving that decision to the Maiden of my coven, Lizzie Grey, who is giving the young man what one might term an 'oral' as we speak. If she find him worthy, she will invite him. Please do not mention the matter to him if she has not done so."

"How can I discover whether she has mentioned it to him without mentioning it myself?"

"You must say to him *Alu Nemani*; he should reply *Alu Tura*. If he does not, then you will know that Lizzie has not approved of him."

"I imagine that she and Mr. Crowley will be getting on like a house on fire. What time should we be here?"

"Eight o'clock sharp, please. People will be arriving between half-past seven and half-past eight, but obviously I don't want everyone to come at once—that would look suspicious. Though to-morrow night at least most folk will be too busy with their Hallowe'en festivities to spare much thought for us."

"The people of this Island still burn Witches in effigy, I believe. I have seen pasteboard Witch-masks in the shops."

"Yes. I suppose it's better than burning us in reality, but I still don't like it. Many of the children make effigies, and bring them to School on that day, so that they may beg for coppers with them on the streets

242

during breaks and after school. I have asked Dr. Strange to prohibit the practice, but he will not do so, for fear of offending the Provost, and other powerful men who love these old traditions. The Grimson girls have a habit of making their effigy to resemble me, which I find quite upsetting. They earned themselves another detention to-day, so I shall probably have to share my classroom with the horrid thing for an hour or so after school to-morrow. Och! It's not nice to be hated, is it, Mr. Holmes?"

"To be hated by the ignorant and deluded is no shame, my dear Miss Reid; what matters is that one should have the respect of the wise—and I am sure that you have that."

She gave him a loving look. "I shall think of your words to-morrow, as I sit in my classroom staring at an ugly caricature of myself, and wishing for you to come to the Game."

* * *

On the road back into town, Holmes felt the want of an umbrella. It had been a remarkable evening; he would be glad to get out of the rain so that he could calmly consider the astonishing things that Miss Reid had said.

A Policeman stood on a corner, and held up his lantern. "This is a nasty night for walking, Mr. Holmes!"

"I'm afraid you have the advantage of me, Constable—?"

"Irvine, sir."

"Oh, I have heard of you, Constable Irvine! Tell me, when you went to Mr. Tollemache's cottage, did you see anything of his black notebook?"

The Policeman looked surprised—and, Holmes thought, a little guilty. "No, sir, I did not."

"He must have taken it with him when he went out for his fatal midnight stroll, then. Curious behaviour, is it not, for a man to take a book to a place where he could not have hoped to read it?"

"Very curious, sir."

"Indeed, Constable, this is altogether one of the most baffling cases which I have ever investigated. I have been for a solitary ramble in the hope of clearing my thoughts, but I can still make no sense of it. I fear that I shall have to return to London and inform Miss Tollemache that my investigation has failed to throw any light upon this mystery!"

"To-morrow, sir?"

"Perhaps; or perhaps the day after. I have a little business to conclude here."

"It's hard to believe that you're retiring baffled, Mr. Holmes. From Dr. Watson's stories I had supposed you to be ever-victorious."

"Oh, I have had my failures; but Dr. Watson does not generally write about them, for obvious reasons! Some problems simply cannot be solved."

"Ah, that makes sense, sir. The best of us is but a man, after all; and only the Lord can do all things."

"Anyway, Constable, I should be glad to be indoors. If you will forgive me, I must bid you good night."

"Good night to you, sir; and God bless you!"

* * *

The desk-clerk gave him a candle in a holder to light his way to bed. In the corridor outside Crowley's room he paused for a moment, listening to the muffled sounds of pleasure coming from within. It made him a little sad to consider that he was excluded from such enjoyment—'better than Wagner!' young Crowley had said. Still, there were worse afflictions: one might be blind, for instance, and robbed of all the beauty of the visible world! That would have been far worse. His own affliction had been a good thing in many ways, as it had left him with more time and energy for study. And he had not been solitary, for he had enjoyed the love and constant companionship of his dear Watson.

Only partially consoled by these reflexions, he took a dose of laudanum before turning in for the night. He wondered if he dared to attend the Game, and was still turning over the *pro*'s and *con*'s when sleep overtook him.

CHAPTER XIV.
THE DARK ARTS.

When Crowley opened the door, his face was happier than Holmes had ever seen it. The young man was naked beneath his long dressing-gown. The curtains of the room were open, showing sunny skies outside; but one had to be grateful for the jolly coal-fire.

Lizzie was still in bed, and apparently naked too; but she was sitting up and smoking one of Crowley's cigarettes, holding the sheets to cover her breasts. She was very beautiful, in quite a different way to Miss Reid: small and dark-eyed, with straight, dark-brown hair which now hung loose about her pretty face. If Miss Reid was the Fairy Queen, this girl was a mischievous Pixie. She raised a hand and waved to him. They exchanged *Good morning*s as Crowley shut the door.

"Well, Mr. Crowley," Holmes said, "I'm afraid that this question might seem a little odd to you, but indulge me, I pray. How would you respond if I were to utter the cryptic words *Alu Nemani?*"

Lizzie looked pleased. With theatrical slowness, Crowley responded: "Why, Mr. Holmes, I should be inclined to respond by saying something along the lines of... *Alu Tura!*"

Lizzie clapped her hands, letting the bed-clothes fall for a moment. She had very pretty little breasts. "So we are all Witches!"

"Hmm," said Holmes. "I shouldn't quite say that. I am certainly sympathetic to Miss Reid's variety of Witchcraft, which seems to me quite as good a religion as the Buddhism of Ceylon, for example; but I shouldn't necessarily describe myself as a Witch."

"But you are coming to the Game, aren't you? Just taking part in that is enough to make you a Witch—or a Warlock, if you prefer."

"What's the difference, Lizzie?" asked Crowley.

"Well, 'Witch' covers both sexes; but 'Warlock' is only for men. They both mean the same: someone who worships the Goddess."

"I have not yet decided," said Holmes, "whether or not I shall attend Miss Reid's seasonal celebration. I am certain, however, that I have no objection to the secret rites which she practices in her cellar. She and her followers are doing no harm to anyone, and they seem to be generating a good deal of happiness."

"So I take it that you would have no objection to *my* attending the Game, sir?"

"Not unless something unexpected comes up, Mr. Crowley, and I need your help on the case. But frankly, at the moment I think that my investigation is pretty much at an end: I don't see what more I can hope to achieve here."

"Who do you think was responsible for the disappearance of Mr. Tollemache?" asked Lizzie.

"I really don't know, Miss Grey; but if I were forced to choose the most likely suspect I should have to say the Provost, acting with the aid of the Sons of Grim. The evidence tends to suggest that the fraternity was somehow involved in this matter."

"Yes," she said. "That's what I think, too. They wanted to keep the true story of the Reign of the Crow a secret, and they killed Mr. Tollemache to keep him from publishing his work, just as they used to kill us Witches. They knocked him on the head and threw him into the sea."

"That is indeed a plausible hypothesis. I believe that you once met the Reverend gentleman, did you not?"

"Only very briefly, in the shop. When he asked me about the tale I was alarmed, thinking that no minister of the Christian Church could be a friend to Witches. Now I wish that I'd told him more, so that he might have gone back to Devonshire alive, with the story that he wanted so much. But we can only do what seems best to us at the time, can't we?" She stubbed out her cigarette in an ashtray that lay on the coverlet. "What do you think can be done now, Mr. Holmes, in order to bring the guilty men to justice?"

"Probably the best thing would be for me to return to London and tell my brother Mycroft all that I have learned here; I expect that he will initiate an official investigation into the case. Meanwhile, the Trowley Police Force could be brought under the governance of the Home Office, and the Sons of Grim declared a proscribed association."

"You'll not tell your brother about our little Coven, I hope; I'd hate to see *that* organization proscribed."

"No, I don't believe that there's any need for me to do so; and there's no chance of that happening anyway. Only the guilty men of the fraternity need have anything to fear."

"Hmm. They may still get away with what they've done."

"Yes, Miss Grey; but they will be unlikely to do it again; and surely that's the main thing, is it not?"

"I suppose so." Despite the grudging form of words, she did actually seem convinced.

"Anyway," said Holmes, "I am feeling a little... out of place here. Shall I return when you are dressed?"

"Would you like to join us for breakfast, sir?" asked Crowley. "I have only just ordered, so it should be no hardship for the kitchen to increase the quantities. Should I ring and ask them to do so?"

"Yes, that sounds most agreeable."

"Return in half an hour then, sir, and you will find us washed and clothed and in our right minds."

Lizzie giggled. "I don't know about the last one—not while there's any of that Temple Ball left!"

* * *

When Holmes returned, he found that a low, square table had been set up before the fireplace; it was covered with a white cloth, and places had been set for three people. There were two large covered dishes, a teapot and a silver coffee-pot. Lizzie, in skirt and blouse, was decoratively seated in one armchair, and Crowley insisted that Holmes take the other, while seating himself on a low stool. The young man played the *rôle* of host most graciously, serving his guests a typical Scotch breakfast. This consisted not only of the usual eggs and bacon but also of various other fried foods: bread, potato-cakes, and thick slices of various sausage-like things: black pudding, white pudding, and even a sweet fruit-pudding, such as one might eat in England for dessert, but here sliced and fried like the others. It was all very tasty; but not, one felt, terribly good for one's health. Still, on a cold morning like this it was just what the inner man craved!

It was agreeable to see how friendly the two young people had become. Despite their difference in station, they seemed to like each other very much indeed. Of course it was almost unthinkable that a rich young gentleman like Crowley would actually *marry* a working-class girl like Lizzie—but then Lizzie was hardly the typical working-class girl! The delicacy of her sign-writing was of a piece with the intelligence of her conversation.

She finished breakfast first. Even while the gentlemen were still eating, she began to load a pipe with fragments of the Temple Ball. When they had finished, she lit the pipe and smoked it for a while, inhaling deeply but almost immediately expelling the smoke. She seemed very familiar with the whole process—probably her old Head-Mistress had introduced her to the drug, thought Holmes.

"Miss Grey and I have discovered a common enthusiasm for the poetry of Mr. Swinburne, sir, although in Lizzie's case most of her approbation is confined to a single poem, *Hertha*. Do you know it?"

"No, I'm afraid not. As a young man I read some of his *Poems and Ballads*, but I found it so little to my taste that I resolved to read no more of him."

"Who *do* you like among the modern poets, sir?"

"Hmm. Browning, I suppose."

Lizzie passed the reloaded pipe to Holmes, giving him an intense look as she did so. He held a match to the hasheesh, and inhaled. It was a rougher smoke than Miss Reid's water-pipe, but it did the job.

"Well, I can understand that," she said. "Mr. Browning was an intellectual. He thought about things, and came to interesting conclusions. Mr. Swinburne's not like that: he doesn't have many ideas, and most of those he does have aren't very interesting, being about things like the beauty of the sea or the pleasures of perverse sexual practices, about which there's really not much to say." She grinned charmingly. "Not that I'm denigrating the beauty of the sea, or indeed the other thing, Mr. Holmes: my point is that they're more interesting to experience than they are to talk about. So nobody would read him for the ideas, and I can understand that an intellectual gentleman like yourself wouldn't read him for anything else. But you have to admit that he's technically very accomplished."

"Yes, he is skilled at the art of verse-making. Certainly more mellifluous than Mr. Browning."

"Well, we're agreed then: Mr. Swinburne was a good craftsman with nothing much to say. But, once in his life, he found something rather interesting to say, and he said it beautifully. The poem's called *Hertha*, which is said to be the Old Germanic name for 'Mother Earth', and in it he gives a voice to Nature. It's a kind of prophetic book—a bit like the Koran, only shorter, thankfully. In the poem, Nature speaks to us in a female voice, like a mother talking to her children. I used to know the whole thing, but at the moment my memory's none too good, on account of Mr. Crowley's excellent hasheesh. I think that I can recall the first three stanzas, though, which will give you some idea of it:

> *"I am that which began;*
> *Out of me the years roll;*
> *Out of me God and man;*
> *I am equal and whole;*

God changes, and man, and the form of them bodily; I am the soul.

"Before ever land was,
Before ever the sea,
Or soft hair of the grass,
Or fair limbs of the tree,
Or the flesh-coloured fruit of my branches, I was, and thy soul was in me.

"First life on my sources
First drifted and swam;
Out of me are the forces
That save it or damn;
Out of me man and woman, and wild beast and bird; before God was, I am."

Lizzie was good at reciting poetry, and she knew it. She paused, looking at the gentlemen for approval. They applauded briefly.

"Oh, that's capital!" said Holmes. "A Materialist *Genesis*! I was a little dubious about 'flesh-coloured fruit', but of course I can see what he meant: the human race, as the fruit of the Tree of Life. It's just that 'flesh-coloured fruit' sounds a trifle disgusting to my ear."

"It sounds all right to me, sir," said Crowley.

"Then it is obviously a matter of taste, Mr. Crowley, and *de gustibus non est disputandum.*" He passed Lizzie the pipe, which she began to refill. "We are not all made alike. My other reservation concerned the use of the word 'soul' in what is purportedly a Materialist poem; but no doubt this is just poetic language, meant to convey the idea of selfhood."

Lizzie looked up. "Yes," she said, "I think that's exactly what it is. You understand the poem very well, sir. I'm glad that you approve of its sentiments, for they are very dear to me." She handed the pipe to Crowley.

"It is Miss Reid's theology in a nut-shell," said Holmes.

Lizzie nodded. "So she herself has often said. I don't know if Mr. Swinburne met a Witch, or a Tantric initiate, or someone of that sort, who gave him Knowledge of the Goddess; or if the Goddess just manifested herself in his hasheesh-intoxicated brain one night, as can happen, I believe. Anyway, he wrote it down on paper, and he got it just about right. But nothing that he wrote before or after *Hertha* seems half so interesting to me. Yatter, yatter, the mighty ocean; yatter, yatter, masochism; yatter, yatter, Mary Queen of Scots—it's all very pretty, but really, who gives a damn?"

"Sacrilege!" said Crowley. She looked at him with her big brown eyes. "On the other hand," he conceded, "you do have a point. 'Yatter, yatter,' indeed! *Hertha* really is something special, especially as you recite it."

"Thank you, darling." Like Miss Reid, Lizzie visibly enjoyed being praised.

"Now I think about it," the young man continued, "you're quite right, of course: it's not the intellectual content of Mr. Swinburne's poetry that delights me, but the beauty of his language. That and his general anti-Christian attitude, I suppose. 'Thou hast conquered, o pale Galilæan, and the world has grown grey from thy breath.' That kind of thing really strikes a chord in me—always has done, since I was a boy."

Holmes smiled. "I do not think that you would have admitted this so freely yesterday, Mr. Crowley."

"You're quite right, of course, sir. Is it not strange to consider that we who began this adventure as a pair of Witch-Hunters should conclude it by attending the Sabbath?"

"Indeed." Holmes smiled. "But I think that you were already half a Warlock in your heart."

"To be honest, sir, in my heart of hearts I have always been entirely a Warlock."

"Hmm," said Lizzie, pleased and interested.

"Yes," Crowley said, "I was brought up in one of the strictest of Protestant sects: the Exclusive Brethren. Even as a little boy, I hated our sect's oppressive God, and longed to join the movement opposed to this tyrant, whoever they were. When I first heard stories about Witchcraft, I thought, 'That's the religion for me!' But how was a schoolboy going to find Witches? Only when I arrived at Cambridge was I able to begin a little research of my own. I asked my trusted bookseller for anything that he could recommend on the subject."

"What did he show you?" asked Lizzie.

"It was a book by Mr. Arthur Edward Waite, promisingly entitled *The Book of Black Magic and of Pacts:* a collection of extracts from old *grimoires*. I came away from it with the idea that the whole business was a piece of contemptible folly. There was nothing in the *grimoires* like the noble, poetic Satanism which I had imagined: only pusillanimous attempts to manipulate the Universe in one's selfish interest by means of idiotic rituals—which, to make it worse, were all performed in the name of the Christian God! Here and there in the book, though, Mr. Waite did make cryptic remarks to the effect that, although the magic of the *grimoires* was indeed contemptible, he knew of a more genuine kind of occultism, preserved by the initiates of a secret Order. To cut a long story short, that's how I came to be a member of..."

He hesitated, and Holmes solemnly interjected: "The Hermetic Order of the Golden Dawn!"

Crowley laughed. "However could you know that? You are good, sir!"

"Yes, well done, sir!" said Lizzie. Then, to Crowley, she added: "But what a pity that your bookseller didn't find you a better book— something like Mr. Gomme's, or Mr. Wright's, for example. You might have found your way to the Goddess sooner."

"My spiritual journey has been most interesting," said Crowley. "I really don't regret any of it. But I do feel that perhaps now, on this Isle of Witches, I have at last found what I was looking for."

Holmes noted the *perhaps*. He could see why the young man was attracted to Miss Reid's little Cult; but also a couple of reasons why it might not suit him for very long. Yet it seemed not quite the time to remark on these possible sources of future discontent. Holmes searched for another topic of conversation, and readily found one.

"Miss Reid has told me that her Temple is decorated with hypnotic patterns. May I deduce that you had a hand in its decoration, Lizzie?"

"Yes, I did most of the painting down there."

"You have a great talent for such work. What are these patterns like?"

"Some of them are the old sacred signs that have been handed down through Miss Reid's family; and some are of my own invention."

"Can you show us some?" asked Crowley.

"Just a couple, of the very simple ones, darling. I shall have to be back at the shop soon. Can I have a pencil and paper?"

Crowley took out his notebook, carefully opened it to a clean page, and passed it to her along with a pencil.

"This should really be red on black, to get the full effect," she said. "I take it that Miss Reid has told you about Tura, and the Wheel of the Year—the pattern of the Equinoxes and the Solstices?"

"Yes."

She drew a circle, and then an equal-armed cross, quadrisecting the circle and projecting outward a little beyond its boundaries.

"This is the sign that we draw in memory of that. We draw it and we think about Tura: how her life fitted onto the Wheel of the Year, and what that life of hers was like. Sometimes we might sing one of the old songs while we remember her."

To a strange but rather pretty pentatonic tune, she sang the name "Turabel" over and over, seven times in all.

"Of course, there are more complicated versions—like this one, for example."

She drew the cross again; then another cross, at an angle of forty-five degrees, superimposed on the first, to form a figure of eight branches diverging from a common centre. Around that centre she drew a small circle, quite as neatly as if it had been done with a pair of compasses. Its diameter was about a quarter of the total width of the design. At the mid-point of the lowest branch, she drew a short line at right-angles to that branch, then another similar line above it, and one below. At the bottom end of the branch she drew a downward-pointing semicircle, of equal radius to the one at the centre. All the other branches were then embellished in the same way, producing a design of considerable æsthetic interest.

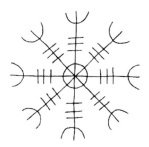

"My word!" said Crowley. "That *is* impressive! Looking at it for only a few seconds is enough to cast a spell upon the mind."

"You should try a few minutes sometime, darling—or even a few hours! Miss Reid has a big one of these above her altar, painted in red and edged with gold on the black wall. When she says the Black Mass down there it really does become radiant with the presence of the Goddess."

"Do you associate the different branches with events in the life of Tura?"

"Yes, that's one of the ways we use it as an aid to meditation. For example when I draw this line, or look at it"—she touched the top left point—"I remember how she first made love, in early May; and here I think about her dancing for the head of Grim. Or I might look at the design and think about the seasons of the year more generally; or the points of the compass, with East here," (on the left), "South here, (at the top), "West here," (on the right), "and North here," (at the bottom). "It's the opposite way round to a modern map, I know; but it makes sense, because the top part is associated with summer and mid-day, and the bottom with winter and midnight. So I suppose you might say that the outer part is what philosophers call 'phenomena': things extended in space and time. This part, at the centre is... well, the timeless essence of everything, I suppose. And the two are one."

"Thank you for sharing this remarkable design with us," said Holmes." Can you show us one of your own, Lizzie?"

She grew appealingly bashful. "Och, no—mine are all very complicated. You'll see some to-night." She glanced at the clock. "I really must be on my way. What are you planning to do when I am gone?"

"I am torn, Miss Grey. I should like to visit the Public Library and read Professor Pearson's lecture, *Woman as Witch*; but I am also curious to visit the Ring of Brogan."

"Why the Ring of Brogan, sir?" asked Crowley.

"Last night, at Miss Reid's, I experienced some rather vivid mental images of incidents which supposedly occurred in the vicinity of that monument. I am interested to know how far my vision of the place might correspond to reality."

Lizzie was putting on her shawl. She looked as if she quite understood. "Well, then, there are two things that you should know, sir. The first being that *Woman as Witch* is quite long: Miss Reid said that it lasted about two hours when she heard it at the Somerville Club, although a scholarly gentleman like you could probably read it in half the time. The second thing is that, by the look of the sky, this good weather isn't going to last all day. So you have just time enough for both your projects, and you'd probably do well to visit the Ring of Brogan first."

"How long does it take to get there in a carriage?"

Lizzie smiled. "About an hour, I should think. I don't ride in carriages very much."

* * *

"Isn't she wonderful, sir?"

"That seems to be the *mot juste*. We are on an Island of remarkable women."

"An Isle of Witches indeed!"

"So, Mr. Crowley, will you accompany me to the Ring of Brogan?"

"Should I be more of a help or a hindrance to you there, sir?"

"A little of both, probably. It is easier for me to concentrate my thoughts in solitude; but in lonely places one is in constant danger of attack, and from that point of view your presence would be most welcome. Yes, certainly: provided that you do not distract me with your charming conversation, you will be a great help to me."

"Shall we come back here for luncheon?"

"I thought that we might eat out. Fish and chips, perhaps?"

* * *

259

Holmes took the carriage back from Storwick on his own, leaving Crowley chatting to his greasy *innamorata* in the chip-shop. The day had turned much darker, and the first drops of rain were beginning to fall, proving Lizzie a true prophet—of the weather, at least.

The Ring of Brogan had been impressive for its size and its unknowable antiquity; yet even more striking to Holmes was how closely it matched what he had seen in his inner visions of the previous night. Still, he reasoned, it was the kind of place that men loved to photograph, and he had read many publications on the subject of Archæology, so it was highly probable that he would have seen photographs of the Ring, even though he retained no conscious memory of them. He knew from his research in the fledgling science of Psychology that the subconscious mind could store such impressions for decades.

But whence had come those other images, of the people by the stones? Of Turabel dancing in a smaller circle drawn at the centre of the stone ring, and the joyous crowd ranged about her? It was still vivid in his mind, like a memory of something that he had actually witnessed; and so were other scenes, less pleasant to contemplate. Perhaps it was all down to the properties of that particular variety of Bengali hasheesh. He resolved to purchase some from Lowe's, on his return to London, and begin a series of experiments of his own. He would ask Miss Reid for the precise name when he saw her that night.

Or he would ask Mr. Crowley to ask for it, if he decided not to attend the Black Sabbath; but at the moment he was rather inclined to go—mainly for anthropological reasons, and out of scientific curiosity, of course. But, if Miss Reid's enchantment worked on him,

260

he would be by no means averse to staying for the end of the party. He was glad to know that the Witches and Warlocks extinguished their candles, and performed the 'act of darkness' in the dark. How embarrassing to be observed at such a time! Strange to think that he might to-night become, in the full sense of the word, a man—at the age of forty-five! If the potion and the ceremony failed of their effect, that was all right, too; he could simply leave after the feast, with his curiosity satisfied and his reputation intact. The only conceivable danger was that of being photographed and blackmailed; but, given what he knew of Miss Reid, he could not imagine that she would be party to such a thing. Yes, he decided, he would certainly attend. He knew that, if he did not, he would always regret the missed opportunity.

* * *

As arranged, he went from the Library to a little tea-shop nearby, where young Mr. Crowley was already waiting for him. They had a table in a secluded alcove, out of earshot of the other genteel customers. A neat little waitress stood by to take their orders.

"You'll be wanting tea, I expect, gentlemen."

"Whose tea do you have here?" asked Holmes.

"Twinings', sir."

That was always a guarantee of good quality. "Earl Grey, then, if you please."

"And the same for me."

"Can I fetch you anything to eat, gentlemen?"

"I have a fancy to try the Scotch crumpet," said Crowley.

261

The two gentlemen looked at each other. It was hard to repress an unseemly giggle. Mr. Crowley affected to cough.

"I, too," said Holmes.

"Fruity, sir, or plain?"

Crowley coughed again.

"Fruity, please," said Holmes.

"And the same for me, please."

When she had gone, the young man softly exclaimed: "What an Island for beauty!"

"I know. You would find a visit to the Library interesting, on account of their Miss Deck; but I suspect that we may see more of her to-night."

"You are definitely going, then? Good-o!"

"The affair is extremely interesting from an anthropological point of view."

"Yes," said Crowley, and coughed again. "Speaking of anthropology, sir, what did you think of the Professor's lecture?"

"It's good, Mr. Crowley, but it didn't leave me entirely satisfied. Professor Pearson should write a whole book on the subject, and properly explain some of the things at which he could only hint in so short a piece. But what he has written is most interesting."

"What does he say?"

"Hmm. He maintains that mediæval Witchcraft was the survival of a very old religion, which worshipped the Goddess of Nature with sensual rites. Although he does not use the term 'Neolithic', he clearly places the origin of Witchcraft in the Neolithic period. In those days, he says, it was the only religion; but in later times, and particularly

262

after the conversion to Christianity, it became a despised and persecuted faith. He argues that the sexual licence of the Witches' assemblies was quite normal in Neolithic times, and only became remarkable later. He lays great stress on the Witches' worship of a Goddess, rather than a God, as one of the proofs that their religion had its roots in the primæval age of Mother-Right. And he produces a good deal of testimony, mostly from Germany, which tends to prove that assemblies of Witches actually took place as recently as the sixteenth century, and were pleasurable rather than sinister in character."

"Did he convince you, sir?"

"Yes, on the whole I think that he did. His lecture is an impressive piece of reasoning backwards, from the phenomena which we can observe to their unknown origin: a technique which I myself have used in solving many a mystery. I shall certainly read more of his work."

The waitress returned with a tray.

"Thank you, my dear." Crowley contrived to touch hands with her during the disposition of the items.

The options for the crumpets were butter, jam, and maple syrup. Holmes went for the first and the last; Crowley for all three. The crumpets had the same pitted surface as their English namesakes, but were larger and flatter, more like pancakes; one ate them with a knife and fork. They were very pleasant.

The gentlemen sat, eating their crumpets and drinking their tea, while the world outside the window grew darker and wetter. Afterwards they smoked, and looked at the tea-shop's newspapers.

They talked for a while of the war in South Africa, about which they both had serious misgivings.

Then they took a carriage back to their Hotel, where baths were being prepared for them.

* * *

The clock on the wall behind young Forsyth's desk indicated the hour of six. Holmes was wearing his tweeds; Crowley his cloak and top-hat.

"What form do the popular festivities take?" Holmes asked, after handing over his key.

"Well, sir, you'll have gathered that fire-wood's a commodity in short supply on this Island; we have so few trees here that all our timber has to be imported. A few rich men have fires in their yards, but most folk go to see the Municipal Bonfire on Gallows Hill. That's where we used to burn the Witches, in olden times; and it's where we burn them still, although only in effigy. The Provost presides over the burning, just as his forefathers did in days of yore. These days we have a firework display as well, and a big ox-roast. Whoever brings a Witch to be burnt is given a free portion of roast meat."

Crowley said: "I don't know how it strikes you, Mr. Holmes; but to me that last part has disturbingly... anthropophagic overtones."

"Hmm." Holmes looked at him and nodded. Then, to Forsyth, he said: "When do these interesting ceremonies take place?"

"They'll have started the ox-roasting by now, sir, but the burnings and the fireworks won't begin until half-past seven."

"So what happens until then?"

"The young folk go about the town with their Witches, asking for treats or money. Some of them sing a few old ditties, appropriate to

264

the festival. Sometimes they carry lanterns made out of turnips, carved to look like dead men's heads. And there'll be fireworks going off already, in gentlemen's gardens. Frankly, sir, it's nothing very wonderful, but it's probably worth seeing while you're in town. This is one of the last places to keep up the old custom, I believe."

"We shall certainly take a look; should we find it tedious we shall soon come back. But we have an appointment later this evening; so, if we do not return soon, we may not do so until the small hours."

"That's not a problem, sir: whatever the hour, there'll be somebody here to let you in." By his expression, young Forsyth suspected them of some venereal delinquency, of which he did not disapprove. He smiled. "I hope that you gentlemen enjoy your Hallowe'en in Cunningsborough!"

CHAPTER XV.
THE UNTHINKABLE HORROR.

The rain had almost stopped, although there was a moderate wind blowing. The main streets of Cunningsborough were thronged with people. Apparently many local men regarded the festival as an excuse for heavy drinking. As yet, however, no one seemed to have reached the bellicose stage, and the atmosphere was jolly rather than threatening. The two gentlemen strolled southward along the main street of the Old Town. The street was rather narrow, and flag-stoned all over, without any distinction of road and pavement. From time to time one had to stand by the wall to let a carriage pass by. The town's few shops were open, of course, and so were the public houses.

Around the relatively well-lit entrances to such buildings, small groups of young people stood with their Witch-effigies. Other youngsters were taking their Witches about in wheelbarrows or on chairs, the latter carried just as the old Sedan chairs had been, on two poles. The effigies were all female, life-sized, and of varying quality, the best of them quite realistic. Most had the same face: a chalk-white pasteboard mask with hooked nose and jutting chin, the very image of a story-book Witch. Some of the poorer effigies had only a crude face drawn on a paper bag.

The lamps that hung outside the shops and public houses provided a useful supplement to the Municipal street-lights, which were also oil-burning. He wondered idly why the town had still no gas-lamps, and supposed that the Provost's conservative attitude might have had something to do with it. The nineteenth century had made little impact on this Island; surely the twentieth would change it beyond recognition. There would be electric lighting here, soon; there would even be motor-cars—aye, and (despite the Provost's hatred of the things) there would be mutoscopes too—or whatever fantastic twentieth-century entertainment-machines might take the place of the mutoscope. There was already a barrel-organ, he noted, some distance ahead. Predictably, it was playing *Soldiers of the Queen*.

Next it would be *Goodbye, Dolly Grey*, he felt sure. Those were the two most popular songs everywhere at the moment, with the troops on their way to South Africa. Why, he asked himself, were people always so enthusiastic about the beginning of a new war? The reality of such affairs always involved a good deal of human suffering and death, however just the *casus belli*. How many young men would perish miserably before this conflict was over? How many women and children?

The smell of gunpowder made him think of battlefields; but it also brought back childhood memories of Guy Fawkes' Night. There were occasional explosions of rockets in the sky on the landward side, to the left; some of them so beautiful as to draw expressions of awe from the crowds. There was still within Holmes the innocent child who had gone into ecstasies of æsthetic delight at such displays; he found it rather touching that inside all these rather tough-looking men and women, the innocent child survived too.

Here came four little girls with a Witch-effigy in a red wheelbarrow. People seemed to be impressed by their Witch. The girls were singing a mournful old song, of which this was the entire lyric:

> *"This very night, this very night,*
> *The Witch shall meet her end;*
> *By candle-light and fire-light*
> *To Hell-fire must she wend."*

The speed of Holmes's thoughts was very rapid; as the girls sang the first two lines he looked at their effigy, and made a number of deductions.

The figure lay slumped in the barrow with its head lolling back between the handles, its arms dangling over the sides, and its skirts sticking out above the wheel. It was well-made: probably the best that he had seen to-night.

Its long, loose hair was of an auburn colour, very similar to Miss Reid's. Surely that had to be a wig, made of real human hair—an expensive thing! Presumably the girls would remove it before the burning, for use again next year. Still, whoever had made this effigy could not be poor; a poor person would have sold the wig.

The battered, conical hat looked like an heirloom; so no doubt that would also be saved for use in later years. The face, however, was a common pasteboard mask that would surely be consigned to the bonfire, along with the rest of the figure.

The body was clad in a man's patched black jacket, which looked as if it had once adorned a gardener, and a long black skirt which might until recently have formed part of a maid's uniform.

A black scarf was tied around the figure's neck and tucked into the jacket's opening. The hands were stuffed black gloves. These old clothes had been stuffed rather skilfully to approximate the shape of the female form. Even a pair of dainty high-heeled boots poked out from beneath the hem of the skirt, in just the right location. He supposed that the boots would also be saved from year to year; and he wondered how they might be attached to the body. Stuffed stockings, stitched to the bottom of a bolster—that would do it! Yes, he discerned the shape of them beneath the skirt. This effigy had been made with some skill—more probably by maid-servants than by these children.

From the figure's resemblance to Miss Reid, he deduced that it was intended as a spiteful representation of her. From the details of its construction, he could tell that the girls accompanying it came from wealthy households, and had servants. So, rich little girls who hated Miss Reid: these, he deduced, had to be the Grimson twins, and those their friends, the Sinclairs.

At this point in his thought-process the girls had reached the mid-point of their song. He verified his deduction observationally while they sang the last two lines.

With their round faces and their curly blonde hair, the Grimsons matched his memory of their photograph. In reality, though, their faces seemed less angelic, and rather more... brutal. Yes, a harsh word; but it seemed the *mot juste*. They did not look like nice little girls; they

269

looked like bullies. The other twins were thin and mousy, just as Miss Reid had described the Sinclairs.

One of each pair of twins each bore one of a pair of Indian clubs. He remembered those clubs from the girls' bedroom at Monksdale. Presumably, as well as singing and displaying their effigy, the girls also solicited donations by putting on a display with their clubs, whirling them about, or even juggling them; it was a popular fad among young people. But there was no room for such a display in this crowded street. They must have done their act in more open spaces, like the one outside the Cathedral and the one by the Harbour; it seemed a fair deduction that they were currently on their way from the one to the other. Probably later they would come back from the Harbour to the Cathedral; and thence, at last, to Gallows Hill, to surrender their Witch for burning and collect their free portion of roast meat.

The Sinclair girl who was carrying a club also carried a ceramic jam-jar, into which people were dropping coins. The other Sinclair twin was pushing the barrow; the other Grimson girl was brandishing another jam-jar—at him, now.

"A penny to burn the old Witch, sir!"

He fumbled in his pocket for a sixpence, wondering if he dared to engage the girl in conversation.

"I expect that you four are great friends," he said, holding the coin, "on account of your all being twins."

"Yes, sir," she said, holding out her jar expectantly.

"You must have some jolly romps together, eh?"

"Um." She rattled her jar.

270

He resolved to try another line of questioning. "Tell me, child, did you ever meet with an old gentleman from England, called Mr. Tollemache?"

She was the picture of outraged innocence. "I don't know what you mean," she said, loud enough for others to hear. "I never did nothing with no old gentleman from England, nor from nowhere else!"

People were looking angrily at Holmes. He heard some muttered dialect speech which seemed to be about old lechers and young girls. Somebody uttered a sentence in which "thirteen" was both the last and the loudest word. Thinking that an explanation would only make matters worse, Holmes dropped the sixpence in the jar and said: "I beg your pardon, Miss; you must have misheard me."

They moved on.

"Awkward," said Crowley, sympathetically.

"These things happen. Let us give it no more thought."

* * *

Up on the flat top of Gallows Hill the ox-roasting was under way. In the firelight, a fiddler was playing reels, and a few people were dancing. Holmes wondered whether that would continue when the Provost arrived. The fiddler's technique was remarkable for its simplicity: he used no *vibrato*, and very little ornament. Everything on Trowley was plain, it seemed—except for the women, of course! Young Crowley was gazing with interest at some of the dancers, and Holmes could not blame him. Their skirts flew about in their dancing, so that a provocative amount of calf was revealed.

The view in the other direction was quite good, too: one could see the whole of the little town, and the fireworks being set off in its gardens.

There was not much more of interest on the hill-top: only the as yet unlit bonfire onto which the effigies were to be thrown, and the great heap of lumber from which it was to be replenished. The place must have looked much the same in the previous century, he thought, when real human beings had been burnt on the fire. It was unsettling to reflect that what he and Mr. Crowley were about to do would have been enough to earn them the same ghastly fate. The horror of those executions seemed very real here; one could easily imagine oneself back in the days of the Witch-hunts, about to witness a burning. He shuddered.

"This wind grows tiresome," he said. "I think that we have seen enough, don't you?"

Crowley turned swiftly away from his contemplation of the dancers. "Right-ho, sir!"

* * *

"Ah, Mr. Sherlock Holmes: my liberator, my redeemer, and my friend!"

Although it was only a quarter past seven, Mr. Marwick seemed already to have drunk a great deal of whisky. He was smartly dressed, however, in pin-striped trousers and a dark jacket, with a collar, tie, and soft hat—not quite a Homburg, but something of the same *genre*. He had just come out of a public house, accompanied by a blowsy woman wearing a good deal of make-up.

"May I present my friend Jenny?"

Holmes bowed and touched his hat.

"Pleased to meet you, I'm sure," said Jenny.

"And may I present Mr. Aleister Crowley?" They exchanged bows and courtesies.

"How are you enjoying our little festival, gentlemen?" asked Marwick.

"It has," said Holmes, "a certain folkloric interest, I suppose; but what it celebrates is the burning alive of human beings, and that rather grates on my sensibilities."

"Och," said Jenny, "but is it not nice to see how the bairns have worked sae hard to make their Witches bonny?"

"I don't know that I should call any of them 'bonny', but I have seen a few which might be described as impressively realistic."

"We just saw one—did we not, Jenny?—down by the Star and Garter. There's four little school-lassies have made it, the Provost's daughters and their friends, and they've made it to look like their Head-Mistress, Miss Reid—apart from the face, that is, because Miss Reid's still young and pretty, and they'd given her the face of a proper old Witch. But apart from that, it looked just like her, with hair and everything."

"Yes, we've seen that one too," said Crowley.

Marwick chuckled. "There was a funny thing, actually, sir. As they were coming past us, just as I was dropping a penny into their pot, the wheel must have gone over a rough place in the paving, for the Witch's arms wobbled about as if she were coming to life. The lassie who was pushing didnae look very bright, but she was quick enough on the uptake then, for she said straight off to the lassie with the club, 'Bash her again. I think she moved.' Dearie me—how we laughed!"

A chill gripped Holmes's heart. "And did she do it?"

Marwick looked blank. "Do what, sir?"

"Bash her with the club."

"Bash the Witch, you mean? Och, no, sir. I expect that would have knocked all the stuffing out of her." He giggled. "It was just a bit of fun, yi' ken. I thought that it was clever." He seemed a little disappointed that his anecdote had fallen so flat.

Holmes's mind was reeling. Marwick's interpretation could be correct, of course. On the other hand, the girl's words might have been seriously intended, and the implication of that was terrible indeed: that in their wheelbarrow the girls had, not an effigy of Miss Reid, but the unconscious body of the lady herself! There was an even worse implication in the word *again*: that she had been rendered unconscious by the crudest method imaginable—a blow to the head from a club! Perhaps she had been struck more than once. Holmes knew enough about the brain to understand how easily it could be damaged by such an assault. Even if the lady were to survive, she might be a life-long imbecile, or blind, or paralysed! He felt as if a ghastly abyss had opened up beneath him.

Yet this horrifying interpretation did make sense; and if the Grimson girls were capable of doing this to Miss Reid, then they might have been capable of killing the Reverend Mr. Tollemache. The girl's protestations about 'never having done nothing' took on a sinister significance. The question that naturally arose was that of why

274

they would do such a thing; but he considered it to be of less pressing importance than the question of what they might do next.

"Are you feeling all right, Mr. Holmes?"

"No, not really—but thank you, Mr. Marwick. Tell me, which way were the girls going when you saw them?"

"Down to the harbour, sir."

"Walking fast?"

"No, sir, just dawdling."

"Well, Mr. Marwick, I'm afraid that we too must go."

"If there's something afoot, sir, I hope that you'll let me help you. I owe you a great debt for what you did last night."

"Very well, then: I could use an extra man. Come with us down to the harbour, and keep an eye out for those girls."

"'Bye, Jenny," said Marwick, without hesitation.

Crowley caught Holmes's eye. "What—"

Holmes raised a hand. "Please let me think for a minute or so."

They walked in silence while he pondered. If the girls had done this terrible thing to their Head-Mistress, they could have had no intention of letting her recover. They did not seem in any great hurry to make an end of her, however. Since they had presumably assaulted her during their hour of detention, between half past four and half past five, they must have been wheeling her senseless form around the Old Town for something like two hours. He imagined that it would be a source of pleasure to them to have a formidable adversary so completely in their power. They did also seem to be collecting a good deal of money by exhibiting their well-shaped Witch. At some point, though, they would have to dispose of her—but when, and how?

275

Could it be that the plan was for Miss Reid to be publicly burnt on Gallows Hill, as so many of her fellow-Witches had been, in years gone by? The thing could be done, just about. The effigies and the lumber might be used to conceal her body on the pyre, while the roasting meat might cover the smell of her burning. But was the Provost insane enough to devise such a plan? And, even if he were, could his influence over his underlings be strong enough to induce them to take part in murder? It was hard to believe. Holmes saw another, perhaps more likely, possibility: that Miss Reid was destined to burn on a private bonfire, perhaps at Mickle Winning, or at Monksdale.

If the plan were to dispose of Miss Reid in some other way than burning, the most obvious course would be to cast her into the sea, just as the Sons of Grim had done with suspected Witches in former times. If that were the plan, the girls might be waiting for the firework display to distract public attention from them—and the display was due to begin shortly!

This whole thing seemed like a nightmare! He recalled with nostalgia the old, sane world in which he had been living a few moments earlier: a world in which the figure in the wheelbarrow was just a lifelike effigy, and Miss Reid was safely at home with Tanith, making preparations for their evening's entertainment. That might still be the real state of things, of course. If only this Island had a telephone service! There was no way for him to check if she were at home without actually going there.

"We must track down those girls, gentlemen," he said, "and examine their effigy."

"You seem," said Crowley, "to suspect that it may be Miss Reid herself."

"I sincerely hope not; but I cannot discount the possibility."

"What a ghastly idea! Should we not inform the Police?"

"Unfortunately, Mr. Crowley, we cannot entirely trust the local Constabulary in this matter; nor do I consider that we have enough evidence to convince even an honest Policeman such as Sergeant Flett. It would be a waste of time to attempt such a feat; and we have no time to waste. We must find that Witch and examine her. If a lovely woman's face should be found behind the mask, every man in the crowd will be on our side, and we shall need no Policeman to assist us."

Marwick was sobered by the news. "You mean that when I was laughing at the lassie's words there was an injured woman lying helpless in front of me? And I just stood there laughing like a fool and didn't even see her!"

"Don't be too harsh on yourself, Mr. Marwick. The thing is simply too horrible to be believed. I have looked at the effigy myself and never suspected that it might be a living woman. Please note that I say that not that the effigy *is* a living woman, but that it may be so. There are grounds for suspicion, and so we must investigate. I hope very much that our efforts will uncover a being of cloth and paper, rather than one of flesh and blood, because the consequences of the latter discovery would be terrible indeed."

They fell silent then, apart from the necessary polite phrases which they used to make their way through the crowd. When they came out into the open space by the harbour they were somewhat separated.

Crowley was the farthest to the left. "View-halloo!" he shouted, waving. Holmes ran toward him.

Yes: over yonder, beneath the lamp-post, were the girls; and there was the Witch. One of the Grimson girls was whirling the Indian clubs about, rather awkwardly. That was good, because it meant that there was an innocent explanation for the girls having the clubs; although it did not rule out their having been used for a more sinister purpose.

Holmes was in front now, close enough for the girls to see and recognize him. The juggleress threw her clubs into the barrow, and the Sinclair girls grabbed its handles; they all moved off quickly, in the direction of the embankment. Holmes heard them say something to the passers-by about a "dirty old man" that was following them. He found himself confronted by a couple of beery young fishermen in cloth caps.

"Best leave the lassies be, sir," said one, suddenly very close on the right, and brandishing a fist. There was no time for explanations. Holmes placed the palm of his right hand under the man's chin, and put his own right foot behind the man's heels. A swift upward pressure of the hand was all that was needed to topple this self-appointed Galahad.

The other attacked from the left, with a powerful kick, which Holmes sidestepped. He caught the fellow's ankle, placed a hand between his shoulders, and pushed there while kicking at the other leg. Another spectacular fall!

There seemed to be no others eager to defend the girls. Holmes turned his attention to their vanishing forms, and had gone some distance towards them when he felt an arm around his neck, attempting to strangle him. One of his fallen assailants was coming back for more. Holmes leaned slightly forward, gripping the man's wrist and elbow. By bending his knees, he lowered his own centre of gravity beneath that of his assailant; then, by bending his whole body sharply forward, sent him flying through the air. Holmes watched how the fisherman landed, and was pleased to see that he did not appear to be seriously injured—although he would certainly be discouraged from renewing his attack.

Holmes ran towards the embankment. The girls had already gone some distance along it, with Crowley and Marwick not far behind. It was darker here, with only the little moon for illumination; the waves broke angrily below them on the seaward side. As he caught up with his comrades he saw that the girls had stopped. They must have realized that there was no escape for them. Were they planning to surrender? No: they were lifting their Witch out of the wheelbarrow; and from the apparent weight of her she seemed to be a real woman rather than a dummy. They swung her from side to side, building up momentum.

"Stop!" cried Holmes, although he felt that it was useless. "Stop in the name of—"

Before his horrified gaze, they flung the Witch out from the embankment; and, in a perfectly Newtonian arc, the limp body of a lovely woman fell into the dark sea.

* * *

"What a terrible end for Miss Reid!" exclaimed Dr. Watson. He seemed deeply moved, Holmes thought, as he looked at him across the fireside of 221B Baker Street. It was the afternoon of Friday, the third of November, 1899. Rain beat on the windows, and the wind howled in the chimney like a crying child; but the warmth of the fire, and that of Dr. Watson's affection, were very comforting to Holmes after the horror of these recent events. The Bourbon that they were drinking was proving helpful, too.

"You are mistaken, Watson."

"What do you mean, Holmes? Was it some other woman in the wheel-barrow? I hope that it wasn't Tanith: I rather liked the sound of her."

"No, it was certainly Miss Reid."

"She did not perish, then—you rescued her. Well done!"

"I do not deserve your praise, old friend. In my judgment it was virtually suicidal to plunge into that cold, rough sea. Although I had a great admiration for Miss Reid, I considered that the chances of her surviving this ordeal were very slim; and that even if she could, improbably, be rescued alive, she would most likely be little more than a shadow of her former self. I made a rational comparison of costs and benefits, and I decided that I should do more good by staying alive to fight crime for a few years more, than I should by risking almost certain death in such a hopeless cause.

"Mr. Crowley, meantime, was taking off his outer clothing, and his boots.

"'Get a boat, sir!' he cried, with a hint of Leamington in his accent; and so Mr. Marwick and I went off without a word to do so, as he plunged into the sea. We took a rowing-boat without the owner's permission, I'm afraid—but circumstances alter cases, as you know.

Even half-drunk, Marwick was an excellent seaman. We found Miss Reid quickly enough; Mr. Crowley was holding her in his left arm and just managing to keep both their heads above water by paddling frantically with his other limbs. The hat and the mask had come off. We pulled her in first, and then him. The brave, foolish lad was chilled to the bone, but he was still alive. Whether there was any life left in Miss Reid's body was harder to determine. When we landed, Mr. Crowley went back to his room to recover—a process which, I gather, involved drinking a good deal of brandy."

"Probably the best thing in the circumstances," said the Doctor. "But what about Miss Reid?"

"Down in the lobby, we applied every known technique of resuscitation to her beautiful, limp body; and at last she did begin to breathe again, although she did not regain consciousness. The Doctor who came to attend her was the same young Dr. Snoddie whose work she had praised. He took her to the local Hospital, promising to keep a constant watch on her, and to do whatever was necessary to preserve her life. I formed the impression that he was more than a little in love with her."

"Understandably! So what did you do then?"

"I took a carriage to Gallows Hill, to see the Provost. At my suggestion we conversed in the carriage on the way back to Monksdale. I told him that his daughters had been witnessed committing a felony: the attempted murder of their Head-Mistress. I also told him that I suspected them of the actual murder of Mr. Tollemache, explaining my reasons—the footprint evidence, and so on. He was appalled, but he believed me, on both counts.

"In the course of our conversation I became convinced that, up until this point, the Provost had genuinely believed that Mr. Tollemache had been killed by an act of God, as a judgment on his blasphemous project. Mr. Grimson admitted that he had been responsible for the destruction of Mr. Tollemache's note-book, and of the documentary evidence in favour of his theory, but that was all. The girls it seemed, had acted entirely on their own; and this was confirmed when we entered the house and found them already there.

"He made them swear to tell the truth, and they confessed the whole thing. One of them had gone to Mr. Tollemache's cottage after dark on Wednesday, and lured him to the cliff-edge with a tale of an injured child; once there they had both struck him with their clubs and pushed him over into the sea."

"The little monsters!"

"Victims of circumstances, like all of us, Watson. 'There but for the grace...' —you will recall the quotation."

"What were the circumstances in this case?"

"They had grown rather wild after their mother's death, and their father had filled their heads with tales of the Sons of Grim and their fight against Witchcraft. In my opinion the Provost is still guilty of these crimes, although not directly, because he put the notion in his daughters' minds that it was heroic to go out with a club and kill Witches. He had also denounced Mr. Tollemache to them in the strongest possible terms, describing the Reverend gentleman as an enemy of God. Of course, he never expected that they might do what they did, and he was properly appalled to learn of it; but, even so, they would not have done it had he not given them the idea."

"He is not culpable in law, however; and they, I suppose, are faced with the prospect of a life-sentence, like poor Constance Kent."

"A terrible prospect for a child! I should not want it on my conscience that I had condemned four little girls to such a fate."

"Then what is to become of them?"

"That we did not decide until the next day, when Miss Reid regained consciousness."

"Oh! How was she?"

"Remarkably well, considering the abuse that she had suffered. She had a bad headache, and no recollection of the afternoon preceding her injury, but her memory was otherwise unimpaired. Her senses were all normal, too; and she was able to discuss the situation very sensibly. I think that there is a very good chance of her making a full recovery in a matter of days."

Watson was delighted. "She is very lucky."

"I told her as much. She replied that the Goddess had been good to her."

"It seems to come to much the same thing."

"Indeed."

"So what arrangements have been made to punish these horrible crimes?"

"Mr. Grimson's daughters have been committed to the local Asylum. Yes, I know that sounds frightful; but in fact the place is rather pleasant, and run to the best modern standards by rational and compassionate people. The girls are to remain there until such time as they are deemed to be reformed; and are not to be released without

Miss Reid's consent. Mr. Grimson has given that lady a cheque for a thousand pounds, as a mark of his sympathy."

"And the Sinclair girls?"

"Seeing that they did not instigate the attack on Miss Reid, and apparently did not strike her, we have agreed that they may remain at home, provided that they have no further contact with Faith and Hope. Mr. Sinclair has given Miss Reid a cheque for five hundred pounds, however."

"That seems only fair. But where does this leave Emily—Miss Tollemache?"

"Better off than she might have been. I have brought her another thousand-pound cheque from the sympathetic Mr. Grimson, and also a death-certificate, which will enable her, and all her father's heirs, to inherit his property immediately. The story which we have agreed to tell is that his body was washed ashore on Wednesday, and buried in the graveyard. There is a plot upon which a memorial may be erected, although of course the grave is empty."

"The official cause of death being 'misadventure', I suppose."

"Quite so, Watson. There seems little point in distressing the lady with the horrific facts of the case."

They sat in silence for a few moments, listening to the wind and the rain.

"Young Mr. Crowley must be quite the darling of the Cunningsborough Witches."

"Yes; he is no doubt making the most of his opportunities. He may even attend a few of their Games, but I can't imagine that he will be a member of the Coven for long. Unlike the Hermetic Order of the

Golden Dawn, Miss Reid's Cult promises its adherents no præternatural powers—and I know how much Mr. Crowley wants to perform miracles. Nor does he seem quite the type to enjoy being bossed about by a lot of women!"

They laughed together.

Watson said: "So it seems that you have missed your own chance to enjoy the pleasures of the Sabbath."

"Yes. It's probably for the best: I might have developed a taste for such things—and then what would have become of my work as a detective? I might have become prone to fall in love with every damsel in distress that crossed my path—like you, old chap! What price objectivity then?"

Watson looked a little guilty.

"What—" said Holmes, "not you and 'Emily'?"

"Well, I must admit that a certain... closeness, has developed between us, over the course of the last seven days. She is a charming girl, Holmes; and very intelligent. All her life she has lived to serve her father; I have been helping her to conceive of a different way of living, in which her own desires may sometimes be gratified."

"Have you actually gratified any of her desires yet?"

Watson coughed, and blushed slightly. "Don't worry, old man; it's nothing serious. I've no desire to be married again; and Miss Tollemache could find a far better husband than me, I'm sure, particularly with a thousand pounds in her bank-account. I won't desert you again; you may be sure of that!"

Holmes filled his old briar-pipe with shag tobacco from the Persian slipper, and lit it with a glowing ember from the fire. "Thank you, Watson," he said at last. "I tease you sometimes, but you know that I should be quite lost without you."

"Hmm." Watson nodded. "What do you suppose the future holds for Miss Reid's revived version of the Old Religion?"

"As to that, we must wait and see. It might flourish in the coming century, as a form of spirituality peculiarly suited to the 'New Woman'; but I rather suspect that the world is not yet ready for a revival of Goddess-worship. Anyway, from an anthropological point of view I am glad that I have had the opportunity to learn so much about the ancient Cult whilst investigating this most surprising case."

"Surprising indeed! Who would have guessed that, at the end of the nineteenth century, you might be called upon to investigate a case of Witchcraft?"

THE END.

Also from MX Publishing:

Close To Holmes.

A Look at the Connections Between
Historical London, Sherlock Holmes
and Sir Arthur Conan Doyle.

Eliminate The Impossible.

An Examination of the World of

Sherlock Holmes on Page and Screen.

www.mxpublishing.com

Also from MX Publishing:

The Norwood Author.

Arthur Conan Doyle and the Norwood Years (1891 – 1894).

In Search of Dr Watson.

Wonderful biography of Dr.Watson from expert Molly Carr.

www.mxpublishing.com

Also from MX Publishing:

Arthur Conan Doyle, Sherlock Holmes and Devon.

A Complete Tour Guide and Companion.

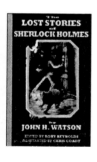

The Lost Stories of Sherlock Holmes.

Eight more stories from the pen of John H Watson – compiled by Tony Reynolds.

www.mxpublishing.com

Also from MX Publishing:

Watson's Afghan Adventure.

Fascinating biography of Watson's time in Afghanistan from US Army veteran Kieran McMullen.

Shadowfall.

Sherlock Holmes, ancient relics and demons and mystic characters. A supernatural Holmes pastiche.

www.mxpublishing.com

Also from MX Publishing:

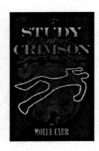

A Study in Crimson.

The second adventure of the 'female Sherlock Holmes' with a host of sub- plots and new characters joining Watson and Fanshaw

The Chronology of Arthur Conan Doyle.

The definitive chronology used by historians and libraries worldwide.

www.mxpublishing.com

Also from MX Publishing:

Aside Arthur Conan Doyle.

A collection of twenty stories from
ACD's close friend Bertram Fletcher
Robinson.

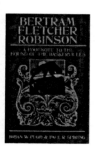

Bertram Fletcher Robinson.

The comprehensive biography of the
assistant plot producer of The Hound of
The Baskervilles.

www.mxpublishing.com

Also from MX Publishing:

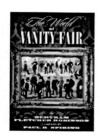

The World of Vanity Fair.

A specialist full-colour reproduction of key articles from Bertram Fletcher Robinson containing of colour caricatures from the early 1900s.

Tras Las He huellas de Arthur Conan Doyle (in Spanish).

Un viaje ilustrado por Devon.

www.mxpublishing.com

Also from MX Publishing:

The Outstanding Mysteries of Sherlock Holmes.

With thirteen Homes stories and illustrations Kelly re-creates the gas-lit, fog-enshrouded world of Victorian London

Rendezvous at The Populaire.

Sherlock Holmes has retired, injured from an encounter with Moriarty. He's tempted out of retirement for an epic battle with the Phantom of the opera.

www.mxpublishing.com

Also from MX Publishing:

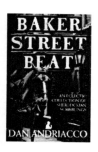

Baker Street Beat.

An eclectic collection of articles, essays, radio plays and 'general scribblings' about Sherlock Holmes from Dr. Dan Andriacco.

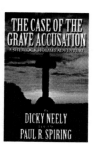

The Case of The Grave Accusation.

The creator of Sherlock Holmes has been accused of murder. Only Holmes and Watson can stop the destruction of the Holmes legacy.

www.mxpublishing.com